PROMISE OF REVENGE

PROMISE OF REVENGE

Two Western Stories

by

LAURAN PAINE

Skyhorse Publishing

First Skyhorse Publishing edition published 2014 by arrangement with Golden West Literary Agency

www.skyhorsepublishing.com

10 9 8 7 6 5 4 3 2 1

Library of Congress Cataloging-in-Publication Data is available on file.

Cover design by Brian Peterson

ISBN: 978-1-62873-630-4
Ebook ISBN: 978-1-62873-988-6

Printed in the United States of America

Table of Contents

Tomahawk Meadow

I

It was one of those situations a man sometimes rode into without warning, without expectation, and without any desire or taste for. The range men fired a volley just as Buckner's horse turned up out of a dusty, bone-dry cañon, and the sound startled Buckner as much as it surprised his horse. They hunched toward the top-out because they were already committed to the extent of this trail, but the moment they got up there where foggy dust lay here and there and where men were locked in a fierce little savage battle, they both wished they were almost anywhere else.

It was easier to make out the range men than it was to see their adversaries, but in this territory at this time Ladd Buckner had no doubts about the identity of the wispy, raggedly firing people across the arroyo-scarred grassland in among the thin stands of pines. In fact, when the range men seemed to be in the act of converging, in the act of mounting their common effort and peppered the first and second tier of trees, several of those bushwhacking individuals, stripped to moccasins, clout, and sweatband, whisked back from tree to tree in a shadowy withdrawal. They were Apaches, which meant they were also Ladd Buckner's enemies. They were in fact the enemies of everyone, even including certain subdivisions of their own nation.

Buckner swung off, drawing out the Winchester as he stepped to the talus rock soil, then turned his horse out of the cleared place in the direction of the trees, and sank to one knee as a bronco Apache swung free and darted up an exposed stretch of highland trail, racing for cover. Ladd Buckner fired, along with four or five range men who had also been awaiting just such an opportunity, and the fleeing man turned over, headfirst, like a ball and rolled into a tree where he unwound and lay sprawled and lifeless.

Another pair of bronco Apaches suddenly turned back, and Buckner, who was on higher ground than the other range men and for that reason had a better sighting, tracked the lead Indian and fired. The Apache gave a tremendous bound into the air as though bee-stung and lit down, racing harder than ever. Among the range men someone shouted encouragement in a pleased voice. Buckner tracked the second Apache, and fired. That time he'd held slightly downhill instead of uphill, and the Indian's legs tangled, then locked, and he fell in a limp heap.

Finally now the Apaches had guessed they had an enemy on their right flank where they had expected no one, and began cat-calling back and forth as they attempted to shift position, but the range men were after them now like hawks. The stranger's arrival and deadly shooting had completed the necessary unity among the bushwhacked range men; they systematically fired at every movement up along the foremost ranks of spindly forest, keeping the attacking Apaches on the defensive.

A man's powerful, deep voice sang out in English: "You up there . . . keep watch! They'll get behind you if they can! Keep down . . . keep low!"

Ladd Buckner heard without heeding. He knew as much about Apaches as any of those range riders down yonder. He was not worried about himself; he was worried about his horse. Apaches would kill a man's horse if they possibly could, although they much preferred stealing it.

But this time it appeared that the Indians had had their belly full. In a space of minutes when they'd had no reason to think it possible, since this had been their careful bushwhack, they had lost two warriors, shot dead on their feet, from a direction that their previous scouting had shown them there was no danger.

The range men began hurrying, finally, passing up along the gritty bottom of an arroyo, booted feet grinding down hard as they hastened ahead, knees bent and never straightening as they came on toward the nearest stand of pines. They had been caught completely unprepared by the first Apache volley, and they'd taken a couple of casualties, but that momentary surprise did not last and now the range men, coldly and mercilessly angry, were going after their attackers. They made such good progress that a brace of broncos who had boldly—and foolishly—advanced well ahead of their companions to jump down into one of the arroyos and attempt a stalk closer to the range men could hear them coming. The range men made no attempt to be silent; they talked and cursed and scuffed dirt and stone and rattled gun stocks along the sides of their arroyo. They did every careless thing that to Apaches was a sin, but they kept coming and eventually the Apaches could no longer remain in the arroyo.

Ladd Buckner was straightening around after having brushed some belly-gouging sharp small stones from beneath him when the first raghead appeared, head and shoulders like a rattler lifting more and more and more as they twisted left and right. Ladd held fire. The Indian jumped out of the cleft in the grassland and turned up across the open territory in a desperate race for the upland shelter where his tribesmen were already withdrawing. Ladd settled the gunstock closer, snugged it back until it became almost a part of his slowly twisting body, and was ready to fire when the second bronco sprang up out of the earth and also began wildly running. It was a distraction but only a momentary one, then Ladd fired.

The foremost Indian gradually slackened pace. He seemed to want to continue to rush along but the harder he tried the slower his gait became, until the other bronco ran up and without even a glance shot past and kept right on running. From far back a number of range men sang out, then an immediate ragged volley ensued. The unhurt, swiftly speeding buck went down and rolled end over end. His uniquely slowing, stumbling friend was not fired upon. The range men, like Ladd Buckner, lay there frankly interested in just how much longer the wounded buck could keep up his charade. Not much longer. He stopped, legs sprung wide, used his Winchester for a support, and turned very slowly to look over where Buckner had fired from. He could not see the man who had hit him but he tried to locate him. Then his knees turned loose and he fell, first into a sitting posture, then he rolled over.

The Apaches had failed in their attempt at a massacre that would have provided them with horses, pocket watches, pistols, and shell belts as well as cowboy saddles that brought a great price deep in Mexico. The reason they had failed had simply been because someone who could shoot accurately had appeared suddenly over where there was not supposed to be anyone, and he was still over there, prone in the rocks. As the broncos withdrew, wraith-like into their shadowy world, one bitter man went back and aimed into the talus where Buckner was, and fired. The slug ricocheted like a furious hornet. Buckner pressed lower than ever and tried to find that Indian. He never succeeded.

The bronco sent in another probing shot, doubtless hoping to come close enough to make Buckner move, but he was not dueling with a novice. Buckner felt the sting of stone without moving any part of him except his eyes. He tried as hard to locate his adversary as the bronco did to locate him, and the end of it occurred when the range men got up to the northernmost end of their arroyo and suddenly, recklessly sprang out and raced for the nearest trees. The Apache had to end his manhunt and race up into the shadows in the wake of his retreating companions.

The range men blazed away where there were no targets, which was not as futile as it sometimes appeared. Apaches could be anywhere, prone under leaves, up trees watching for stalkers below, or even stealthily coming back to fight again. They weren't. They had failed, and, although the numbers were equal, they did not fight pitched battles. It was not their way and never had been.

They were specialists in ambush, in stealthy mayhem, in wispy comings and goings. By now, wherever they had hidden their horses back upslope, they would be springing aboard to haul around and race away. Their casualties were already forgotten. At least three were dead, which they could not have helped but notice, but that bronco Ladd Buckner had shot down last was wounded. Still, the broncos did not have room, or time, for chivalry. If a man dropped, wounded or simply out of air or perhaps just stunned, he was counted a fatality because the enemies of the Apaches rarely took prisoners. The Apaches did not take them, unless they were half-grown children, and neither did their enemies.

Those charging range men burst past the first tier of trees, red-faced and in full throat. They wanted blood. In their environment there was no such thing as a worthwhile Apache. If they could have got up where the broncos had their tethered horses, they would have killed every man jack of those Apaches. It was hot out upon the grassland; that meant it was even more breathless in the humid foothills; those range men unlike their foemen were not accustomed to running on foot, and the Indians had achieved a speedy head start.

The gunfire ended, and after a while even the futile chase ended. The Apaches had disappeared, so the range men turned back, whip-sawing their breath, shirts plastered flat with salt sweat, their legs and hips aching from the mad charge up from the grassland into the spindly forest. They cursed between deep-drawn breaths and tried to guess which way the ragheads had gone so that perhaps later on they might be able to go in pursuit. Until they were low enough again to see beyond the forest's fringe to the range beyond, they seemed to have forgotten that man over in the talus rock who had so perfectly confused the Indians by appearing on their right flank with his deadly gunfire.

"Whoever he is," a youthful, wispy, tall rider said, "he sure as hell deserves a medal."

"Came up out of the cañon just before the fight started," stated an older man. "I seen him. I figured, by God, he was another raghead, except he had a white man's way of settin' his horse and all. You're dead right . . . he sure come up out of there in the nick of time."

"We'd've cleaned them out anyway," grumbled another man.

"Yeah, most likely," conceded the older rider. "But he came up out of there and sure made a hell of a lot of difference."

There was no way to dispute this statement even if the other riders had wanted to dispute it, which none of them did. Then they came out of the trees and saw Ladd Buckner squatting beside that wounded bronco, and angled off in that direction. The sun was high, the air smelled of burned powder, and far out several saddled horses grazed peacefully along.

II

Buckner was not an exceptionally tall man. He stood six feet, and in heft weighed about twenty pounds less than a couple of hundred, but if this amounted to an average man in physical respects when the three range men ambled up and halted as Ladd Buckner arose from beside the wounded Indian, it became clear to the observing survivors of that raghead ambush that Ladd Buckner was something more than simply a range rider who had inadvertently come down out of the northward hills and up out of that gravelly cañon at the precise best moment for him to appear upon Tomahawk Meadow.

A dark-eyed, black-haired, stalwart man shoved out a soiled hand and said: "I'm Chad Holmes, range boss for the Muleshoe cow outfit. This here is Buster Dent, Jack Caruthers, and Pete Durbin."

They pumped hands once, then let go, and Chad Holmes looked long at the unmoving, snake-eyed Indian on the ground whose middle had been bandaged. Then Chad turned from the waist to look elsewhere and said: "You fellers better see if you can catch those damned horses, and, if so, you'd better tie Morton and Devilin across their saddles." As the cowboys turned away, Muleshoe's range boss turned back for a more thoroughly assessing study of Ladd Buckner. "You sure came up out of that cañon at the right time," he said.

Buckner sounded indifferent as he replied: "Mister Holmes, I'd have given a lot to have been ten miles easterly in some other cañon, but once we started up out of there, we didn't have room to turn around to head back down."

Holmes looked at the Apache again. "Where did you hit the son-of-a-bitch?"

"Through the body," replied Buckner. "It's one of those wounds you don't know about until some morning you look at him, and he's stiff as a ramrod or else he's grinning back at you."

"He isn't going to grin," said the dark-eyed range boss.

Ladd hooked thumbs in his bullet belt and considered Muleshoe's range boss. Chad Holmes was dark, 'breed-looking, stalwart, and physically powerful. He was about Buckner's age, thirty or thereabouts, but he was thicker and not quite as tall. Muleshoe had plenty of reason to hate this particular raghead. Most northern Arizona range men had abundant reason to despise most Apaches.

Ladd Buckner also had reason to hate ragheads, but, although he understood exactly how the range boss felt, he was opposed to murder even when it was committed against ragheads, so he said: "Mister, this one belongs to me."

Holmes shot a dark glance upward. "What does that mean?" he demanded.

"I saw him, I fought him, and I shot him. I also patched him up. He belongs to me. That's how they call their shots."

"Yeah, but we're not ragheads," stated the range boss. "This son-of-a-bitch was in a bushwhacking band and I got two dead cowboys to prove it. We got laws about something like that."

Ladd sighed. "You don't lynch this one, mister."

Holmes began to look less baffled than antagonistic. "You're going to stop the four of us?" he quietly asked. "What's your name, mister?"

"Ladd Buckner. No, I'm not going to stop the four of you, Mister Holmes, I'm only going to stop you, because you and I are the only ones standing here." Buckner paused, traded looks with the 'breed-looking Muleshoe boss, then gently smiled. He had a very nice smile. "Mister Holmes, I don't deal in favors, but this time I guess I got to. I did you boys a little favor coming up out of the cañon when I did. Do you object to settling up small debts?"

Chad spat aside and glanced again at the venomous-eyed, prone Apache. "All I got to say to you, Mister Buckner, is that, if you insist on being foolish over one stinking raghead . . . all right. Just don't be around here when my riders come back because they aren't going to stand for this, if you're still here." He looked sulphurously upward. "What in the hell sense does this make? You're risking your life keeping one of those underhanded, treacherous bastards alive. You patch him up and the minute he gets a chance he'll slam a knife to the hilt between your shoulder blades."

Buckner disputed none of this. He knew Apaches as well as anyone else knew them. "If he gets behind me, it'll be my own darned fault," he told Chad Holmes, and looked up and around. "You know, Mister Holmes, I was on my way southward to a place called Piñon when I came up out of that blasted cañon. How much farther is it?"

"Twelve, fifteen miles," stated the range boss. "It's our nearest town. In fact, it's the only town anywhere around the Tomahawk Meadow range country." Holmes assumed an interested look. "You acquainted down there?"

Ladd wasn't. "No, sir, but I read in a newspaper up at Cache Le Poudre about a harness works being for sale down there."

Holmes dryly said: "Mister, if you can sew a trace or rig a saddle as well as you can shoot, I'd say you'll make a fair living in this territory."

The Indian attempted to sit up and Chad Holmes turned stonily to watch. Ladd Buckner stepped back and set a big leg behind the bronco for support. It was a rough but a generous gesture. The Indian settled back and glared. "Subbitch," he snarled at Chad Holmes.

Neither of the range men moved nor replied. Far out one cowboy had managed to catch one of those loose saddle animals and was now astride it going in search of additional stampeded saddle horses. It would be inevitable that some of the loose stock had not stopped after being abandoned when the Indians had first struck. By now those horses would be two-thirds of the way back to the home ranch of Muleshoe.

Ladd Buckner leaned to hoist the wounded Indian up to his feet. Chad Holmes, arms crossed, stood and watched. If the raghead's life had depended upon some merciful act by the range boss, there would have been another dead Apache.

Ladd encircled the Indian's middle with a strong arm and turned to head in the direction of his saddle animal. Chad remained, arms crossed, bitterly watching, but he did nothing to interfere.

Buckner had to waste time because the wounded Indian sagged badly a couple of times. When he got to the horse, eventually, the Indian looked back and grunted.

The Muleshoe men were clustered around their range boss. They were mounted, but there were no spare horses. That meant the two dead cowboys would have to make the trip to the home place flopping behind someone's cantle.

Ladd propped the Apache against a sickly pine with yellowing needles, held the reins to his drowsing horse, and waited a long while leaning upon his Winchester. But the range hands did not come. Maybe Holmes had given an order that the men had obeyed, or, more likely, he had not given any order at all but had simply pointed out that Ladd Buckner was no one to fool with, if he chose to oppose them, and they did not need any more casualties, certainly not over one lousy raghead who was probably going to die anyway.

The Muleshoe men turned off southwesterly after loading their dead men and rode off without a rearward glance.

Buckner continued to wait. The Indian watched him and seemed to get weaker as the moments passed. By the time

Buckner thought it was safe now to head out, the Apache weakly held aloft a hand and wagged his head.

"No good," he muttered in mission English. "No more good for me."

Ladd knelt, leaned aside the Winchester, and pulled back the bandage he had created from the raghead's shirt. There was almost no external bleeding, but the flesh around the point of entry of the perforating bullet was turning a bad shade of blue. It was not as noticeable on the Indian's hide as it would have been on a hide with less basic pigment, but it was still clear enough. There was no swelling, though. Perhaps there would not have been swelling in any case since the bullet went into the man's mid body in the soft parts and emerged out of his back the same way, in the soft parts.

Buckner put the bandage back in place and said: "You give up awful easy, Apache. I've been hit harder than that in the mouth and never even stopped talking."

The Indian was sick, which he had every right to be, but it amounted to more than a reaction to being injured; he was also demoralized and beaten. His type of people died very easily, almost handily, when these conditions combined against them.

Buckner went to his saddlebag and returned with a pony of brandy that he poured into the dull-eyed Indian. The Apache choked and almost gagged, then his eyes copiously watered, but their brightness momentarily returned, and, as he panted, his stare at Ladd Buckner remained quizzically bleak but interested. He clearly could not imagine why a range man would go to this trouble over him.

Ladd stoppered the pony and hunkered opposite the Indian as he said: "Now listen to me, strongheart. We're going out of here, you on the horse, me walking ahead of it. Do you understand what I'm saying?"

The Indian understood. "I ride, you lead."

"Yeah. Now tell me where your people are, because I can't take you down to the cowman's town and I'm not going to sit around up here in among the trees for a couple of weeks until you can make it on your own. You tell me, and I'll take you pretty close to where they'll find you, then we'll part. You understand?"

This time the Indian said: "Why?"

Ladd considered the bottle he was holding. "Because I don't like murdering folks. You wouldn't understand." He arose and glanced over both shoulders. The land was totally empty as far as a man could see in three directions. It was probably equally as empty northward back up through the forest but there was no way to be sure of that since visibility was limited to the first tangle of trees.

The Indian jutted his chin. "Cowman go there," he gutturally muttered, indicating the southwesterly distance Chad Holmes and his Muleshoe men had taken. Evidently the Apache knew this territory well enough, and evidently he thought Ladd Buckner would be interested in where the nearest ranch might be.

Ladd did not care in the least where the Muleshoe Ranch was. He leaned to hoist the Indian. Without a word he roughly reared back and boosted the Apache across his own saddle. The Indian locked his jaws and fumbled for the saddle horn, then held on with his face averted. He was in great pain.

Ladd did not replace the Winchester in its saddle boot. It was another burden to be shouldered as he walked ahead, leading the horse, but close to fainting or not, that raghead up there was still capable of making a murderous effort. They skirted around the nearby cañon and angled up into the foothills where the muggy heat was noticeably oppressive, and once the Indian almost turned loose all over and fell, but Ladd caught him, swore at him, and roughly straightened him up again. Then he handed up the pony of brandy, waited until the bronco had taken down two more swallows, and struck out again.

Finally the Indian dripped sweat and got light-headed, so Ladd had to rest beside a deep little narrow creek. Here, he upended several full hats of cold water over the raghead, and, when the Indian recovered and was able to be moved again, Ladd asked where the Apache ranchería would be.

The bronco would not confide in him. He simply pointed vaguely and said: "Put me down four, five miles. Put me down out there."

Ladd used up the last of his brandy getting his ward ahead that far, but he made it just ahead of full darkness, and, as he eased the bronco down and was leaning over, he said—"Good luck, you murderous son-of-a-bitch."—and swung up over leather to retrace his way back down toward the grassland again.

He had no feeling of having done a Christian deed, if indeed that was what it had been, since an awful lot of non-Christians had done similar things. All he thought of as he picked his way through the darkness to the last of the uplands and emerged back upon the rangeland was that he'd done what he'd felt needed doing and that was the end of it—and from now on, when he came up out of a cañon in the Tomahawk Meadow countryside, he would look first before he rode right on out.

III

They were having a fiesta of some kind the day Ladd Buckner reconnoitered Piñon, then rode on in and put up his horse at the livery barn. There was a lot of that reedy kind of lilting Mexican music over in the cottonwood grove east of the town plaza, which usually went with celebrations in the Southwest. At the livery barn all a little bandy-legged oldster had told him was that one of those traveling troupes of pepper-belly play actors had driven into town the night before last and had set up their stage over between Mex town and the business section of Piñon. It did not have to be a fiesta then at all.

It was late in the day. Ladd needed a bath, a shave, and a place to stay, and he was in no big hurry, so he went first to a café opposite the jailhouse for a meal, and after that he walked the roadway on both sides, familiarizing himself with the town of Piñon, and finally he strolled to the shaded front of the harness and saddle works to stand out front, hands clasped loosely behind him, and gazed at the manufactured goods on display beyond the wavery glass window. The work was excellent. In fact, even people who did not appreciate the full expertise of the Piñon harness maker would have been impressed. Whoever he was, he was no novice; he had not been a novice according to Ladd Buckner's guess in perhaps forty or fifty years, and this was not only the truth, it also happened to be the reason he had his harness works up for sale.

An open-faced, tousle-headed young cowboy walked up, leaned to see what Ladd was admiring, and amiably said—"Sure is the best, ain't he?"—and passed southward without awaiting a reply.

Ladd stepped to the doorway, but the shop was locked. There was no one at the workbench or behind the counter inside. It was not really that late, but evidently this particular merchant thought it was, because he clearly had closed up shop for the day.

Across at the saloon there was a spindly little coming and going, mostly it seemed of townsmen who were coming from the direction of the Mex music and play acting, as though perhaps whatever play was being enacted over there induced thirst. Ladd went in search of the hotel and found that Piñon had instead a boarding house. He got a room, then paid an extra two bits for a chunk of tan lye soap and a scorched old towel. He followed the arrows to the bathhouse carrying his one and only change of attire from the bags on the saddle he had brought up with him from the livery barn. Bathing was always work, unless a man did it in a creek, and then it was usually uncomfortably cold. At least this time he got warm water from the great brass kettles atop the old cook stove, and could draw the cold water by pulling a corncob out of the hollowed log that served as a pipe from some distant spring.

When he was clean and freshly dressed and even neatly shaved, he hung the gun and belt around his middle, emptied the tub, and trooped back inside with the towel and soap. Darkness had settled. Piñon was ready for one of those fragrant, bland summertime nights, and the Mexican musicians were at it again over at the cottonwood park east of town where nearly all local celebrations and fiestas were held.

He had a drink at the saloon, then ambled over where light from a long row of guttering candles at the foot of an improvised stage helped him select which vacant seat among the hand-squared big old cottonwood logs, arranged in ranks like benches, best suited his requirements. He did not have to get as close to the footlights as some men did; he could see well enough from midway back. And it was awfully hot down that close to those burning candles. Nor did anyone actually have to get that close anyway, unless they wanted to. There was a full moon this night.

Mexican urchins passed soundlessly back and forth on bare feet showing vast smiles as they sought to sell pieces of candy—chunks of squash soaked overnight in brown sugar water. Several cowboys who had already made too many trips back to the saloon were behind Ladd making remarks about the buxom leading lady, a sturdy woman in her thirties with a magnificent downy mustache, who swooned into the arms of the hero at regular intervals, but only after he had got his legs braced. In fact, as Ladd sat there eating his chunk of candy watching the performance, he noticed that the tall, handsome hero of the play in his elaborate but not very clean soldier's uniform knew exactly when the buxom woman would throw herself at him. The hero began preparing himself moments in advance. Even then, several times she made him stagger.

The musicians were exceptionally gifted. The difficulty arose from the fact that, although they never once left their darkened places beyond the lighted stage as most of the male audience did, from time to time the musicians kept getting out of tune and off-key as the evening advanced. They had bottles of pulque and tequila discreetly cached close around where they sat.

The plot of the drama had to do with the buxom lady's enormously difficult struggle to retain her virtue against the lecherous machinations of a rather portly civilian twice her age who knew every way to achieve his dastardly ends. She wavered between yielding, and rushing into the arms of the heroic soldier who was her true lover but who kept going off to join in wars and revolutions, until, near the end of the play, with all the participants perspiring profusely as a result of the heat generated by all those candles, the buxom heroine was finally caught out by the evil, leering, portly villain. In her subsequent despair, self-loathing, abysmal agony and anguish, she used up the entire third act that culminated in her suicide.

Ladd had another piece of the sugar-soaked squash and wandered away from the cottonwood grove. But most of the other spectators lingered until the final act when the big woman plunged a shiny dagger into her ample cleavage, and sank with many outcries and lamentations to the stage at the feet of her heavily perspiring soldier lover. She required almost a full five minutes to expire, during which the portly villain, standing just out of the candlelight in gloom and shadows, leered and dry-washed his hands and chuckled, something that prompted all the Mexicans in the audience to hiss fiercely at him. A number of the non-Mexican audience also joined in and someone hurled a carrot that missed but that nonetheless inspired the villain to move back a little farther into the shadows.

Ladd finished his candy and rolled a smoke while standing near a huge old cottonwood tree where a number of other men idly stood. One of them said: "Last year someone fired a shot over his head"—meaning the villain—"and the troupe was mad as hell next day because they could not find their villain for the next play."

Ladd grinned and looked at the speaker. He was a graying, tall man with a droopy mustache and a nickeled badge on his shirtfront. As Ladd lit up, he said: "That lady's pretty stocky to be hurling herself into the arms of the general . . . or whatever he is."

The lawman agreed. "Yes. She's been piling it on for the past three, four years. I recollect her first performance here in Piñon. She was a slip of a woman. Well, the Mex taste runs to hefty ones." The lawman looked around with a wry twinkle. "I sort of agree with that myself. I just never cared much for mustaches, though."

They grinned together, then Ladd wandered off back in the direction of the town's main business area. It was a very pleasant night, and probably because it was midweek there did not appear to be many range men in town. Maybe that helped the town remain calm and relatively quiet and peaceful.

A man driving a dusty top buggy rolled past with his little lamps lighted and merrily glinting. The man had on a dented plug hat and a rusty old frock coat. There was a small black leather satchel visible upon the seat at his side. He was a somewhat stocky individual, round-faced, and not very old-looking. He saw Ladd and nodded as though they were acquainted, then kept right on rolling in the direction of the livery barn.

Southward and upon the east side of the road there was a small office sandwiched between two larger buildings with the legend Doctor Enos Orcutt upon the window in elegant gold letters. Ladd guessed that had been Dr. Orcutt who had just driven past. Not many other occupations required a person to haul a little leather satchel around with them. Also, plug hats seemed to go with the frontier medical profession.

At the saloon a snub-nosed, red-faced, bull-built older man brought Ladd's beer and nodded genially at him as though he knew a stranger when he saw one and was perfectly willing to welcome strangers to Piñon. His name was Joe Reilly and at one time he had been a career soldier, but a musket ball at Antietam had cut short that career, something Joe had sworn up and down ever since was the best, and most painful, thing that had ever happened to him. Perhaps because there was not much trade right at the moment he lingered at Ladd Buckner's end of the bar to talk a little. When Ladd explained who he was and why he had come to Piñon, the saloon man grew warmly expansive. It seemed that Joe Reilly was by nature an accommodating, friendly man.

"It's the rheumatics," he explained, "that made old Warner put his works up for sale. Some days it's so bad he can scarcely close a fist. Other days he can sew a harness tug without any pain. He told me just a couple of days back that if he couldn't sell out directly, he'd just have to hold an auction, then head on out to his daughter in California." Reilly was also interested in Buckner's ability. "You been a saddle maker long, then?"

Ladd replied without sounding as though he felt a compulsion to explain: "Best way for me to demonstrate, I expect, would be to work a few weeks with Mister Warner. All the bragging in the world wouldn't make me a harness maker, would it?"

Joe smiled. "You're right. And in these parts, Mister Buckner, folks judge a man by what he can do, for a fact."

Ladd said: "It's a nice town. Pretty and all . . . with trees and flowers."

"We got water," stated the saloon man. "That's what makes the difference, you know. A town can have the prettiest view and the nicest settin' and the friendliest folks, and without water it's nothing." He could have added "especially in Arizona" but he didn't, probably because anyone who knew anything at all realized that water, or rather the shortage of it, had always been Arizona's biggest dilemma. "You'll like folks hereabouts," stated Reilly, who had been in the Piñon country for eleven years now.

"How about Indians?" asked Ladd mildly, and Reilly's geniality vanished in a second. "Them lousy sons-of-bitches," he boomed. "Yes, we've got 'em. Sneakin' little murderin' raghead scuts, they are. They can steal the horse right out from under a man without him knowin' it, they can. Slit throats of fellers who are lyin' in their bedrolls. They're the curse of the territory, Mister Buckner. I got to admit we got 'em. Wouldn't be honest not to warn folks against the bandy-legged little mud-colored bastards." The matter of Apaches usually brought up a related subject in the territory. It did now, with Joe Reilly. "And the bloody Army!" he exclaimed. "What does it do, I'd like to ask you? Not a darned thing, that's what. It goes chasing Mex horse thieves all over the countryside, and doesn't even acknowledge the ragheads. I tell you, Mister Buckner, when I was soljering, we looked at things a lot different. In those days we'd hunt them down and scrub them out down to the nits. Nowadays the Army's soft and riddled with politics."

As soon as the saloon man paused for a breath, Ladd moved in swiftly to change the subject. "What time does Mister Warner open his harness shop in the mornings?"

Reilly had to wait a moment until his adrenalin diminished before replying. "Oh, I'd say about eight o'clock. Yes, usually about eight. I see him over there about then."

Ladd paid for his beer, smiled his thanks, and left the saloon carrying away with him a critical bit of local lore. Never mention Apaches around Joe Reilly unless you wanted to be skewered to the bar front while Reilly got it all out of his system.

IV

Three weeks of sleeping on the ground followed by one night of sleeping in a boarding house bed seemed to signify a change in the life style of Ladd Buckner. When he went forth in Piñon the following morning, early, and walked both sides of the town before heading in the direction of the café, he was beginning to feel that he belonged, and yet he hadn't even known Piñon had a bank until he paused in the new day chilly dawn light out front of a square little ugly red brick building to read the sign: The Stockgrowers' Trust & Savings Bank of Piñon, Arizona Territory. There was someone's name beneath all that fine lettering but Ladd looked in at the barred windows ignoring the name, then continued on his way to the café.

Five or six laborers were already at the café counter, wolfing down breakfast, and one of them who was called Abe by the others had a magnificent black eye that was the unavoidable butt of all kinds of rough comments among the others. Evidently they all knew one another. It was impossible for Ladd to believe those other men would have teased the man with the black eye if they hadn't all been friends, especially since the man with the black eye stood better than six feet tall and weighed well over two hundred pounds.

The café man did not come for Ladd's order. He instead brought coffee and a platter of steak, hashed spuds, and a piece of warm apple pie. The pie in particular was unbelievably delectable, and yet to look at the slovenly café man it was hard to believe he could have made such a thing.

An older man arrived, sat next to Ladd, and, as he reached for the tinned milk to weaken his coffee, he winced and exasperatedly said: "God damn rheumatics."

Ladd handed over the tinned milk and gazed at his neighbor. The man was at least sixty and in fact probably was seventy years old. He was tall and gaunt and scarred. His hands were stained and work-roughened. Ladd said: "You wouldn't be Mister Warner, would you?"

The old man finished washing down his coffee, then looked over. "I'd be," he admitted.

Ladd introduced himself and smiled. "I been on the trail three weeks getting down here after seeing an ad you had in a newspaper up north."

The old man's eyes brightened. "Is that a fact? About the harness works?"

"Yes."

"Well, well," stated old Warner, and pushed out a hand. "Shake, son, then we'll finish eatin' and walk across the road." Warner reached for his knife and fork. "You married by any chance?"

Ladd wasn't. "No, sir. I'm single."

"That's good," stated the harness maker, "because the shop'll make a decent livin' for one person, but it won't support no woman, too, and no kids." Warner studied Ladd a moment as he chewed. After he swallowed, he asked another question. "You got enough real money to buy me out?"

"Depends on how much you got to have," stated Ladd.

"Well . . . five hundred dollars?"

Ladd took his time about answering. He drank coffee, hacked at his breakfast steak with a dull knife, looked around, then smiled at old Warner. "Kind of hard to eat and talk business at the same time," he murmured.

Old Warner had to be satisfied, then, until their meals were finished and they passed out into the new day sunlight. The town marshal was passing and unsmilingly nodded at them, his gray gaze flickering in recognition over Ladd Buckner. Across the road in the harness shop the smell was pleasantly familiar; it was an amalgam of tobacco smoke, new leather, and horse sweat, but mostly it was of new leather.

Old Warner puttered, handling tools, talking as he moved from workbench to cutting table to sewing horse and finally to the counter and the hangers where repair work hung, each article with a scrap of paper on it giving a name and a price in cryptic longhand. It required no great power of observation to see how difficult this day was for the old man. He had spent a major portion of his life here, good years and bad, wet years and drought years. He had buried a wife while operating this business, had raised two children, only one of which, a daughter, had survived, and from that front window he had watched dozens of friends he had known most of his life pass by for the last time.

Finally he went over to poke some life into a small cast-iron stove and to place a dirty old graniteware coffee pot atop it, and to remove his hat and scratch, then resettle the hat as he said: "What can you stand, son?"

Ladd had one thousand dollars in Union greenbacks in a belt around his middle. Five hundred of it was in old-style notes, five hundred was in later, and crisper, greenbacks. He said: "Mister Warner, I can't buy it and sell it, too. You put on a price, and, if it's too much, I'll just walk back out of here, and if it's not too much, we'll shake on it."

Old Warner was aged and lined and stooped but his eyes were as clear as new glass while he made his judgment, then said: "Five hundred dollars, Mister Buckner." He smiled a trifle sadly. "It's worth more, but I'd a sight rather see you succeed than have to operate hand to mouth only to get cleaned out if a bad year hit the range and folks didn't come in very much. You keep back what you got to have to operate on and give me five hundred, and tomorrow morning I'll be on the stage to California."

They shook hands, then Ladd went to the workbench, reached inside his shirt to unbuckle and remove the money belt, and under the frankly interested gaze of old Warner he counted out $500. In turn, the harness maker wrote him out a painstakingly clear and inclusive bill of sale, then, after handing this over, Warner turned and looked around, and turned back with a grim-faced little nod.

"Treat it good, son, and it'll do as much for you. It's a fair and decent livin' and it's got a reputation for doing right by folks."

Ladd went out to the shaded overhang with the harness maker, feeling poignant and sad for the old man.

Warner turned and smiled as he said: "Good luck, son. Someday you'll come to this day, the same as I came to it, and I sure hope you can turn it over to the next young buck with a plumb clear conscience."

Ladd watched old Warner trudge northward in the direction of the stage station, watched him turn in up there, then he also turned and walked away, heading for his new business. He was experienced. He was a good saddle maker. In fact, he had more experience at saddle making than he had working up sets of harness. For a couple of hours, until the liveryman brought in four broken leather halters, Ladd examined the patterns and templates. The liveryman looked surprised. After a moment of explaining what he wanted done to the halters, he looked up with a squint and said: "You're the new harness maker?"

Ladd introduced himself. "Yeah. Mister Warner sold out to me."

"You're young," said the liveryman, who was not quite old Warner's age but who was fast approaching it.

Ladd smiled. "I'll hang around Piñon until I can remedy that," he said. "Tell you what. I'll repair your halters, and, if you don't like my work, you don't have to pay for it. Fair?"

The liveryman nodded. "Fair." He walked out without offering his hand or smiling. In a place no larger than Piñon where most residents had been there all their lives or at least for over a dozen years, newcomers were never viewed with frank delight, first off. Barring Joe Reilly, Ladd did not expect to be taken to the town's heart by its established residents until he had earned that kind of recognition. He was willing to work for it. He had his reasons for being willing to work for respect and acceptance. If even Joe Reilly had known the reason for his willingness to do this, Joe would probably have been just a tad more reserved in his association with Ladd Buckner. As it was, Joe got his first outside opinion of Buckner three days after old Warner had departed forever from Piñon, and the new saddle and harness maker was organizing his time and materials to turn out his first riding saddle as the newest businessman in Piñon.

Chad Holmes of Muleshoe rode into town with two of his cow camp men on the seat of a ranch wagon, and, while the rig was being loaded around back at the dock of the general store, Chad and his range men went up to the saloon for beer. There, Joe Reilly mentioned the new harness maker, only to discover that the men from Muleshoe already knew him. In fact, as the range men told the story to Reilly, Ladd Buckner was a dead shot with his carbine and one of the best fellows in the entire territory to have on your side in a skirmish with ragheads.

Joe inevitably broadcast this tale. Ladd did not know the Muleshoe men had been in town. Neither Chad nor the others came across to the harness works to see him. The first Ladd knew that his episode on Tomahawk Meadow had finally reached town was when two teenage embryonic cowboys who lived with their parents in town arrived at the saddle shop one afternoon to stare and smile a lot, and finally to blurt out that they had heard Ladd was a professional Indian fighter, and that he had come along and had single-handedly routed an entire war party of Mescalero Apaches, the worst of the lot, with only his Winchester.

Ladd laughed, then came over to the counter to lean there and explain exactly what had happened out there, beginning with his own very strong desire to be anywhere else when he rode up out of the cañon and found himself in the middle of a fierce little gunfight. The boys left, finally, to spread the word that along with being probably the most formidable Indian fighter since Al Sieber, Piñon's new harness maker was also a man imbued with that most valued of all frontier ethics—modesty.

It all helped. Joe Reilly did his share, too, and whatever some people, most particularly womenfolk, thought of Reilly's profession, people were inclined to trust his judgment of humanity. Joe favored Ladd Buckner, so it became a lot easier for folks to smile a little, and to nod. The liveryman, too, admitted that old Warner hadn't been able to sew as well in years, when he got his busted halters back. "And he's makin' a saddle," stated the liveryman to his cronies out front in tree shade at the loafers' bench near the stone trough. "He's an honest workman. No danged copper rivets in the rigging. It's every bit of it hand-stitched and buckskin-threaded. That's how I tell an honest man. When he does something right, even when he knows it ain't going to show when he's through with it."

"But he's young," muttered one of the townsmen who regularly sat down there out front of the livery barn chewing cut plug and whittling on soft cottonwood chunks.

"Well, God dammit," stated the exasperated liveryman, "so was you, once, Al, although darn' few of us can remember it now. Anyway, give him enough time and he'll outgrow that."

"He'll probably raise the prices," grumbled another older man. "They all do. Let some new feller come to town and buy in, and the first thing he'll do every time is raise the blasted prices."

The liveryman had a retort for that, too. "Tell you how I feel about that. He fixed up four busted halters for me and hardly charged enough to cover the thread let alone the time. I figure I'm that much ahead right now, so the next few times he could even charge me a mite more and I'd still be breaking even."

The other older men went silent and remained that way for a while about the new harness maker. Therefore, what possible good could come out it if the liveryman, who was favorably impressed, continued in pressing this discussion? None, of course. Eventually one of the old men got back upon a topic that they never wearied of, and that they never agreed upon, either, but that they could discuss and swear about and denounce one another over without much danger of actually hurting anyone's feelings—politics.

No one else in Piñon cared a whoop about politics, and generally for a very good reason. They did not live in a state of the federal Union; they resided in a territory, and since all the territorial areas of the U.S. were administered by the Army, there was very little of the elective process to make politics interesting. Otherwise, of course, there were the national elections, but out in Arizona someone could run for President and even be elected, and Arizonans would not even know who he was for several weeks after he'd moved into the White House. It usually took that long for the news to reach isolated cow communities like Piñon.

V

For Ladd Buckner there were a number of concerns to take precedence over such things as politics, and he was not, and never had been, very politically aware. Like most people out in the territories, living from day to day with hardship, privation, and real peril, politics like a lively social involvement constituted a luxury. It would be a full generation yet before the cow country would be able to afford a socialized strata or a politically active environment. Presently as Ladd told Town Marshal Tom Wharton when the lawman strolled in for coffee and a visit one morning, perpetuating a habit he had established fifteen years earlier with old man Warner, if a person could just eat three times a day, keep dry, and pay his bills, he was probably doing about as well as folks could expect to do in Arizona Territory.

Tom Wharton, who was quite a bit older than Ladd Buckner, who had run the gamut from Indian scout to buffalo hunter, to range man and lawman, sipped coffee over by the stove and slowly nodded his head. "And keep out of trouble," he added, watching Ladd buck stitch a bucking roll. "Eat, keep dry, pay the bills, and keep out of trouble." He eyed Ladd Buckner thoughtfully. "You haven't met Doctor Orcutt yet, have you? Well, sir, he told me one time that it was his opinion that, if folks out here didn't get shot or snake bit or horse kicked, they'd probably live longer than the national average. It's healthy out here. The air is clean, the food is natural, the water's not bad from too many years of folks abusing it."

"Just keep away from ragheads," said Ladd whimsically. "Don't set in any drafts, and maybe mind your own business a little."

Tom Wharton sparingly smiled. He rarely smiled any other way. "You've got it about right." He watched the strong, deft hands working at the sewing horse. "You sew well," he said. "That's sure going to be one hell of a good saddle when you're finished with it. You know, when old Warner was younger, I didn't think there was a better man with leather in the territory. I'm beginnin' to figure you might be just as good." Marshal Wharton finished his coffee, rinsed the cup, and draped it from the nail above the cutting table where it had hung suspended beside old Warner's coffee mug for years. "I'll break the habit," he told Ladd, "if it bothers you to have a person bargin' in first thing each morning and having a cup of java. It's just that old Warner and I had that arrangement for many years, and now I got it as a habit."

Ladd looked up from the sewing horse. "Nothing's going to change very much in the shop," he told the lawman with a little warm smile. "I'll keep putting the pot on first thing, Marshal."

"Tom," said the lawman, winked, and strolled out into the sunlight of a new day.

Ladd had an opportunity to meet the man Marshal Wharton had spoken of that same afternoon when the medical practitioner walked in to have the grip on his satchel repaired. It had broken loose. As Dr. Orcutt said, they just didn't put handles onto things like they did when he was first in practice a number of years back. Then he laughed at himself. Up close, Ladd got his first good look at the doctor, and came to the conclusion that, although Enos Orcutt looked quite young, he was probably in his forties. Ladd also made another judgment of the doctor. Enos Orcutt talked and acted, and even looked like a man who marched to the cadence of his own drummer. It was a good judgment; if there was one thing Dr. Orcutt was known for around the countryside, it was an independent mind and manner. When other medical men were prescribing purgatives for appendicitis, Dr. Orcutt was applying ice packs and performing swift surgery. He left Ladd with a feeling that he would be a good man to put one's trust in.

When Ladd handed over the repaired satchel, the doctor said: "Perfect match for the first time it was ever done, after I bought the satchel up in Colorado, Mister Buckner. That time it lasted six years, the longest it's ever lasted."

Ladd smiled. "Doctor, try putting it down and lifting it up. No leather on earth can stand too much roughness."

Enos Orcutt smiled back, but skeptically. "Mister Buckner, in my business you don't always have time to put something down or lift it up. Sometimes you have to toss your satchel into the buggy, and sometimes you also have to yank it with you when you jump out of the rig. But I'll try. How much?"

"Ten cents," replied Ladd, and watched the doctor count out the small silver coins.

As Orcutt headed for the door he said: "You come from Colorado, did you?"

Ladd nodded, then puzzled a little over that question. Why had the doctor asked it, and why hadn't he said Idaho, Oregon, Wyoming, or Montana? It did not matter. Ladd went back to do some of the repair work that had trickled in over the past week or so. He had learned long ago that the articles folks brought to be repaired were important to them on a day-to-day basis and the surest way to antagonize people was not to have their articles ready when they called for them.

The liveryman returned, this time with a woman's side-saddle that had slipped under a horse, had dumped its rider but without serious injury, although the agitated horse had proceeded to kick the saddle unmercifully until someone could control the beast and remove the outfit. Ladd looked at the remains without commenting, and the liveryman, who was watching Ladd's face as some sort of gauge as to what the repair bill might be, finally said: "It's genuine old Kentucky spring seat, Ladd. It'd be a blessed shame to toss it into the rubbish heap. They don't make spring seats any more."

Ladd avoided a definite commitment by saying: "Come back day after tomorrow." The reason he gave no commitment was because he was unsure of the actual condition of the tree beneath the leather. If the tree were still sound, then all he would have to do would be replace a lot of leather. If the tree were smashed . . .

Tom Wharton, in one of his pre-breakfast morning coffee sessions, told Ladd how the accident had occurred that had resulted in the ruin of the side-saddle. "Darned kids walking down the alley with a big old yeller mongrel were pitching rocks for the dog to chase. They rolled a stone directly under the damned horse and it took to bucking. The cincha was loose anyway. The lady wasn't hurt." Tom's gray eyes assumed their near smile as he said: "Maybe she'll be eating off the mantel for a few days, though."

Ladd put the side-saddle upon a workhorse and showed Tom Wharton the extent of the damage. He also showed him how a genuine spring seat was constructed, and, although Marshal Wharton was interested, up to a point, in the articles of a trade that had been as much a part of his life as anything else, the saddle was a woman's rig, and Ladd Buckner discovered a probable reason for Tom Wharton's single status. He did not show the least interest in the Kentucky saddle because it had been made for women; he clearly did not have much regard for womenfolk.

"The father of the lad who owned the yellow dog," Marshal Wharton related, "was going to whale the daylights out of the dog. I stopped him on the grounds that the dog didn't do a blessed thing he wasn't supposed to do . . . which was obey his master. Then the damned fool was going to larrup his lad, and I stopped that, also. The boy had no idea the rock would roll under that darned horse."

Wharton sighed, refilled his cup, and stood, wide-legged, where he could see past Ladd across in the direction of the roadway window. Out yonder in the yellow-lemon summertime heat, roadway dust arose from the slightest motion, and as near as the far side of the road there were dancing heat waves. Full summer had arrived. There probably was no place on earth where full summertime could be as unnerving, as generally debilitating, as it could be in Arizona Territory.

"If I'd learnt a trade instead of always having to rush over and see what was on the far side of every blessed mountain," mused Marshal Wharton, "I'd probably right now be doing what you're doing, Ladd, and the good Lord knows it's a sight better than being a lawman." He paused to sip coffee, and to say it afterward exactly as he had been thinking it. "As an aging lawman."

Later in the day the foreman of the forge, which was near the south end of Piñon on the opposite side of the road, brought up a torn running-W to be repaired, and lingered to explain what had happened. It was a highly unusual horse that could not only survive a bout with a running-W, but that could break one of the things. This horse, according to the sweat-stained blacksmith, had not only broken the taming rig but he had also turned back, charged through the shop, put six grown men to flight, and had hit one old loafer with his shoulder, knocking him into the black water of the cooling barrel. The blacksmith smiled broadly. Ladd laughed along with the blacksmith. He promised to fix the rig so that it would not break again.

After the second week it was beginning to be predictable, how he would conduct the business, how much trade would come through his doorway, what the possible livelihood would net him, and, since the living quarters off the back of the little wooden building was his home and his only outside expenses involved supplies from Denver and an occasional drink across the road at the saloon, or breakfast and maybe supper at the café, he could pretty well estimate what the years up ahead held in store for him. Many men would never have settled for that. Many men would have felt stifled by the sameness of the routine and the predictability of the days, week in and week out. Ladd

Buckner not only did not feel stifled; he settled into his routine with clear comfort and pleasure. And he was a good leather man. Even those skeptical old-timers who hung around the bench out front of the livery barn and who had for the most part been critical of every newcomer as well as every change and innovation ultimately decided after closely inspecting the new harness maker's work that he was not just good at his trade but that he was also a credit to the community.

Homage came slowly, but not as slowly as it could have come. Ladd accepted it like he learned to accept a lot of things in the Piñon countryside. Mainly he became passive because he had his work and he enjoyed every day of it. Other things could fit in, or not, as they chose, or as the people around him caused them to fit or not; he didn't care in particular, perhaps because as the weeks and days passed he became more and more aware that his work was approved of not only by the townsmen, the blacksmith, the doctor, and the liveryman, but also by the outlying cow outfits. He had repaired saddles, bridles, even boots and chaps, suspended all along one wall awaiting the irregular return trips to Piñon by men of the distant cow ranges.

Bert Taylor who owned and operated The Tomahawk Valley General Mercantile & Dry Goods Emporium was also Ladd Buckner's source of credit information, but as a matter of fact most of the people who brought in articles to be repaired, or who purchased new items, had a definite use and a need for them. Cow country was seldom where people defaulted on debts to merchants. Occasionally a cowboy would ride off and never return, or perhaps be killed out on the range somewhere, but harness makers rarely lost money. The repair bill on just about any saddle, bridle, pack outfit, or pair of boots never exceeded its saleable value. Ladd, in fact, made more money than old Warner had been making the last few years before he had sold out and left the country. The reason, according to Bert Taylor, whose store was across the way, was simply that old Warner's eyes had been failing him and his hands hadn't been up to the demands made upon them, with the inevitable result being that his work had suffered. Much that ordinarily should have come to Piñon went elsewhere to be rebuilt or repaired. Now it was beginning to trickle back to Piñon again.

Ladd was busy, and he was good at his trade, and once when Dr. Orcutt and Marshal Wharton came together at Reilly's bar for a nightcap, the doctor made a remark about someone as young as Ladd Buckner being as experienced and skilled at his trade being extremely rare, and Tom Wharton had leaned there, studying his empty shot glass for a long while before saying: "Enos, you don't just figure he's a natural leather man."

Dr. Orcutt agreed. "No, I don't. He sewed the grip on my satchel exactly the way a man from the Colorado penitentiary sewed it one time. I've only seen that kind of loop-through knotting done by men who've learned their trade in prison."

Marshal Wharton looked up with a sardonic, vague smile. "Funny you should say that, Doc. A while back I was over there, having coffee and watching Ladd work on a busted side-saddle. He made the identical routine moves a feller did I once sent to prison in Colorado, and who also learned his trade there, and came back to the territory years later, where I visited him in his harness works over near Tombstone. Funny we should both notice that, Doctor."

VI

Tom Wharton wrote to the authorities of the federal penitentiary in Colorado. It was a routine letter of enquiry by a man who was usually curious about people and things without ever being excessively interested. Wharton was pretty much of a live-and-let-live individual. But he was tough and thoroughly capable when he was required to be. He had that kind of a reputation and he had not acquired it by just talk.

When he had his morning coffee at the harness shop one clear, still, and azure early morning about a month after Ladd Buckner had taken over as harness and saddle maker, he had the reply to that letter he'd sent up to Colorado in a shirt pocket, folded neatly and buttoned out of sight. He made no mention of it. As a matter of fact for as long as Tom Wharton lived, he never mentioned that letter.

He stood and watched Ladd at work, and, when he'd finished his coffee and was ready to go forth into the rising morning heat, he turned at the door and said: "Ladd, Chad Holmes was by the jailhouse yesterday. We had us quite a talk. Your name came up."

The harness maker did not raise up from the cutting table but he lifted his eyes in a quizzical way. "He mentioned that little tussle at Tomahawk Meadow, did he?"

Wharton nodded. "Yeah, seems him and the other Muleshoe fellers are still talking about the way you handled that Winchester. They were also still talkin' about you holding back a hurt raghead. They wondered whatever became of him."

Ladd could understand that because he'd occasionally wondered the same thing. "I took him up within shouting distance of his ranchería and left him, and that's all I know," Ladd told Marshal Wharton. "I sort of figure he probably died. He was hard hit through the carcass."

The lawman was not convinced. "They're tough. They're tough enough to survive just about anything but a direct head or heart shot. I know, I've seen my share of 'em down a rifle barrel, and I've gone up afterward only to discover that the feller who was supposed to be dead had gone and crawled plumb away." Tom leaned in the doorway. Out in the roadway, northward to judge from the sounds they made, a number of horsemen entered town at a hard lope. Shod hoofs made a ringing sound over either rock or hardpan and this late in the summertime Piñon's roadway was purest hardpan. The lawman casually looked, then just as indifferently turned to gaze back where Ladd was leaning. "Muleshoe's making a legend out of the way you came up out of that cañon and busted into those ragheads like you was the cavalry." Wharton showed that vague, faint sardonic smile of his and straightened around to stroll away.

Ladd saw him take one step, then whip straight up in what looked from the rear as complete astonishment. He whipped straight up and hung there for perhaps five seconds, then he ripped out a muffled curse, and Ladd saw his body loosen, begin to settle flat down as Marshal Wharton went for his gun. Two carbines erupted. It sounded to Ladd Buckner as though one carbine was northward upon the opposite side of the roadway while the other carbine was on the same side as his harness works, but northward about as far as the stage station.

Tom Wharton went back drunkenly against the front wall of the harness shop, then loosened the grip on his six-gun, and turned very slowly with Ladd frozen in place, staring. Wharton continued to turn until he was staring straight at Ladd, then he turned loose all over, and collapsed in a heap.

Up the road someone sang out in a sing-song sort of chant with his words being indistinguishable. Ladd pulled back, laid aside his cutting knife, wiped both hands on the apron, then reached back and systematically untied the thong, pitched the apron atop the table, and walked toward the doorway. He picked the six-gun from its holster upon a wall-peg just inside his shop, and walked out where the lawman was lying.

Up in front of the bank three armed men faced outward across the roadway with carbines cocked and held two-handed, ready. Another rifleman was indeed up in front of the stage station upon Ladd's same side of the road. Otherwise, the roadway was totally empty. Whether this happened to be a natural condition, or whether those two gunshots had emptied the roadway, was anyone's guess. Ladd studied the men at the tie rack out front of the bank, then moved slightly to step past Tom Wharton. Nothing happened. He saw all he had to see, up yonder, then slowly turned and gazed downward.

There was nothing anyone could do for Marshal Wharton. He had caught both of those slugs high in the body. He was either dead or within a breath of being dead. Ladd swung forward again, sank deliberately to one knee, and called ahead: "You at the tie rack!"

That was all; he simply called forth as though he meant to catch the attention of those men up there, and the next moment when one of those bank robbers stepped ahead to take his stance, Ladd shot him through the chest. The man fell, his carbine bounced against the plank walk, and those other outlaws swung to begin firing. Ladd was not the best target in the world, in shadows out of the bitter sunlight in front of his shop and beneath its overhang, but they could see him clearly enough if they made the effort, and they were certainly attempting to do that as they began firing.

It sounded like the Indian skirmish all over again. Gunfire built up to a fierce crescendo, then another of those horsemen up yonder dropped on his face, and the man over in front of the stage station suddenly panicked and raced as hard as he could over to join his companions out front of the bank. Ladd tracked this running man, aimed lower than before, and squeezed off a shot. The outlaw fell with a ripped-out scream, rolled and writhed with a smashed hip, then suddenly blacked out and flopped back with blood darkening his trousers and the dusty roadway around him. He needed immediate aid but no one offered to go out into the center of the roadway and give it to him. He died.

Two men darted from inside the bank. At the last moment one of them swung back around in the doorway and systematically fired. The echoes from within the brick building were deafening. Finally, now, there were other townsmen belatedly entering the fight, but it was over the moment the surviving outlaws flung up across saddle leather, sank in rowels, and raced wildly northward out of Piñon.

Ladd got to his feet, moved out to the center of the roadway, took two-handed aim, and emptied his six-gun without bringing down a single fleeing bank robber. Someone from Reilly's saloon darted to the bank doorway, halted, and yelled into the acrid-scented hush that followed Ladd Buckner's final gunshot: "Jesus, they killed 'em!"

People emerged, furtively and tentatively at first, peering up the roadway in the wake of the outlaws, and went over to join that horrified man in the bank doorway only when it was no longer possible to see the escaping outlaws because of their pillars of dun-colored dust up the stage road in the direction of the far-away hills.

Ladd Buckner remained out in the roadway, hatless in the violent heat and sun smash, shucking out spent shells from his six-gun. He had no other slugs to replace the casings with, so he walked back into the overhang shade where the lawman was lying, and knelt with the empty gun while he made a closer study of Tom Wharton. It had all happened just too fast. Wharton must have been the most thoroughly astonished individual in town when those bank robbers appeared and boldly fanned out to cow the town as their companions went inside to loot the bank. Wharton's death had also been too sudden and too thoroughly unexpected. Even the peaceful expression on his face had an underlying expression of total surprise. Sightless eyes stared up through Ladd Buckner and through the warped overhang ceiling above Ladd Buckner.

Enos Orcutt came out from between two buildings a few doors southward, did not speak, walked up, and sank to his knees, little patched black satchel at his side. Ladd pulled away, stepped inside to fish out six fresh loads for his useless six-gun, and re-armed the weapon while Dr. Orcutt went through his necessary but futile routine. Orcutt twisted to look up at Buckner as the harness maker slowly took down his belt and holster and buckled them on. "Are you all right?" the doctor enquired.

Ladd said: "Yeah, I guess they couldn't aim as well when someone was firing at them as they aimed when Marshal Wharton first got ready to brace them. He's dead?"

"Within moments of the time he hit the ground," confirmed Dr. Orcutt. "They cut him down as neat as marksmen cut them down back during the war. Like they were waiting for him to step out so they could do it."

Up the roadway someone began shouting for Dr. Orcutt to hurry to the bank building. Whoever he was he not only had a powerful set of lungs and a resonant voice, but he also had no intention of being quiet until Enos Orcutt appeared.

The doctor got to his feet and hurried forward, clutching his satchel, leaving Ladd Buckner standing there, looking a trifle quizzically after him. Why would the doctor say Tom Wharton had died as though those outlaws had expected Tom to step forth from the harness works, exactly as Tom did step forth. Orcutt had made it sound as though it were, in one way or another, a kind of prearranged killing. He had made it sound as though someone had deliberately set the lawman up to be murdered.

Joe Reilly and Bert Taylor came across from the opposite side of the roadway and stepped up into overhang shade to stand mutely staring. Reilly, the former soldier, said: "God damn, they nailed him right through the brisket. He didn't have a chance at all."

Bert Taylor lifted a troubled face to Ladd. "He didn't even get a chance to draw, did he?"

Ladd looked at the holstered Colt for the first time. "Doesn't look like it," he replied. "What did they do up at the bank?"

"Killed the head man and shot hell out of the cashier!" Reilly exclaimed. "My God, they didn't just come to town to rob us. They rode in to kill as many folks as they wanted to."

"Renegades," stated the storekeeper. "I can't believe it happened this way. There wasn't a word of warning. I was at my desk in the back room when the firing started." Taylor looked blankly at Ladd Buckner. "You turned them out. What else might they have done if you hadn't shot it out with them?"

"Nothing," said Buckner. "They got the money. That's all they came for."

"But . . . look at Tom," protested the storekeeper. "My God, look at what happened inside the . . ."

"God dammit," snapped the harness maker, "I told you . . . all they came for was the darned money." He holstered the recharged six-gun and turned back into the harness shop, leaving the two older men out there gazing after him, until eventually they looked at one another and Reilly said: "Leave him be. It's darned upsetting, shooting it out like that."

They trudged back in the direction of the opposite side of the roadway where people were beginning to throng up in the direction of the bank's bloody and rummaged interior. It was a hot day; the raid had occurred shortly before noon; there was settling dust far up the stage road for a half hour after the attack, and for most of the residents of Piñon what had occurred had in fact happened exactly as the storekeeper had implied—too suddenly, too unexpectedly, and too swiftly for them to see any of it although all but the stone deaf had heard the gunfire.

The legends began even before the dead men had been hauled feet first down to the doctor's buggy shed for preservation until graves could be dug. Eventually Tom Wharton was also carried down there, and, during the subsequent course of Enos Orcutt's preparation of the Wharton corpse for burial, the doctor extracted that letter from the marshal's shirt pocket. He also read it.

VII

The outlaws were identified from dodgers in the late town marshal's office as three members of a renegade gang that normally operated farther southward, down closer to the international border. Bert and Joe Reilly composed a letter to the Texans and the New Mexicans who had worked up those dodgers, informing them that three of the wanted men had been shot to death at Piñon, Arizona Territory, and gave the date of those killings as well as the circumstances surrounding them. Then they put in requests on behalf of Ladd Buckner for the bounty money and neglected to tell Ladd that they had done this. It was a plain oversight; neither Taylor nor Reilly had experience as lawmen. They only did what had to be done, then they went among the other townsmen to urge the appointment of some kind of interim committee, or perhaps a vigilance organization to keep the peace and enforce the law until a new lawman could be appointed. None of it was precisely according to the law, but all of it was according to the community's immediate needs and desires.

Dr. Orcutt embalmed the three outlaws and Tom Wharton, then one evening he came down to the harness shop after closing hours and pummeled the door until Ladd emerged from his rear quarters to admit the medical man. Orcutt had three separate bundles, pitifully small and woefully insignificant. He offered the bundles to the harness maker, and, when Ladd suspiciously pointed to the counter top, Enos put the bundles up there.

"Everything which was in the possession of those three outlaws you shot," he told Ladd Buckner. "But there was actually nothing much to be used to identify the men." Enos shrugged and leaned upon the counter. The only light in the shop was coming through the rear doorway that led into the harness maker's living quarters. "There are pictures of two of them among the flyers Tom kept at his jailhouse office, and an excellent description of the other one," Enos Orcutt added. "They were vicious, unprincipled sons-of-bitches, Ladd, if that makes you feel any better."

Buckner changed the subject. "Care for some coffee? I just made a fresh pot out back in the kitchen."

Enos shook his head and continued to lean and study the younger man. "You're not troubled, then, about having killed those three men?"

Ladd's expression flattened a little, smoothed out in an expression of cold, unfriendly regard of the medical man. "There isn't any way to kill people and not be troubled, Doctor. Even men like those three. But if you mean . . . has it ruined my appetite or did I lose sleep, or have I begun to fear retaliation from their friends or kinsmen . . . the answer is simply not one blessed bit." When Orcutt was about to speak again, Ladd held up a hand to silence the older man. "But there is one thing that's been bothering me, Doctor. You said while you were on your knees beside Tom Wharton that it looked to you as though someone had given a signal or something when he stepped out of my shop, that he had been shot down deliberately like maybe it had been planned that way."

Orcutt did not drop his gaze as he replied to what sounded very much like an accusation. "That's roughly what I said, indeed. Ladd, he was hit twice. You could place a playing card over both those holes, they are that close and that deadly."

"What of that?"

"Ladd, all those men fired at you and they didn't even come close enough to nick you."

Buckner scowled. "You'll have to make it plainer than that, Doctor."

"Well, how would it have looked to you? Wharton walked out of your shop into the shadows under your wooden awning, and there was no reason for those outlaws up in front of the bank to expect him to do that, or to know he was the law, or even to see him in that shade the way they did at that distance. But, Ladd, they were completely ready, as though they were expecting him to appear and had their guns ready. Tom was shot down methodically. That is the only conclusion I can come up with. I've written it up in my medical report that way."

Dr. Orcutt continued to lean and gaze at the younger man for a while, then he slowly hauled upright and fished in a pocket, brought out a crumpled, much-folded piece of paper, and shoved it across the counter toward Ladd Buckner.

"Read that," he said. "It was in Tom's right-hand shirt pocket when I prepared him for burial."

It was the letter from the prison authorities up in Colorado and Ladd Buckner only read the letterhead and the first couple of paragraphs, then he slowly replaced the letter upon the counter top. "You believe I was somehow involved in that bank robbery?" he asked in a voice made reedy by his own incredulity.

Dr. Orcutt looked at his hands for a moment. "I don't see why, if you knew those men were going to raid our bank, you would have deliberately sent Tom out to be shot down, and then why you would have followed him out to shoot it out with those renegades." Orcutt raised his eyes. "Unless you are a homicidal maniac, Ladd. Unless you are the kind of human being I cannot possibly understand." He pointed to the letter lying between them. "You served seven years in the federal penitentiary in Colorado for bank robbery . . . There is the whole record in black and white. And just in case you need to know how Tom got interested in your possible background, we both noticed that you stitched, knotted, and sewed exactly the way the rehabilitation people teach their pupils to work at the prison up in Colorado."

Ladd glanced again at the letter, this time at the date it had been sent. "How long had Wharton had this information?" he asked, and the doctor did not know except to surmise that, since the letter had been dated two weeks earlier, and the usual mail delivery required only one week, that perhaps Tom Wharton had had that letter at least a full week.

Ladd was doubtful. "He didn't so much as even hint about what he knew when he came in for coffee each morning."

Orcutt conceded that. "You didn't know Tom as well as some of the rest of us knew him. He wasn't a man who would use something like this to hold over your head, and he never would have intimidated you with it. He would just keep it in mind, and, if you never forced him to make a case against you, he would never have mentioned it." Dr. Orcutt's voice changed slightly, turning brisk and more incisive as he went on. "But he's dead, and so are a number of other people including our bank president. Maybe the cashier will die. It's too early to determine that."

Orcutt paused and Ladd, who was certain there had to be more coming, leaned there, waiting.

"If we had enough time maybe I could say this diplomatically," averred the medical practitioner, and ruefully smiled a little. "Although I've never really had the knack for diplomacy."

"Say what?" asked Ladd.

"Say that there is an old saying, Ladd. It takes a thief to catch a thief. We no longer have a law officer. No one I can think of offhand has your ability to face guns and to use them as well as you can."

Ladd stared. "Me? Are you asking me to go after those renegades?"

"I'm asking you on behalf of the town council, which includes Reilly and Taylor and myself, to do something like that. The alternative is for the town to send out to the cow outfits for volunteers, and by the time they arrive back here those murderers will be out of the country . . . It's your town, Ladd. You came down here, set up in business, and adopted it."

"And a member of the town council believes I had a hand in the murder of Piñon's lawman."

"No," stated Enos Orcutt, "I at no time said I believed that. I said it looked as though someone had set Tom up, and I still think that may have happened. On the other hand he could have simply walked out there coincidentally. Ladd, we can discuss this anytime, later." Orcutt reached to pick up the letter lying between them and fold it. "Right now we have some dead men to avenge by law, and we have an awful lot of money, mostly the savings of folks around town, that needs to be recovered, and we need your help to accomplish those things." Orcutt slowly pocketed the letter without taking his eyes off Ladd Buckner. "I'm making an appeal. You can refuse."

Ladd nodded in the direction of the pocket Enos had just used. "Sure, just an appeal . . . and, if I don't help you, the letter will be circulated around town."

For a moment longer Enos Orcutt stood motionlessly, then he reached, withdrew the letter, tossed it over in front of the harness maker, and said: "Burn it, if you want to, do with it whatever you want." He started to turn. "I'll be down at the livery barn with the others saddling up, if you change your mind."

"What others?" asked Ladd.

"Joe Reilly and Simon Terry, the blacksmith."

Ladd scowled. "That's all. Just the three of you?"

"Well, no, we were kind of figuring there would be a fourth fellow," said the doctor, and walked on out of the shop.

Ladd looked from the empty doorway to the letter, picked it up, and read it, then balled up the letter and crossed over to pitch it into the little iron stove. He got his booted carbine and his belt weapon with its shell belt. He took his time about rigging out, and, when he moved across the room to pick his hat off the antler rack near the workbench, and a hostler from down at the livery barn walked in carrying some torn chain harness, Ladd pointed. "Dump it in the corner there," he said, then, booted carbine across one shoulder, he herded the liveryman back outside. The hostler offered absolutely no objection. He looked from Ladd's face to his weapons, then scuttled southward without a word.

Several cowboys were just stepping to the ground from their saddles up in front of Reilly's place. Ladd saw them without being the least bit interested. Elsewhere, as he walked forth, then turned back to lock his roadside door, he also saw those two gawky teenage pseudo-cowboys who had questioned him one time about the fight at Tomahawk Meadow. He ignored them, too, but they certainly did not ignore Ladd Buckner, who was armed to the teeth and who looked bitter-faced as he swung to hike southward down the roadway.

Apparently Dr. Orcutt had told his companions something about his conversation with the harness maker, because, although Joe Reilly would have normally been his customary loquacious self, this time, when Ladd appeared, all Reilly did was look up, nod his head, then look down again as he finished rigging out his saddle animal.

Dr. Orcutt was back nearer the wide front barn opening. He had been watching the northward roadway so Ladd's appearance did not come to him as a surprise. He allowed the harness maker to get close, then he casually gestured toward the burly, dark, and bearded man. "Simon Terry," he said by way of a curt introduction. "Simon, this is Ladd Buckner."

The blacksmith shook Ladd's hand in a grip that could have crushed bones, then unsmilingly went back to saddling and bridling his animal. Simon Terry was a powerfully muscular man, dark as a half-breed Indian, thick and hard as oak, and usually taciturn. He had been known to go for days at a time without ever more than grunting. But he was not a surly man, the way many taciturn individuals were. He was just not fond of talking.

The liveryman himself brought out Ladd's animal and rigged it in silence. When he handed over the reins, he still said nothing, but he winked as he walked away.

They did not head northward up through town. Simon Terry, the blacksmith, led out, and Simon did not like ostentation of any kind, so he led them up the back alley out of town. That way they would not be viewed by the townsfolk as grim and relentless upholders of the law, which, although they might be, Simon did not like to have folks say about them. Also, if they came slinking back perhaps in the night having failed at their undertaking, it would be a lot easier to live with the failure if they hadn't pretended to be mighty manhunters on their way out of town.

As far as Ladd Buckner was concerned, he wasn't involved in any of this; he was only interested in studying the distant countryside and the even more distant mountain slopes, and trying to imagine where exactly those surviving outlaws had gone. The only thing he was certain of, as they angled back around and got atop the stage road northward beyond town, was that there had been only three survivors who had fled out of Piñon with their canvas sack full of bank money.

VIII

Because it was a moonless night with plenty of watery star shine, it was inevitable one of them would comment upon the visibility. Joe Reilly said: "I remember back during the war going out on a special patrol one night like this." Maybe Joe had not meant to say more but the others waited and finally Joe finished it. "There was a bunch of Rebels in a spit of trees and they chased us two-thirds of the way back to our lines, shooting and hollering their darned heads off." Joe smiled in the gloom. "I was never so afraid in my life."

Dr. Orcutt smiled but neither the blacksmith nor the harness maker showed appreciation of Joe Reilly's little tale.

"In the dark can't no one see you very far ahead," stated the blacksmith, and kept on leading the way up the road in the direction the outlaws had gone.

"Yeah," said Ladd dryly, "and we can't see very far ahead, either, Mister Terry. If those men turned off left or right, we'll still be riding north come sunup."

The blacksmith turned his bearded countenance to gaze darkly at the speaker before saying. "They didn't turn off left or right, Mister Buckner."

That was all he said; he did not explain how he knew they had not turned off, nor even whether he actually knew this or was simply guessing about it. But Dr. Orcutt offered an explanation. "A stage driver coming south only a couple of hours after the robbery saw three hard-riding men, one with a canvas sack slung over his shoulder, going northward up into the pass through the yonder hills."

That was no certainty, but Ladd settled for it, and, if it turned out to be a fact that those had been the surviving outlaws, why then the posse men from Piñon were indeed on the right track and were also unlikely to be seen. Something had to be right; everything that had been done since the robbery and the killings could not have been wrong.

Simon and Joe Reilly knew the onward countryside the best, but Simon did not elaborate upon what lay ahead. Joe did. The nearest town was at the foot of the yonder hills upon the far side. Otherwise, there was nothing but cow country on both sides of the mountains, and the actual mountains themselves were of little value except for hunting and sometimes, at the higher elevations, also for fishing. Unless one considered their value as a hide-out. Joe Reilly recounted a tale of two fugitive renegades who had existed in the mountains by simply changing camps every four days, for three years, and even then, he said, they probably would not have been taken except that one of them developed appendicitis and his partner brought him out. The ill man died anyway, and his partner had been tried and sent to prison. Joe concluded this recitation with his own homily: "Since a man never knows what might happen to him, I guess the best thing is not to get into trouble with the law, eh?" No one answered.

The night turned chilly as they entered the distant foothills and began a steady ascent. It got colder each hundred yards or so they climbed toward the gunsight notch that served as the route from south to north, and from northward to southward in the direction of Piñon. Enos Orcutt dropped back to ride beside the fourth posse man, and to offer a cigar that Ladd refused in favor of a rolled cigarette of his own manufacture. With looped reins and a turned-up collar, he said: "Doctor, what do they have in this town we're coming to directly? Boarding house, saloon, place for folks to put up tired horses?"

"All those things," agreed the doctor. "And a town constable named Brennan who is . . . well, so I've heard anyway . . . purchasable."

Ladd lit up and exhaled smoke. "Purchasable?"

"If you were three outlaws with nine thousand dollars in a sack and needed some rest and a place to put up your horses for a while, maybe for five or six hours, you could offer him a handful of greenbacks and he'd see to it that you got those things."

Ladd's gaze was saturnine. "Sure takes you a long while to say something, don't it?"

Dr. Orcutt's teeth shone in the silvery night. "I suppose it does." He continued to grin. "Let you in on another of my secrets, Ladd. I'm probably the worst marksman in the entire Arizona Territory."

"In that case, I'd appreciate it, Doctor, if you'd stay in front of me," said the harness maker, and grinned back for the first time since seeing that letter Enos Orcutt had brought down to the harness shop with him.

Ladd glanced up ahead a few yards where silent Simon Terry was slouching along beside loquacious and burly Joe Reilly. He was slightly amused. If there were ever opposites on the trail, it had to be those two. Orcutt, guessing Ladd's thought, sighed and softly spoke: "Different as they are, we couldn't be riding on a mission of this kind in better company."

There was an opportunity to ask for an elaboration of this statement but a distraction arrived in the form of a very large cougar whose tail alone was as long as most other cougars were in the body. All four horses reacted to the powerful scent of that killer cat in the same way, by shying violently and keeping their riders very busy for a number of uncertain moments, or until the astonished and frightened big cat had fled westerly across the road to disappear silently into the darkness without looking back.

Later, as they pushed steadily upward toward the top out of the pass, and the cold became more noticeable than ever, Joe Reilly produced a bottle of malt whiskey that he magnanimously passed around. It helped a little to keep chilled bodies warm.

Ladd considered asking how much farther they had to go before getting down upon the far side of the pass, but in the end said nothing for the fundamental reason that knowing how many additional miles he had yet to traverse was not going to minimize them, and, whether there were a lot more of them, or a lot less, he was still going to keep riding along until they had been covered. On this kind of a ride, about the only thing that truly mattered was that the men did not stop any more often than they had to, and that they steadily and doggedly persevered, which they did, and were still doing when the cold, hushed, and rather dismal world through which they were passing in wraith-like silence began to pale out a little at a time until visibility improved enough for them to be able to look back and see the uneven, spiky rims behind them, and to look outward and downward and see a partially fog-shrouded immense valley and prairie ahead of them. They could not see the town at all but it was down there. As Joe Reilly said: "The folks that built Paso, the town we're coming to, had their reasons for not advertising that they had a settlement out here. Back in those days these hills were alive with crawling bands of ragheads."

"They still are," grumbled the blacksmith, and as usual did not elaborate after making his statement.

Eventually, as the daylight began to strengthen even though there would be no sunrise for another hour or two, it became possible for the men dwarfed to ant size upon the high slope winding their way downward to see roof tops and uneven roads and several sets of more distant ruts heading toward the clutch of buildings, mostly made of logs, lying at the very base of the pass on the westerly side where the land was more open and amenable to settlement and to the kind of labor that went with creating a town, such as garden patches, little postage-stamp-size milk cow enclosures, and horse corrals. Paso, for all its relative age in this raw, new world, had not grown as had Piñon. Of course there was a reason for this, but to Ladd Buckner the reason was anything but obvious. In some ways he could see that Paso had advantages that Piñon did not possess. For example, Paso was sheltered in the lee of the mountains behind it from winter's worst storms. Also, since it was shaded by those same peaks and slopes, it would be much cooler in summertime, which was always a major consideration in Arizona Territory.

Then Simon Terry made a short remark and Ladd was enlightened a little on this topic. The blacksmith said: "Never had enough water down there. Dig wells all the time and never get more than a trough full a day out of each well."

All the other blandishments in the world would not make up for that kind of a fault. Ladd rode along alternately watching the town shape up below him, and also watching for the sun to appear over in the hazy-blurred east. They were cold and beard-stubbled from being in the saddle all night. They were also rumpled and somewhat red-eyed and doggedly bleak and rugged in their general appearance. If someone saw them riding along like this, at such an ungodly hour armed to the teeth and scarcely more than grunting back and forth as they came down closer to the rear of the town at the foot of the pass, it would be almost impossible to consider them as anything other than renegades of the same variety as the men they were pursuing.

Dr. Orcutt alone could make some claim to respectability because of his frock coat and his curly-brimmed derby hat, but as they progressed these adjuncts of a civilized existence became less and less respectable in appearance, and by the time they were coming down across the last mile or so toward Paso, down where the trail flattened out for an agreeable change, Dr. Orcutt more nearly resembled a raffish, sly, and conniving gambler, or perhaps a peddler of paste diamonds or water-divining rods, than a genuine physician and surgeon.

Ladd Buckner looked at his companions when the light got better and decided to himself that if the people of Paso had any reason to be suspicious of strangers, he and his associates were going to become targets of some hard and probably hostile looks. It also troubled him a little that the lawman of Paso might be a badge-toting renegade. After all, the men from Piñon were shortly going to be entering this individual's bailiwick only four in number, seeking three proven murderers and bandits, and, if the town marshal chose to resent the interference of the men from Piñon . . .

Joe Reilly straightened a little in the saddle and called their attention ahead down the roadway where a stagecoach had just wheeled clear of the Paso station to head up into the pass. "Morning coach bound for Piñon," he said. The way he made that announcement set his companions to eyeing the oncoming vehicle as though it might be their last best opportunity to send back word to Piñon of their whereabouts.

Then Ladd put their position into perspective by saying: "You string out across the road to stop this stage, gents, looking as mean and dirty and gun handy as we look in this lousy gray light, and that gun guard up there is going to start shooting as sure as I'm a foot tall. We look more like highwaymen than posse men."

The stage came on, without slackening pace, and both the men upon the high seat reached for weapons that they balanced across their laps. They had indeed seen the four horsemen from Piñon and had indeed turned very wary of their presence upon the road so early in the day, armed as they were. Then the stage swept past without anyone on either side waving, which was customary, and Dr. Orcutt twisted to look after the coach as his horse headed back for the center of the road again in the thin dawn dust. Dr. Orcutt had never been stared at in quite that way before. It was both a revelation to him, and a distinct discomfort.

Finally they came down behind the town and smelled breakfast fires in the making, which reminded them that they as well as their horses had been without food for a very long while. All night long in fact. Nor did it help arrest this realization that, as they passed down through several crooked little back byways, they could distinctly smell meat and potatoes frying and coffee boiling.

Paso was still only partially stirring when they walked their horses into the yard of the combination horse trader and liveryman, dismounted wordlessly, and handed over their reins to the round-eyed night hawk who was about to go off duty. They said nothing to the night hawk, who was suddenly very wide-awake, and he said nothing to them. Up the road a man with an ample paunch stepped forth and hurled a dishpan of greasy wash-water out into the center of the roadway, then retreated back into his place of business, which had the legend Café emblazoned across one wavery glass window.

Simon Terry led off as usual, this time making a beeline for that beanery. The sun still had not appeared over in the hazy east.

IX

The café man looked as askance at his odd assortment of very early diners as that worried night hawk had looked at the same crew out front of the Paso livery barn. But the café man was older, more scarred and worldly, and therefore less likely to open his mouth either in front of those four men, or behind their backs. He differed again from the night hawk; as soon as the liveryman showed up along with his day man, the night hawk fled up in the direction of the constable's office in the ugly little functional log building up at the extreme north end of town. Otherwise, Paso did not notice or record the arrival in town of a massively powerful dark, fully-bearded individual whose silent lips were almost completely hidden by his black beard, or his companion upon the café man's bench who was wearing a shoved-back little gray derby hat that at one time had been an epitome of frontier elegance but that now had a dent in front where it had connected with a low tree limb in the dark of the previous night, and another dent in the back where it had struck the road after falling from Enos Orcutt's head when the tree limb had made its connection.

The other two, Joe Reilly and Ladd Buckner, also differed. In fact there was almost nothing those four men seemed to have in common as they sat in strong silence, eating like wolves, except that each one of them was heavily armed and each one of them had evidently been in the saddle all night. The café man concentrated upon filling them up and keeping the coffee coming. He did not open his mouth unless he was spoken to, and he did not stare. He, too, had at one time many years ago arrived in

Paso like this, except that he had come down from the north and the posse men who had hunted high and low for him had been told a deliberate lie by a Mexican shepherd, and had ridden off to the east into the mountains on a wild-goose chase. That had been twenty-one years ago, and unless they had finally given up the pursuit in disgust to return homeward, by now they probably were walking their horses across the underside of the earth somewhere, but, wherever they were, the café man had done well in Paso and proposed to continue to do well in Paso—by seeing nothing, knowing nothing, and above all else by saying nothing. Even when Joe Reilly asked about the town constable the only retort he got was when the café man leaned down, peered over Reilly's head out his fly-specked roadway window, then grunted and pointed in the direction of a burly, graying man strolling along upon the opposite plank walk in the direction of his log jailhouse.

"That's him," announced the café man. "Constable Lewis Brennan." Then the café man became very busy gathering up empty plates and cups.

The men from Piñon went out front just as the first rays of sunlight appeared over in the distant west up along some night-shrouded high peaks, creating an effect of breathtakingly soft beauty. They saw only that daylight was coming as Ladd Buckner, who had been turning their situation over and over in his head, offered a suggestion: "Four of us beard this crooked constable, and it'll be like a bunch of ducks in a rain barrel if he decides to be troublesome. You three circulate around town, apart from each other so's it won't look so much like we're invadin' this place, and I'll go see the constable." He looked around as though anticipating an argument. None came, so he finished it: "I'll walk down the roadway here, to the livery barn, out in plain sight when I've finished with the constable. You watch, and meet me down there for our next palaver." Again he looked around. "Someone know better?"

Even Joe Reilly shook his head. Ordinarily Joe would have had something to say. Already Joe had sought out and located the local saloon.

They split up. Two men watched this, the café man behind them in his place of business, who was very interested but who would never to his dying day say that he had seen anything out front this morning, and the weasel-faced little wispy livery barn night hawk, who would, on the opposite side of the same coin, never stop talking about this affair and his part in it as long as he lived.

Ladd rolled a cigarette upon the far side of the roadway and wagged his head a little. This situation was exactly like the one he had been involved with almost nine years ago in a place only slightly larger than Paso where he had been sent ahead by the outlaw crew he was riding with to reconnoiter the town. That time, all hell had busted loose, too. He lit up, blew smoke, and tried to guess what was going to happen in this place a half hour or so from now, for while there was no bank in Paso, and the town itself was still more drowsy than awake, cow country communities had an ability suddenly to awaken with guns in all the fists on both sides of a roadway in the twinkling of an eye.

He turned and paced up to the log jailhouse, opened the door, and nodded to the round-faced, lion-maned, coarse-featured man who looked up from behind a littered desk. "'Morning, Constable," he said, and offered a little crooked smile.

The constable nodded, put aside the paper he'd been reading, and gestured toward a wired-together old chair. "'Morning. Have a seat. Care for some coffee?"

Ladd had drunk his daily allotment over at the café and said so as he sat down, then he said: "I come north over the hills last night, Constable."

Constable Lewis Brennan had pale, stone-steady blue eyes and they did not leave Ladd's face. "Is that a fact?" he said in a tone of complete disinterest. "In the saddle all night, then?"

Ladd nodded. "All night. I and some friends were down at a place called Piñon. We . . . got sort of separated down there. My friends were coming up here to Paso. We talked a little about that before we got down there to Piñon."

Constable Brennan pursed his lips in a slight expression of impatience. "What's your name?" he asked.

"Smith. Just plain old Jack Smith."

"Well, plain old Jack Smith," commented the burly lawman, "if you got something particular to say, I wish to hell you'd say it, because I ain't had breakfast yet and I don't do very well on an empty gut."

"Three riders, Constable, coming down over those mountains in a kind of a hurry. Originally there were six of us."

Lewis Brennan's eyes began to mirror caution. "Three left? What happened over in Piñon?"

Ladd leaned to tramp his smoked-down cigarette into the rough floor planking and answered while he was still bending over with his face averted: "The whole god-damned town turned out to welcome us, Constable Brennan." Ladd jumped his eyes back to the lawman's face. "You curious about me knowing your name? My friends and I heard it a long ways from here. We heard that you kept a decent town at Paso, where folks in need of a little lay-over would be plumb safe."

Lewis Brennan's unwavering gaze showed the same shades of caution as he made a quiet long assessment of Ladd Buckner, and finally said: "Well, Mister Smith, every town's got places where men can sort of lay-over and be safe, and in every one of those towns I was ever in it was also sort of expensive to get that kind of privacy."

Ladd smiled without a shred of mirth. "Sure. Well, we got a canvas sack full of money down at the Piñon bank, Mister Brennan. My share is in that sack. You name your price and point me in the right direction, and I'll get the money for you."

Lewis Brennan sat a long while in total silence without so much as changing his facial expression, then, about when Ladd had almost decided Brennan might not speak again at all, he very quietly said: "Turn around, Jack Smith."

It was the tone not the words that conveyed the sense of deadly peril. Ladd straightened in the old chair, then slowly turned.

There was a small cell-room door over across the room, heavily reinforced with strap steel and massive round-headed big black bolts. Wood or not, it would have taken a cannon to have demolished that door, but it wasn't the door that held Ladd Buckner almost breathless; it was the trio of men standing over there, hatless and in their stocking feet as though they might have just been roused from a nap in the dingy cells behind them. Each man had a six-gun pointed squarely at Ladd Buckner.

Lewis Brennan said: "Gents, who is he?"

A venomous-looking man with perpetually squinted eyes and a bluish wound for a mouth said: "Damned if I know, Brennan. I never seen the bastard before. But you'd better disarm him, just in case he's one of them fellers that little runt from the livery barn was in here talking about a few minutes ago."

Brennan made no move to arise from behind his desk. "Disarm him yourself," he told the vicious-looking man, then sat there watching as another of those three men swore and walked over to yank away Ladd's holstered Colt.

At the same time this man, younger than the other two but just as deadly in the eyes, gently shoved Ladd's own gun barrel into his neck at the side, and slowly cocked it as he said: "Start explaining, mister, and you lie just once . . ." He shoved the cold gun barrel harder into Ladd's neck muscles.

The third man in stocking feet suddenly said: "Hey, wait a minute. I know this feller. I saw him plenty of times up north. Give me a minute and his name'll come back."

The man with the cocked gun pressing into flesh said—"He don't have no minute."—and shoved the gun again, making Ladd lean to get away from most of the pressure.

The older outlaw snarled. "Stop playing like you're some kind of lousy executioner and just be quiet for a minute." He stared steadily at Ladd, and finally cursed with feeling because he could not remember the name. "But god dammit, I know that face. That's him all right."

The first man to speak turned a little. "That's who?" he asked impatiently. "Where did you see him before?"

"At Canon City," said the older outlaw. "He was learning saddle and harness making the same as me, but he was in the bunch that went over in the afternoon. I seen him dozens of times when we passed on the way . . . God dammit, Buckner! That's it. His name is Buckner and he was in for robbing stages."

"Banks," said Ladd, holding his head to one side. "Not stages, banks."

The younger man eased off with his pistol barrel a little and looked for instruction to the other older man in the cell-room doorway. That individual put up his Colt and folded his arms while he steadily stared at Ladd.

"Why?" he eventually said, "did you come in here and try that cock-and-bull story on Lew Brennan?"

Ladd risked raising a hand to shove the gun barrel still farther from his neck. The venomous-eyed young outlaw allowed his weapon to be pushed gently away. He in fact even stepped back a little, then passed around toward the corner of Lew Brennan's desk to hoist himself up a little and perch there.

Ladd improvised but he did not overplay it. "I was in the Piñon saloon when you hit that damned bank down there. I saw what happened, and, as soon as I could decently get shed of that town, I tried to catch up to you."

"Wait a minute," interrupted the Paso lawman. "Who else come up with you?"

Ladd scowled. "No one. I met some fellers striking their camp back up the mountains a few miles just ahead of daybreak, had some coffee with them, and rode on down with them. They're freighters on their way up to Denver. At least that's what they said, and I can tell you for a fact they sure as hell aren't range men. One of them even wears a derby hat."

"Never mind that crap," growled the outlaw with the folded arms over in the cell-room doorway. "Why did you try to catch up to us?"

Ladd let his gaze waver slightly. "You got a sack full of money down there in Piñon," he said. "I heard the barman down there telling folks you got nine thousand dollars."

Lew Brennan's pale eyes suddenly jumped from Ladd to the outlaw over in the doorway. The outlaw reddened slightly, then shrugged. "All right, we got nine thousand, Lew."

"You told me four thousand," snarled the lawman. "You louse, you gave me ten percent of four thousand."

"You'll get the rest of it directly," soothed the red-faced outlaw, and looked unhappily at Ladd Buckner. "Damn you anyway. What did you figure to do . . . catch us in our blankets last night and cut our throats and take the sack of money?"

"No," replied Ladd. "I was going to offer to guide you into the westerly mountains where no posse or no one else could find you. For a fee, of course."

X

The youngest of those three outlaws who was still sitting upon the edge of Brennan's desk appeared to have a change of attitude. Earlier, he had seemed perfectly willing to blow Ladd Buckner's head off with Ladd's own gun; now, as he listened and looked, he appeared to be favorably impressed with Ladd's offer to help the outlaws escape.

"There's a hell of a lot of mountains in back of this place," he told the pair of older outlaws across the room. "We'd be foolish to try and keep to the damned roadway."

The bleak-eyed man who was in age between the youngest outlaw and the older one snarled his reply: "Yeah, and you'd take this feller at face value and tomorrow morning you'd be dead as hell out there somewhere, and cleaned out down to your socks."

The oldest outlaw ignored both his companions, as though this kind of bickering was routine between them. He said: "Hey, Buckner, you remember a feller named Reston up there in Canon City? Whatever become of him? We was . . ."

"For Christ's sake," snarled the leader of these men, the outlaw who was still standing over there in the cell-room doorway with both arms folded across his chest, "don't either one of you have a lick of sense? Brennan, we got to find out about those freighters he come down here with."

The constable nodded. "That'll be easy enough. They're likely still around and their horses are down at the livery barn. I'll go look around a little." Brennan swung his attention back to Ladd Buckner. "You got guts," he said, sounding neither hostile nor commendatory. "If you lied, Jack Smith or whatever your name is, you're as good as dead."

Ladd, with enough time to formulate a defensive idea, said: "Constable, I can identify their outfits for you, and lead you up to them. They won't suspect anything coming from me."

Brennan was on his feet as he replied: "If they're just freighters passing through, why should they expect anything? And the liveryman can identify their outfits." He turned toward the cell-room doorway. "I get the feelin' our visitor here wants to get out of here."

"He'll be here when you get back," said the outlaw leader. "Dead or alive, he'll be here."

Ladd watched Constable Brennan leave the jailhouse with misgivings. Brennan would examine the horses, saddles, and effects of his companions from Piñon, and he would also make enquiries around town. Since Orcutt, Reilly, and Simon Terry would be expecting nothing, Brennan would also be able to walk up behind them more than likely. There was no way for Brennan not to return to the jailhouse with a report substantiating his suspicions, unless a miracle occurred, and Ladd Buckner had no faith in miracles.

He rolled a cigarette to occupy his hands, and, when the oldest outlaw filled in the unpleasant silence with another enquiry concerning a man they had both known in prison, Ladd was willing to tell what he knew. He and the oldest outlaw got into quite a conversation. The youngest outlaw listened, then leathered his Colt and yawned, walked around behind Brennan's desk, and sat down back there. The outlaw leader, though, was not nearly as impressed with Buckner's bona-fide outlaw credentials from Canon City. He was evidently one of those lifelong skeptics one encountered more, perhaps, among outlaws than among other kinds of people. He broke into the conversation between his older companion and Ladd Buckner by asking who else had taken the outlaw trail from Piñon.

Ladd told the truth. "As far as I know, there wasn't any pursuit."

The outlaw leader scoffed. "No pursuit? After we busted their bank and shot their citizens?"

"Maybe that's why," stated Ladd. "I can tell you for a fact the whole darned town was stumbling over itself. And you killed their lawman, the only feller around who could organize and lead a posse."

The youngest outlaw smiled for the first time, but not at Ladd, at his leader. "I told you Henry'd fix it for us."

Their leader ignored that statement to say: "By now, though, they sure as hell got a posse on the way."

Ladd was cautious when he answered that. "I'd guess by now they have, but if you follow me off into these mountains back yonder, all the posses on earth can't find you. Mister, I can set you up a camp in a big meadow back in there where the ragheads hid out for ten years without anyone ever finding them."

"Yeah? And suppose they're still in those mountains," stated the head outlaw. "Not too long ago some cattle outfit over around Piñon got hit by a bushwhacking band of 'em."

Ladd brushed this aside. "Weren't more than eight in that bunch. Reservation jumpers, I'd guess. Anyway, I can take you back in there where even the ragheads can't find you. I can set you up alongside a lake in there that's got trout in it as thick as your arm, and all you'll have to do is lie around, fish a little, and get fat, safe as you can be."

There was nothing wrong with the presentation or with the idea; if there was one thing renegades of this kind yearned for, it was a place where they could stop running and hiding, and sleeping with a cocked gun at their side. Ladd knew the psychology of men like these, which was why he had fabricated this alluring prospect. But that man over in the cell-room doorway was not as influenced as were his companions. He said: "Buckner, a feller who would try what you tried by coming after us like a lousy coyote skulking along would work for the law."

Ladd flared up. "What law? Damn it all, you saw him get killed back there."

"Not him," snapped the outlaw. "The law that pays bounties for us fellers."

The oldest outlaw broke in: "Cass, what in the hell . . . ? Listen to me. Let Buckner guide us back into them mountains where we can hide out for a month or two. If he turns out to be double-crossing us some way, we'll simply kill him."

"Sure," assented their leader in a voice heavy with sarcasm, "we'll kill him . . . after he maybe leads us up in front of a lousy posse. Walt, just keep out of this, will you?" The spokesman faced Ladd again. "I wouldn't trust you as far as I could throw you," he stated. "As far as I'm concerned, it'll be up to Brennan what he wants to do with you. You come in here lyin' in your teeth as neat as a whistle. Not only that, but you had to go and say we got nine thousand instead of the four thousand Brennan figured we'd got."

"How the hell was I to know you'd lied to him?" demanded Ladd. "And you don't have to trust me. All you've got to do is keep me in front of you until we're so far back in those mountains the Indians couldn't even find us. Mister, why would I be willing to go back in there with you fellers if I didn't know exactly where to hide you? I didn't come down in the last rain. I know you can shoot me if I don't deliver what I say I'll deliver. Your trouble is, damn it all, you got your tail feathers burned off down at Piñon and now you figure everyone is against you."

The youngest outlaw chimed in with an opinion of his own. "We got our tail feathers singed all right. That lousy town accounted for damned good men. But by God I paid 'em back. I shot their banker and his dog robber, that other feller behind the wicket in their bank. I evened things up a little."

Cass remained over in the doorway, arms crossed, waiting for the younger man to say all he had to say, then the leader of these men asked Ladd a question: "Who was that son-of-a-bitch come out of the jailhouse and cut loose on us out front of the bank?"

Ladd lied as deftly as he'd been lying for the past fifteen minutes. "Feller by the name of Sanders. All I know about him is what I heard in the saloon. He was down there near the harness works when the marshal walked out. Someone said Sanders is a former lawman from down in Texas. That's all I heard."

"We owe him," said Cass gruffly.

Ladd shrugged that off. "All right. But you sure as hell hadn't better try going back over there to settle up with him. Not for a couple of months anyway." Ladd scratched his middle and glanced toward the door. He had been bold up to this point and he might just as well continue being bold, because when Constable Lewis Brennan walked through that doorway again, Ladd Buckner's chances for survival were going to start plummeting immediately.

"Too bad Henry couldn't signal about this Sanders feller, too," said the youngest renegade from his comfortable position in the constable's chair.

That touched a nerve in Cass. "Damn it!" the outlaw leader exclaimed. "Why couldn't he have come up north of town and warned us about that feller, instead of just staying in the lousy store and signaling where the town marshal was?"

The way the youngest renegade sprang to the defense of Henry, whoever he was, seemed to imply at least a friendship. "You yourself told me all he had to do was put on one of those four hats in the store-window so's we'd know where the marshal was. And he done it, Cass, exactly like you said. You can't blame Henry for what happened."

Walt, the oldest outlaw, went to the stove, padding soundlessly across the floor in his stocking feet, and hefted the coffee pot over there atop the wood stove. Evidently Walt's hard existence had inured him to cold stale coffee, because he poured himself a cup of the stuff and went over to a wall bench to sit and sip. He seemed very relaxed now, very comfortable in fact, and the fact that he and his friends were inside a jailhouse evidently did not trouble Walt in the least. At least this particular jailhouse belonged to them as a hide-out, and perhaps that amused

Walt. Ladd had heard a lot of outlaws up in Canon City boast of bribing lawmen. They always seemed to derive enormous satisfaction from their ability to do it. Maybe Walt got the same satisfaction from having the run of a jailhouse whose legal custodian had been bought with some of the blood money from Piñon.

Cass straightened up over in the doorway and walked to a front wall window to stoop slightly and peer out. "What's keeping Brennan?" he growled.

Walt idly said: "Maybe he's the feller we'd ought to worry about instead of Buckner."

Cass turned. "You damned fool," he growled, and went to work rolling a cigarette, scowling unhappily as he did it.

Ladd tried to guess what Cass's weakness was and decided it had to be his inherent mistrust of everyone. But how something like that could be exploited eluded Ladd. Gradually it began also to occur to him that Brennan had been out there an inordinate length of time. The possibilities were tantalizing, and they were also manifold, but Ladd's main consideration was what would happen if Brennan returned, and he thought he had a fair idea about that.

Cass blew smoke at the ceiling, then stepped back to lean and peer out into the roadway again. Paso was quiet, as it probably was two-thirds of the time. A morning stage arrived from across the vast expanse of prairie land northward, and momentarily this appeared to rouse the place a little. A man's hearty laughter up the road beyond sight rang reassuringly.

Walt said: "Brennan better get his butt back here. He's got to fetch us some breakfast yet this morning."

Ladd, remembering what the lawman had told him a half hour earlier, offered a placating suggestion: "He's probably at the café filling up. He said he hadn't eaten."

Cass sighed, and padded back over into the cell-room doorway to finish his smoke and be thoughtful. He ignored Ladd. It was very probable that he had already made up his mind what to do about Ladd Buckner. If this were so, and considering Cass's suspicious, deadly nature, it was not difficult to imagine what his decision amounted to.

That coach that had rattled into town raised a fine dust part way along the central thoroughfare. Ladd did not leave his chair but he could see the dust in the air. He was frankly fearful and he had every right to be that way. Even though Reilly, Terry, and Orcutt would be wary and watchful, they would be susceptible to Brennan's approach; not knowing what had happened inside the jailhouse or what lies Ladd had told, they would be unable to offer believable support for those lies—and that would simply mean that, when Brennan walked through the door of the jailhouse, Ladd Buckner would be living on borrowed time. He had no illusions, either, about Walt, the moderately congenial old renegade who had recognized Ladd from their prison days. Walt, Cass, and especially that venomous-eyed youngest outlaw would gun down Ladd Buckner without a qualm. Inside the Paso township jailhouse, they would not dare use guns, so they would use knives or clubs, whatever came handy, but they would kill Ladd Buckner as surely as the sun would set this evening.

XI

Brennan did not return and Cass was more worried than he allowed the others to see. How Ladd knew this was so was in part a deduction based upon the outlaw leader's increasingly waspish and derogatory comments to his partners, and also by the way Cass paced the room from time to time, always ending up over along the front wall where he leaned down to look out of a barred jailhouse window.

Ladd worried, also, but in a different way. In fact, the longer Brennan remained away, the better Ladd's chances seemed to be. At least they seemed to be better in the area of personal survival. Until Lew Brennan returned and blew Ladd Buckner's story sky high with the simple truth, no one was going to attempt to murder Ladd. Cass no doubt would murder him offhandedly, but now neither Walt nor the youngest renegade was still that deadly minded. Particularly old Walt, who talked to Ladd about the old days up at Canon City as though they were alumni from the same school. Maybe, in a sense, this was a logical spirit since Walt had obviously never attended much school.

Finally someone out front stamping up off the roadway to cross planking in the direction of the jailhouse door brought the three hiding men to their feet. Walt and the youngest outlaw hastened over to be near the cell-room door. All three of them sidled through and Cass reached with one hand, partially to close the door. He shot a savage glare at Ladd and wigwagged with a drawn pistol. Ladd had no difficulty in understanding, even though Cass did not say a word.

The man who entered the jailhouse was not Constable Brennan. He was heavy-set, bald, and slovenly, and he stared at Ladd Buckner as though he had expected to see someone besides a total stranger sitting there. He said: "Howdy, where's Lew Brennan this morning?"

Ladd offered a bland reply. "I reckon he's around somewhere. I haven't seen him in the past half hour or more."

The heavy-set man stroked his chin and continued to gaze at Ladd. "You a friend of Lew's?" he asked, and Ladd smiled a little.

"You might say that," he conceded. "Thing is, you'd be askin' the wrong feller, wouldn't you? Only Lew Brennan could say whether he considers me his friend or not."

The heavy-set man looked a little disgusted with that answer. He glanced toward the desk, around the room, then turned back to place a hand upon the door latch as he said: "Tell him Johnny Wheeler was in and I'll be up at the stage station for another half hour or so, if he wants to look me up." Johnny Wheeler swung back the door.

"Anything else you want me to tell him?" asked Ladd.

Wheeler considered a moment before saying: "I reckon you can tell him I picked up some word on them fellers who shot up Piñon and robbed the bank down there. Tell him I got some information on them boys up at Pine Grove. The law up there went and captured one of them fellers. Well, he can look me up." Wheeler bobbed his head and departed.

Ladd arose, stepped to the door, dropped the bar into place across the back of the door, then turned as Cass and his companions came back into the office from the cell-room corridor.

"Who in the hell," mused Walt, "could some cow town constable have arrested for what we done down in Piñon, I wonder?"

Cass was also interested. In a different tone of voice than he'd used toward Ladd up to now, he said: "You plumb certain those three fellers we had to leave down in Piñon are dead?"

Ladd knew for a fact that each of those men lay dead in Enos Orcutt's shed, but to help his own situation a little by creating more diversion, he said: "That's what they told me in the saloon. They said that Sanders feller dropped all three of them and they was dead." Ladd shrugged heavy shoulders. "But I didn't see their corpses. All I know is what they were saying around the saloon."

Cass turned to the youngest outlaw. "Abner, you was out there in front after we came from the bank. Did you see 'em lying out in the roadway?"

Abner nodded. "I seen them, Cass, blood all over them and the ground. But, like Buckner says, maybe . . ." Abner looked at Ladd for support and did not finish his remark.

Ladd frowned a little. "Why would one of them go north to the next town instead of looking you fellers up here in Paso?"

It was a valid question. Walt echoed it to Cass. "That's not very sensible. They knew we'd paid up in advance to hide out in this damned jailhouse until the noise died down. Cass, why would one of them head on northward and by-pass us here in Paso?"

Before the leader could reply, Ladd said: "Because it's not one of your crew, Walt. It's some other feller up in Pine Grove that the law leaned down on. Maybe it's the law who made up that story so's he could maybe collect bounty on someone. Maybe it was the feller he leaned on acting like he was a lot bigger than he is."

Cass nodded. "That's got to be it. Something like that." He returned to the front window again and stooped down. As he systematically studied as much of the main roadway as could be seen, he said: "That son-of-a-bitch Brennan." He added nothing to this, and a moment later, when he started to turn away, he froze at the window for a moment, then swore exasperatedly. "Two men coming across from the store. Let's get out of sight." He turned, looked at Ladd, and made a small hand gesture. "Get rid of them," he ordered, and retreated with Walt and Abner beyond the cell-room door again.

This time when the visitors walked in, Ladd arose and went to stand over near the gun rack on the far wall, his right side turned away from the pair of cowmen who looked from the desk on around the room and over to Ladd as one of them gruffly said: "Where's Brennan? We got business with him."

Ladd answered forthrightly. "He was here about an hour ago. Since then he hasn't been back. If you've got a message, I'll be glad to give it to him for you."

"There are Apaches on the east range," said the gruff-voiced older man, his expression reflecting the bleak mood he was in. "This here is Jim Morgan. I'm Jeff Longstreet. You see Brennan, you tell him we come by to see if he wants to do anything, and, if he don't, we'll do it for him. We'll make up some riding posses and chase those darned redskins all the way down to the border and across it. You hear?"

Ladd could have heard the angry cowman if he'd been out back in the alley. "I'll tell him when he gets back, Mister Longstreet. By the way, if you really want to recruit riders to go against the Indians, just post a notice that you're paying a decent wage and you'll get all the men you'll need."

Old Longstreet grunted. "I don't need advice, young feller, and us fellers who run cattle on the east range don't need recruits. We got a small army of riders betwixt the lot of us."

Longstreet and his silent companion stamped out of the office. From the cell-room doorway Cass said: "Buckner, I thought you said there weren't no Apaches in the hills around here?"

Ladd did not recall having said any such thing. But he did remember saying he could hide the outlaws so well in the mountains even the Indians could not find them. He repeated this, then he also said: "No better way under the sun to get out of this country, if you want to leave it, than to join a raghead-hunting expedition, and just keep on going. Posse men don't go traipsing after outlaws over territory inhabited by hostiles."

Cass stared. "You're about as smart as Walt!" he exclaimed. "And what would the ragheads do if they seen the three of us out there alone, crossing their damned territory? I'll tell you what they'd do . . ." But Cass did not have a chance to finish his statement. Out front a man swung his horse toward the jailhouse and stepped from the saddle with a loud grunt, and Cass reached again to pull the cell-room door almost closed.

This time, when the stranger walked in, he brought a scent of sage and heat and open spaces with him. He was, like the pair of older men who had previously visited the jailhouse, a range cattleman. His attire spoke volumes about his ability, his rugged confidence, and his cow savvy. He was tall and squinty-eyed and pleasant in the face, although his hide was leathery, lined, and currently unshaved. He smiled pleasantly at Ladd and asked about Brennan. When Ladd said the lawman wasn't around this tall, rugged individual shoved back his hat, fished forth his tobacco sack and brown cigarette papers, and went to work as he laconically said: "My name is Harrison. Brennan will know me if you tell him that name." Harrison lit his smoke and continued to study Ladd Buckner. "I got raided last night and lost maybe thirty, forty steers and heifers on the east range."

Ladd said: "Ragheads. Do you know a feller named Longstreet?"

"We got adjoinin' ranges," said Harrison. "Him, too?"

"Yes. He and a man named Morgan were in here not more than minutes ago. The Apaches hit them, too."

Harrison smoked and gazed at Ladd, then gazed around the office, and for a man who had lost cattle to Indians he did not act nearly as fired-up as Longstreet had acted. "When will Lew be back?" he asked.

Ladd answered cautiously: "I don't know, but he shouldn't be much longer. I think he just went around town somewhere."

"You a friend of his?"

Ladd shrugged. "We know each other."

Harrison did not appear to be in any hurry to leave. Unlike the other visitors who had stopped by this morning, Harrison acted more as though he were paying a social call than as though he were an outraged cowman. In fact he strolled toward a chair and with one hand on the back of it, he said: "If it won't be too long, I could set here and wait."

Ladd had mixed feelings about this. He needed reinforcements but there was no guarantee Harrison would turn out to be his ally in the event of trouble. On the other hand, as long as the range cattleman was there, in the office, even if Brennan walked in, he could hardly afford to denounce Ladd in front of his friend. Ladd decided not to protest, and asked if Harrison wanted some cold, stale coffee. The cowman surprised Ladd. "That's a right good idea," he said, and pulled aside the chair as he sat down facing the side wall and the back wall of the jailhouse office. He seemed never to allow his eyes to widen out of their perpetual squint, nor did it help that cigarette smoke trickled upward, also compelling him to keep his eyes narrowed.

Ladd drew off a mug of the bitter coffee and handed it across. Harrison accepted it gravely. "Much obliged," he said, and shoved out long legs that he crossed at the ankles as he studied Ladd some more. "Seems to me I may have seen you around the countryside somewhere, friend. I run cattle on the north and east ranges." He smiled a trifle. "I also got 'em on the south and west ranges, only they aren't supposed to be in them places."

Harrison rambled on. He was a pleasant man to talk to as Ladd discovered while they faced one another across the room, and it also developed that Harrison was an observant individual. He said: "Mister, did you know you'd lost your six-gun?"

Ladd looked down. He had made a particular point of trying to keep his right side turned to the wall. Evidently he had not wholly succeeded. "Left it with a gunsmith to be fixed," he lied. "The firing pin is so badly chipped it only detonates the bullets about every third or fourth time."

Harrison smoked, sipped coffee, and offered no comment for a while, not until he leaned to drop his smoke and stamp on it. Then he said: "We don't have no gunsmith in Paso."

Ladd reddened a little. "Didn't leave it to be fixed in Paso, friend. I left it up at . . . Pine Grove . . . to be fixed."

Harrison raised skeptical eyes. "And since then you've been riding around wearing that empty holster? Well, amigo, we all got different ideas, don't we? Me, I got no use for guns at all. I wear one because I figure I'd get killed within a week or two if I didn't wear one, but guns are the devil's tools for a fact. Nothing good ever comes of men relying upon guns."

Ladd tried to figure this man out, and he could not even come close to doing it, and he knew he was not coming close.

XII

Cass eased the cell-room door open as quietly and as surreptitiously as he had done with Ladd Buckner, but this time the man sitting before the constable's desk was facing in that direction and saw the three men with their aimed six-guns. Harrison did not lower the coffee cup but continued to sip coffee for a moment, for as long as it took him carefully to determine what was across the room from him. Then, gradually, he lowered the cup and blew a little smoke but neither moved nor opened his mouth. He seemed surprised, but he also seemed perfectly capable of living with this astonishing situation. He leaned to put the cup atop Brennan's desk, then he eased back again as Cass and Walt pushed out of the cell-room corridor, and youthful Abner briskly shouldered past the older men and approached Harrison with his cocked Colt pointed squarely at the cattleman's face.

Harrison turned slightly to cast a sardonic look in Ladd Buckner's direction. "Friends of yours?" he asked quietly.

Ladd did not answer; he simply stood and watched Abner disarm the range man exactly as Abner had also disarmed him. When Harrison was defanged, Walt lowered his gun a notch and said: "Cass, it's goin' to get a little crowded in here directly."

Cass was in no mood for levity and acted as though he had not heard the older man. He cocked his head though, as heavy footfalls approaching from the south out upon the plank walk made a solid, heavy sound. All of them listened, including Harrison. Ladd Buckner was half of the opinion that this time whoever that was out yonder would stride right on past. Cass did not feel this confident, apparently, because he snarled for his companions to retreat again, and led the way into the cell-room corridor. They had scarcely got the door almost closed before Lew Brennan walked in out of the hot sunlight of mid-morning.

Brennan stared from Ladd to Harrison, then over toward the cell-room doorway as Cass stepped forth with his gun hand stone steady and said: "Where in the hell have you been? What took you so long?"

Instead of replying at once to the outlaw's question Constable Brennan pointed: "What the hell are you doing with this feller? He's a local cowman."

Cass turned bitingly sarcastic again. "Yeah, we know he's a local cowman, and we also know that, if you had shagged your butt back here at a decent time, you could have handled the flow of callers been coming in here all morning to complain about some lousy Indians running off livestock on the east range. Instead, you been horsing around over at the saloon, or somewhere, and we didn't even get any breakfast. Brennan, I got half a notion to . . ."

"Wait a minute," protested the law officer. "What was the sense of taking this one? He's harmless. He runs cattle west of town . . . and now you've gone and made a lousy mess of everything."

Brennan looked at the cowman and Harrison smoked, looked steadily back, and, when the silence began to draw out, he dryly said: "Lew, you always were a worthless bastard."

Normally, perhaps, Brennan would have hurled himself upon someone who had insulted him like that, but right at this moment Brennan's thoughts were upon a much more critical phase of what had happened in his absence. Harrison, the respectable local cowman, would be able to identify the Piñon bank robbers and killers as the same men Brennan was hiding in the Paso jailhouse. What Cass actually had done by taking Harrison captive was destroy Brennan's credibility in the town where Brennan was not just the local representative of the law, but where Brennan also lived and enjoyed living. Now, when the outlaws departed, Brennan would also have to depart. Unless something happened to Harrison. But Brennan did not think of that at this moment; he instead turned a brooding gaze on Cass and Walt and the youngest renegade, then jerked his head in Ladd's direction.

"There's just one of those freighters still in town. A big feller with a beard all over his face and he can't talk very well."

Ladd scarcely drew a breath. For Lew Brennan to identify Simon Terry as a freighter implied that Brennan had not as yet discovered the hoax. Ladd was almost ready to start breathing again.

Cass holstered his six-gun. "All right. So Buckner told us the truth about how he got here. That's the only true thing he told us. Now we got to get away from here."

Brennan frowned. "You don't go alone." He pointed. "You fixed it so's I can't stay the minute you let this range man figure things out."

Abner disagreed with this. "Shoot the son-of-a-bitch," he said. "Get away from his chair and I'll do it."

Cass swore. "You crazy devil, Abner. You ease off the hammer of that gun. You pull a trigger in here and, log walls or not, everyone in this lousy town'll hear the shooting and come a-running. Anyway, this cowman isn't our headache. I said ease down the hammer on that damned gun!"

Abner obeyed. He even leathered his Colt but his expression was sullen and he turned away from Cass to face in Buckner's direction.

"What a god-damn' mess," groaned the constable, moving around to his desk chair and sinking down over there.

Harrison dropped his smoke and stepped on it. He shot Ladd a glance, then swung slightly to rake the three renegades with another look. He sighed audibly and waggled his head as though he were monumentally disgusted. "And I thought I had trouble," he muttered, "when I come into town this morning. Lew . . . ?"

Brennan snapped at the cowman. "You do have trouble, Harrison." Brennan turned toward Cass. "Remember, I got money coming. Ten percent of nine thousand." Brennan leaned thick arms atop his desk. Evidently he was beginning to try and ameliorate his dilemma, and, since money was apparently his measure of all things and all kinds of success, he was beginning to reason that he would be paid well for having to flee the country.

Cass did not even answer that, did not even act as though he had heard it. "We'll set around here until nightfall, then we'll have to ride on." Cass said this for the benefit of Abner and old Walt, his fellow renegades, but to Ladd it had the unpleasant sound of something a cold-blooded individual might say whose private decision, whatever it was, had been reached. If this were so, then Ladd felt instinctively that he and perhaps the range cattleman were not going to see another sunrise. If the renegades abandoned Paso and their hide-out, which had become increasingly perilous for them this day, they were probably not going to leave a couple of hostages behind who could not only identify them but who could also recall a number of particular details regarding each renegade.

Walt said: "Take Buckner along and head back into the mountains."

Cass flared back. "You darned fool, haven't you heard what these cowmen been saying all day? There's Indians out there. If they could pick up the tracks of just four riders, they'd be after us like a pack of wolves after a crippled doe."

Walt was not affronted, perhaps because he was by this time well accustomed to being derided by Cass. He shrugged and said: "All right. Then where? We can't go south again. What does that leave?" Walt had a point. If they went northward or eastward, they ran a fine chance of encountering those rampaging Apaches. Southward lay the aroused area around Piñon. Westerly, as the range cattleman had been saying since his arrival at the jailhouse, there had also been an Apache raid. "Stay right where we are," said Walt, looking sardonically at the outlaw leader, "and take us some more hostages." He jerked his head in Brennan's direction. "It'll look like we got Lew here as a prisoner and that had ought to get him out of trouble with the folks here in his town."

"Lew?" exclaimed Cass. "Who gives a damn about Lew? We got just three hides to worry about, and that don't include Lew Brennan." Cass turned upon the constable. "How good is the road west of here along the foothills?"

Brennan didn't answer, the range cattleman did. "Lousy," he said. "In places it hasn't been filled in since the rains of last winter. You don't have trouble on horseback but you can't use it with wheels and teams."

Cass glared. "I didn't ask you!"

Harrison was uncowed. "I know that. But I happen to have ridden in by that road this morning and I don't know when was the last time Brennan was out that way." Harrison continued to look steadily at the glowering outlaw. "You might make it out of here on a stagecoach. So far the ragheads haven't attacked one of them, and, if you could keep 'em from downing the harness horses while you were protected inside the rig with plenty of ammunition, I think you could probably make it all the way up to Pine Grove. There hasn't been any redskin trouble up there yet. Not that I've heard of anyway."

Abner and Walt exchanged a glance, then turned to see what their leader's reaction to this might be. Cass did not keep them wondering very long. He sneered at Harrison. "What the hell do you take us for, anyway? If the ragheads are on the north range beyond Paso, they'd sight anything as big as a stagecoach from a couple of miles out. I think you're trying to get us killed. That's what I think."

Harrison still did not drop his eyes. "Mister, if you got a way out of Paso, and you don't get all the wood and what-not around you when you make your run for it . . . they'll bury you right here. Go ahead and try it on horseback."

Cass went to the window and leaned to gaze out into the sun-bright roadway. Paso lay utterly still on all sides. For a long while the outlaw chieftain looked out and around, then he very slowly straightened up and turned. "Brennan," he said sharply, "there's no one in the damned roadway. Even the tie racks are empty."

Paso's lawman heaved up to his feet and crossed over to look out. Cass was correct; the town was as silent and empty-seeming as a cemetery. Brennan looked more puzzled than anxious as he strained to see up the roadway as far as possible before saying: "It's high noon. This time of year it's pretty much always like this in the middle of the day . . . and later, too . . . for as long as the heat lasts."

But when Lewis Brennan turned back toward his desk, Ladd Buckner got the impression from his expression that Brennan was a lot less puzzled now, that he was just plain worried.

Cass was slightly less anxious after Brennan's pronouncement, but, when he, too, moved away from the window, he shot a cold look around at them all, then echoed the constable by saying: "What a damned mess. The whole blasted thing's got out of hand." He fixed Ladd Buckner with a vicious look. "When you walked in and commenced your lousy lying, the trouble started."

Ladd borrowed a leaf from the cattleman's book by saying: "The trouble started down in Piñon, not up here."

Cass ignored that contradiction to say: "What idea have you got about us pulling out of here?"

"I've been telling you all morning," replied Ladd, "to sneak out the back way when no one is looking and head up into the mountains with me. I don't see that you can do anything else, now that there's a band of raghead marauders on the upper cattle range. Like you said yourself, if you bust out of Paso heading across all that flat, open country, they'll see you sure as hell."

"Not in the dark," said Cass.

Harrison spoke up. "You can't get plumb across it by morning even if you ride fast all night. You'd still be sitting ducks out there."

Abner turned on his chieftain. "Damn it, Cass, quit buttin' your head against a stone wall. These fellers know this lousy country. You heard 'em. We can't get out of here except by Buckner's route."

Cass turned. "Sonny," he said in his most condescending tone, "all these fellers want is to see the three of us get killed. All I'm trying to do is to prevent that from happening. If you want to head out on your own, there is the damned door and good riddance."

Abner did not say any more. He and Walt looked a little more worried as time passed, but they did not again offer to challenge Cass's comments or his judgment.

XIII

Ladd longed to cross the room and look out into the roadway. He was confident that something had happened out there. Perhaps Orcutt, Terry, and Reilly had guessed his difficulty inside the jailhouse, and maybe they had somehow learned that the outlaws they had come north to find were also inside the jailhouse, but whatever people knew around Paso, it most probably had something to do with the men in the jailhouse. If he'd dared, he would have engaged Lewis Brennan in conversation to see if Brennan had even unconsciously seen or heard anything that might have had significance. Instead of doing any of these things Ladd remained over along the rear wall smoking and being unobtrusive. Of one thing he was reasonably certain—this charade was not going to last much longer. If the men outside didn't force the issue, the outlaws themselves would do so.

Cass in particular was becoming increasingly worried and restless as time passed. He walked to the stove to get some coffee and cast a sulphurous glance in Ladd Buckner's direction. "How could we get plumb clear of this town," he asked surlily, "and into those mountains without anyone knowing we'd done it, for as long as we'd need to get a good start?"

Ladd answered bluntly: "You said it yourself. Wait until nightfall, then leave in the dark."

The outlaw lifted his coffee cup. "We got to have horses," he said, "and not just old pelters, either. Riding the mountains requires good saddle stock."

Ladd agreed. "We'll need good stock, no question about it, but they've got it around Paso. Down at the livery barn, maybe, or in the sheds around town. We can take care of that, too, after dark when most folks'll be eating supper."

Walt smiled encouragingly. He had been favoring Ladd Buckner right from the start, and now, when it seemed that Cass was going to adopt Ladd's scheme for getting them out of their predicament, Walt not only felt vindicated, he was also showing by his broad smile that he felt that way.

Abner was sulking and he was bored. The prospect of dying in this mean little village did not appear to trouble him, probably because Abner, who was a totally depthless individual, never considered death as being applicable to him. Death only arrived to snuff out the life of others. And Abner was patently a person who required movement, change, action. Being cooped up in the log jailhouse of a place called Paso brought out his latent restlessness. He probably would have paced, if he'd thought of it or if his partners would have tolerated it. As it was, he leaned upon the wall looking mercilessly at the others and occasionally leaning down to look out of the window. It was one of the times that he was doing this, squinting into the sunshine out in the roadway, that he suddenly said: "There is something going on up at the saloon."

Cass walked over and so did Walt, but when the older outlaw would also have leaned to look out, with his back to the room, Cass growled at him, so Walt shrugged and turned fully to face the hostages.

After a moment of watching and looking, the outlaw leader straightened around, frowning in Brennan's direction. "Take a look," he commanded, "and tell me what it's all about."

The lawman walked over and swung slightly to one side in order to be able to see northward in the roadway. After a moment he stepped back, straightening up. "Looks like one of the cow outfits just rode in . . . something like that."

Cass eyed the lawman. "Can you go up there and find out?"

Brennan said: "Sure, why couldn't I?"

"You was worried a while back about folks knowing you were hiding us in here."

Brennan jutted his jaw. "Harrison there would tell folks, if he got out of here . . . when he gets out of here. But right now they wouldn't know anything. At least I can't see how they'd know anything."

Cass nodded. "Go up and nose around, but be careful. It's too darned quiet out there, it seems to me. Pick up all the information you can."

Abner went over to hold the door open and to say: "Constable, ask about them damned Indians. Find out if they're likely to be into them mountains back there."

As Brennan stepped outside, he nodded his head as though he were agreeing with the youngest killer's interest in marauding broncos, but his eyes were moving swiftly left and right along the empty roadway, too, so perhaps his nodding was simply perfunctory.

Walt turned to Ladd Buckner with an expression of confidence. "We could take that son-of-a-bitch with us for a shield," he said. "I never could abide folks who wear badges, not even crooked ones."

Harrison glanced at Walt, then turned his attention back to Cass and Abner over along the front wall watching Brennan's progress on a diagonal course up the roadway. If Harrison was entertaining some notion of perhaps jumping Walt and trying to get Walt's weapon before Abner and Cass turned around, he had to abandon the idea. Cass abruptly turned to look at the others, then to sigh and walk around to ease down at the lawman's desk and lean back in quiet thought.

There was still a long time before nightfall. Like it or not, for all of them there were a number of long hours yet to be waited out. Cass addressed the cowman. He seemed to have developed a grudging respect for Harrison, perhaps because the cowman had not once been cowed by Cass's evil disposition or menacing attitude. "You figure we'd make it going off with Buckner into the mountains?" Cass asked, and the range cattleman shifted his attention to the outlaw leader but for a long while he seemed to be considering his reply. Eventually he said: "Yeah, I figure you could make it. I know I could . . . providin' I could safely get into the forest cover back there. It's a hell of a big chunk of territory."

"And as soon as we're gone, you'll tell everyone where we went," said Cass.

This time the range cowman smiled. "Sure, that'd be natural, wouldn't it? Trouble is, mister, without Brennan there's no law in Paso to recruit a posse, and, if folks hear that you're the same bunch who shot up Piñon and killed some people, I sort of doubt that anyone could get up a posse. Folks usually figure that, if something don't harm them, why then it's got to be someone else's problem, not theirs."

Cass said no more for a while. He did not seem convinced by Harrison's logic. After all, Cass had already used up two of his lives and only had one life left. Those were the circumstances that made cautious men of a great many outlaws. If things turned out as Harrison thought they might, that would be fine. If they didn't turn out that way . . .

Abner, speaking from the front window, caught everyone's attention: "Brennan's coming back. Looks like no one suspected nothing when they was talkin' to him up there." Abner moved clear of the window and started to form a cigarette.

Ladd Buckner could feel his stomach tightening again exactly as it had when Brennan had returned to the jailhouse the first time. One thing Ladd suspected was that his friends from Piñon were deeply involved in whatever was occurring out there. If Brennan even suspected anything about this, Ladd had no illusions about his own fate.

When the heavy footfalls sounded outside, Abner leaned to haul the door inward and to look through smoke as Lewis Brennan walked inside, faintly scowling. He faced Cass to make his report.

"It's range men from both sides of the road, east and west. There's one hell of a band of broncos raising Cain all around us." He shot Ladd a brief look, then returned his full attention to Cass. "Even back yonder in the lousy mountains."

Walt and Abner straightened up to stare at the constable. Walt in particular had been putting considerable store in their chances of escaping by way of the rearward mountains. Now, he and Abner stared at the lawman.

Brennan did not look very happy either. "The damned Army," he muttered, "drags its butt all over the territory where there aren't no ragheads, and as usual the civilians got to take the bull by the horns."

"That's what all the palavering is about, up at the saloon?" asked Cass, and, when Brennan inclined his head, Cass rocked forward and leaned both elbows atop the cluttered desk. "Damned good thing they don't have a telegraph here," he dryly said to Walt and Abner, "otherwise by now someone would have telegraphed for the Army."

"The hell with the Army," growled Abner. "That's the least of our worries. Just how do we get out of this damned place?"

"Exactly like we figured to do it," stated Cass, smiling flintily at the younger man. "We'll take our chances with the ragheads up in the mountains. My guess is that, if Buckner's any good at all as a guide, he won't lead us anywhere near a raghead camp. And the reason he won't is because his own darned head will roll if he does. If the ragheads don't waste him, I will." Cass smiled over in Ladd's direction. "What you got to say to that?"

Ladd answered wryly: "Not a hell of a lot. You're right. I don't want to die any more'n the rest of you do."

A man rode slowly up past the jailhouse on a large chestnut horse, his hat tugged low and his shoulders lightly powdered with travel dust. He headed up toward a number of range men and townsmen out front of the saloon in the bright sunlight around one of the tie racks. As Abner leaned to watch, the stranger turned in, stepped off, and, while he was beating dust from his clothing, he spoke in an indistinguishable monotone that seemed to be having a very impressive effect upon his listeners. No one said a word while this stranger was speaking. Afterward, though, there were a number of men with questions, and someone stepped forth to take the reins of the stranger's horse, and also to point southward across the road in the direction of the jailhouse. Abner said: "Hell, he's bein' sent down here." Abner hauled around looking at Cass. "We better lock these bastards into the cells, otherwise this stranger's going to suspect something."

Cass was not excited. "Why lock them up? We're all just having a war council in here, is all. The feller's a stranger, isn't he? Then how would he know we're not plumb legitimate?" Cass motioned. "Take the bar off the door so's he can enter."

Ladd agreed with Cass's logic rather than with the reasoning of Abner, but, when the door finally opened and the stranger walked in to nod around at them all, Ladd's breath stopped in his gullet. The stranger was Joe Reilly!

Lew Brennan, looking more hostile than amiable, said: "What's on your mind, friend?"

Reilly turned a surprised look upon the lawman. He gave the impression of a man who had expected a different kind of greeting. "What's on my mind," Reilly answered curtly, "isn't givin' me the headache I figure it's going to give you, Constable. There is a rampaging band of Apaches plumb around your town, and from what I seen up the stage road behind this place, I'd say they're waiting for nightfall to fire you, then shoot your folks down by the light of their own burning buildings." Reilly gestured with one thick arm. "I was just telling this to some fellers over in front of the saloon and they sure as hell verified for me that there's Indians raidin' all around through here."

Reilly removed his hat and beat more dust from his trousers. Harrison, the saturnine range cattleman, sat staring steadily at Joe Reilly, but he was the only one. As far as Ladd could determine, Reilly's statement, not Reilly the man, had made a deep impression.

Cass stood up from the desk and swore with feeling. Lew Brennan looked ready to slam a big fist into the wall behind him. Abner and Walt turned from Reilly to Cass, but he ignored them completely and paced the room, brows knitted. Twice he stopped to look up the roadway toward the front of the saloon where those townsmen and range men were still clustered in grave conversation. Finally Cass said: "All right, we got to stay, then. That's all there is to it." He turned to Joe Reilly. "Where did you ride from, mister, when you come over here?"

Reilly said: "Piñon, a place south through the . . ."

"God dammit, I know where Piñon is!" exclaimed the outlaw, and gestured. "Abner, take his damned gun and push him over against the wall with the others."

XIV

Joe Reilly did not resist when he was herded over toward the rear wall, but he gave an excellent imitation of a man who felt indignant over being treated this way when he had gone out of his way to warn of impending Indian trouble. He finally shook clear of Abner and turned fully to face the youthful killer, and to say: "Constable, just what in the hell is the meaning of this? I'm a legitimate traveler on my way through and . . ."

"Oh, shut up," growled Lewis Brennan. He made it sound enormously disgusted, as though Joe Reilly were the least of his worries, at least the most unimportant of his recent worries.

It was Cass who turned and faced Reilly as he said: "When you was over in Piñon, mister, had they made up a manhuntin' posse to go looking for the fellers who shot up their town and raided their bank?"

"No," said Joe Reilly, staring closely at Cass. "Their lawman was killed in that . . ." Joe let his voice trail off into silence, and he continued to stare at Cass. When he eventually shifted his attention to the only other armed men in the room excluding the lawman, he said: "You three fellers . . . ?"

No one answered him and Ladd wanted to kick Joe in the shins. Reilly knew perfectly well who Cass, Walt, and Abner were. Going through this moment of mock astonishment was making a nervous wreck of Ladd Buckner.

Walt, who had been silent up to now, gazed a trifle doubtingly at Joe Reilly: "Mister, if those ragheads are all around this town and you was up in the pass yonder . . . how'n hell did you get through and past them to get down here without them cutting you down?"

Reilly smiled. "I saw them," he explained. "I saw them first, and that's nine-tenths of any battle, amigo. Once I could see how they were strung out, I only had to make darned certain they didn't look over their shoulders and see me. Then I rode off the roadway and came down through the trees . . . praying every blasted step of the way. It was easy, but by God, mister, I could have died fifty times before I got in among the buildings."

Walt accepted that, probably because it sounded plausible enough. He strolled to the front wall, leaned, and looked out, shook his head, and said: "That's quite a herd of men up in front of the saloon. Why don't they just rig out and get their weapons, and ride out there? If a man can keep ragheads out of the rocks and timber and gullies, he can thin 'em out without much trouble."

Abner sneered: "You and General Custer."

Gradually the men in the jailhouse office lost interest in their latest associate, the man from Piñon, and this allowed Joe to edge over until he was leaning against the same wall Ladd was also leaning against. Joe turned and said: "You got some tobacco, friend?" When Ladd passed over his sack and papers, Reilly methodically went to work.

From a very great distance there came the unmistakable echo of gunshots. It sounded as though there were both carbines and handguns out there. Abner ran through the back of the jailhouse to locate a window and look out there toward the west. Lew Brennan shook his head. "He can't see nothing from back there. There's only one window and it's eight feet from the floor in a cell."

Reilly leaned to return the papers and tobacco sack. "There are no Indians," he whispered swiftly. "It's a scheme to get them out of here." That was all he had time to say as Abner returned, gun in hand as though expecting the Apaches to burst into the jailhouse.

"It was back in them lousy foothills," Abner reported a trifle breathlessly. "You was right, Cass, we das'n't bust out of here tonight and try to make it up into the mountains."

Harrison arose from the chair he had been occupying for a long while and stretched, then turned to gaze from Buckner to Reilly, and smile. He was still the least anxious individual in the log building. For Ladd, the little bit of information Reilly had been able to give him was enough to convince him that his suspicion about his friends from Piñon being involved in whatever was happening outside the log walls of the Paso jailhouse was correct. But that skimpy information had also aroused a lot more curiosity than it had allayed. Cass, speaking again to Lew Brennan, interrupted Ladd's thoughts.

"What the hell will they do?"

Brennan looked up. "The townsfolk? How would I know?"

As though this were someone's cue, a couple of men from across the road walked over and paused out front to argue a little, then one of them raised a hand as though to knock on the office door, and Cass jerked his head for Brennan to go to the door.

When the lawman pulled back the door and looked out, one of those townsmen said: "Lew, we got a meeting called for fifteen minutes from now over at the saloon. They said we'd better let you know."

Brennan scowled. "What kind of a meeting?"

"Well, damn it," exclaimed the other townsman, looking and sounding aggravated, "what kind of a meeting would folks call when their town's surrounded by a bunch of lousy reservation jumpers? A defense meeting, that's what kind!"

Brennan grumbled and began closing the door. Both those townsmen turned back in the direction of the general store, and Cass, with a bright light in his eye, said something hopeful for the first time in several hours.

"I think we got a way out of here," he said, and turned. Everyone was staring at him. He saw this, beckoned Walt and Abner to one side, and whispered to them.

Ladd used this moment to hiss a question at Reilly: "Is there a plan?"

Reilly whispered back. "Yes. Get everyone out of here."

"How?"

But before Reilly could risk answering, the three outlaws were ending their little conference. Abner and Walt also looked relieved and hopeful for the first time in hours.

Lew Brennan seemed to be descending deeper into apathy as time passed. When Cass told him it would shortly be time to attend that meeting, Brennan snarled a reply. "There's not a damned thing I can do over there except to advise 'em to either try and bring in troops or try to recruit the range men, then go Indian huntin'. I can darned well tell you one thing. If they put off settling up with those ragheads until after dark, they won't be able to keep them from sneakin' in and firin' the place. If there's one thing ragheads are right good at, it's sneakin' around in the dark."

"Then go tell them that," urged Cass, and went to open the door for Lew Brennan.

Brennan frowned. "They can't get out onto the range to recruit those cow outfits," he said protestingly. "You heard it . . . the ragheads are completely around us."

Cass accepted this the same way and still held the door. "All right, tell them that, but go attend their meeting."

Cass gestured for Brennan to leave. Ladd guessed this was part of whatever scheme Cass had come up with. He did not want the lawman in the jailhouse. That didn't make much sense, but then Ladd had spent the entire morning thus far listening to things that hadn't made much sense. Brennan stalked out and Cass closed the door behind him.

Reilly leaned and whispered: "One less. Did you ever see one of these log buildings burn?"

Ladd turned and stared, but he had no opportunity to do more than that because Cass called his name.

"Buckner! You know this country so good and you're so sure you can elude the ragheads . . . you ready to go?"

Ladd did not have to pretend to be surprised. "In this damned daylight?"

Cass smiled. "Right now, in this damned daylight. The town's scairt to death over the raghead scare, and somewhere out yonder the Apaches are lying in wait. Well, if we can get out of this jailhouse and over close to the foothills, when dusk falls we'd ought to have good horses and a fair chance of making it." Cass pointed. "It was that traveler gave me the idea. Look at him! Hell, if someone like that can slip through past the Indians, so can we."

None of this was very complimentary to Joe Reilly, but he did not appear to heed the implied insult; he seemed instead to be trying to make some kind of mental adjustment. Perhaps his problem was to try and correlate the outlaw's scheme with some other scheme being perfected by the townsmen. Either way, Ladd Buckner was required to answer Cass. He said: "All right, but I don't like trying this in broad daylight."

Cass was blunt. "You don't have to like anything. All you got to do is lead the way."

It was the range cattleman who broke in to offer an opinion. "The Indians will be watching the town, and the townsmen will be watching the outlying countryside. Mister, you got to be crazy to try something like this."

Cass did not flare up as he had done at other times when his judgment had been challenged. In fact, he continued to smile as he said: "Well, now, cowboy, there is a little more to this. You and that feller who just rode into town this morning, and Buckner there, will be our hostages. If we got to take a few more, we'll do that, too. We're going to walk the bunch of you ahead of us on foot, while we ride, and the townsmen won't dare raise a gun because, if they do, we'll shoot you fellers in the back, one at a time. And the ragheads won't shoot, neither, until we're closer to them than we are to the town. And that's what you'll be for . . . mister . . . shields. If we can't bust around a handful of Indians and make it up through the trees . . . and, mister, no raghead living would abandon his chances of plundering a whole town just to chase after a handful of outlaws who don't have anything but a sackful of greenbacks."

Cass was proud of his plan. Maybe he had reason to be. Ladd eyed the outlaw leader and decided that Cass, whatever else he might be, was not altogether a fool. He knew human nature, apparently, whether it was inside a brown or a white hide. But there was a lot more risk than Ladd Buckner liked to think about.

Walt said: "What about Brennan?"

"Forget Brennan," replied Cass. "That's why I sent him away. He still figures to get the rest of the percentage we owe him."

Cass turned to lean and look out into the empty sun-bright roadway. When he straightened back around, he was still smiling. He drew his Colt and gestured with it toward the back door of the jailhouse office, and, while Walt and Abner stepped back there to lift down the door bar, Cass kicked open the locked lower drawer of the constable's desk to get the sealed bank pouch. Ladd and Joe Reilly exchanged a look, then Joe shrugged thick shoulders and headed in the direction of the doorway. Harrison also turned, looking either resigned or philosophic, and shuffled toward the back wall.

Now that Cass was out of his state of thraldom he was a different person. "Down the back alley," he commanded, "to the rear entrance of the livery barn. We'll take our own animals, if we can't find anything better." He rested his right palm upon the holstered Colt and eyed Ladd a trifle skeptically. "I sure hope you know those mountains," he quietly said.

Ladd didn't know the mountains. He'd never even seen those mountains until he'd crossed through them miles to the west where he'd come up out of one of their cañons to ride into the middle of an Apache bushwhack.

Cass gestured. "Open the door and look up and down the alleyway, Walt, then let's get to moving."

Abner had his six-gun cocked in his hand. He seemed to think in terms of drawing and cocking his gun regardless of the situation. Cass had to warn him to ease down the hammer, but apparently Cass knew how useless it would also be to tell Abner to holster the gun.

Walt pulled back and nodded. "Nothing in sight either way. Want me to lead off, Cass?"

The outlaw leader nodded his head. Ladd got the impression that Cass would probably have sent Walt out first even if Walt hadn't volunteered. Cass viewed the older outlaw as entirely expendable.

XV

Reilly managed to slip in close beside Ladd and say one thing before Cass and Abner, herding along Harrison and carrying the money pouch, stepped through the doorway into the sun-bright and totally empty alleyway. "The whole damned town is watching."

Ladd had sweat running under his shirt and he hadn't even been out in the sunshine yet. Paso was still too quiet. Whether Cass realized this or not, Ladd did. Each time they passed a building on either side that had daylight showing between it and the next structure, Ladd's breathing became shallow. It was in such places that armed men usually waited.

Nothing happened. There were no armed men in sight. There was only a dog scouting up trash barrels in the alley that looked at them, and, after a moment of picking up impressions, tucked his tail and whisked from sight around a warped wooden corner. The livery barn was southward a few hundred yards. There were three empty lots interspersed here and there along Main Street. They may have attested to the lack of enthusiasm on the part of investors in Paso, but right at this particular moment their value to the men in the alleyway was beyond question. They allowed a clear sighting of Main Street, the east side of it where the store fronts loomed, stolid and empty, and the dusty roadway that was also empty. Abner, still carrying his six-gun loosely on the right side, looked out there, then grinned at Cass and continued to walk along.

"Everybody's up at the saloon." Abner chuckled.

Walt said nothing and kept his eyes swinging from side to side. Clearly this kind of thing was nothing new to the oldest outlaw, and just as clearly he was right now functioning at his best.

Ladd used a cuff to push sweat off his forehead. It was one thing to be armed and in trouble and something altogether different to be in trouble and unarmed.

Joe Reilly reached inside his coat vigorously to scratch. His gaze at Ladd was humorous and sardonic. Evidently Reilly had decided that whether he survived this ordeal or not, he was not going to start praying until he had to.

Harrison, the range cowman, usually had a brown-paper cigarette dangling from his thin lips and this moment was no exception. He looked from left to right, cigarette dangling without being lighted, and, when Cass turned and their glances crossed, the cowman drawled an opinion. "You might have it figured right at that. Everyone is so busy worrying about everyone else, you just might make it. Your worst danger'll be beyond town."

Cass answered almost pleasantly. "Yeah, problem will be slipping around the ragheads, but being in the forest, and knowing they're out there and they won't know we're out there, ought to make a difference." Cass continued to gaze at Harrison. "How far's your ranch from here?"

"Four miles due west along the foothills until you come to a big washout in the roadway where a creek comes down, then due north from there another couple of miles. Why? You want to go to work on a cow outfit?"

"If we got to run for shelter out of the mountains," explained Cass, "I want to know where to run to."

Harrison accepted this. "All right. If you can make it to the ranch, you'll be plenty safe. I bought the outfit from a Mex family that built it. The main house and the bunkhouse got walls three feet thick and barred windows. You can sit in there and eat a nice pleasant supper with all the Indians on earth trying to get at you from the yard. They can't even burn it."

Walt made a little trilling sound of warning up ahead. Everyone slackened pace to look. A large, thick, ugly man had just walked indifferently from the rear of the livery barn and was now standing down there in the center of the alley, legs wide, hands on hips, staring up at the group of men walking toward him. As near as could be determined, the man in the center of the alley was unarmed, but he had the truculent appearance of an individual who, guns or no guns, would be disagreeable if he chose to be, and perhaps this kind of attitude arose from the man's size and build; he was large and massive and layered with powerful muscles. His face showed the scars of many brawls, and, when he turned aside to spit amber, his neck muscles were like steel cables.

Walt kept right on walking. When he was less than a hundred feet from the burly, beetle-browed individual, old Walt simply drew and cocked his six-gun, and those two were suddenly complete equals. In fact, old Walt, who could have stood behind the big man without any part of him showing, had the advantage.

The big man looked surprised, then he spat again, and removed his hands from his hips, and that helped a little; at least now he did not look as though he wanted to fight the whole crowd of them.

Walt gestured. "Inside the barn, mister, and just walk nice and easy."

Abner had his gun cocked again, but this time Cass offered no admonition.

The barn's cool, shaded runway had been freshly raked and watered down. The big man turned, finally, to chew his cud in speculative thought as he studied the motley crew in front of him.

Walt said: "You the day man, friend?"

The big man nodded. "Yeah, what do you want?"

Walt smiled and tilted up his gun barrel. "The best strong young horses you got, friend, without no trouble."

The liveryman spat again, looked over Walt's head and Abner's head to Cass, who he had instinctively singled out as spokesman, and said: "Help yourself. But I'm not goin' to lift a hand to help you steal 'em."

From the corner of his eye Ladd saw Abner's gun hand begin to rise. "I've yet to see the horse I'd die over," he told the liveryman, and by this remark drew the hostler's attention to Abner and the look on his face as his gun hand continued to rise. Ladd could do no more.

The day man struggled with himself, and in the end just as Abner's cocked gun settled to bear, the hostler turned with a curse and pointed. "In them yonder stalls on the south wall, gents, is four of the best animals around Paso. They been raced a little, though, so you'd better know how to set a horse." He dropped his arm and turned. "Saddles, bridles, and blankets are behind me in the harness room."

Cass looked at Ladd. "You just saved that feller's life," he said quietly, and turned to study the day man again, and also to say: "And I can tell you right now, Buckner, he's a bully and a lot worse, and there'll be folks around town who'd just as soon see him get shot." Cass for once seemed on the verge of approving a murder, but instead of allowing Abner to kill the big hostler, Cass showed contempt in his voice when he said: "Step inside, mister, pick out the outfits Abner'll show you, and haul 'em out here. You try to get a gun from a drawer or a saddlebag in there, and Abner'll gut-shoot you with my blessing."

Abner waited. When the day man turned to obey, Abner smiled at Cass as though grateful for this opportunity to kill a man. It made Ladd Buckner's hair stand on end. To one side of him Joe Reilly, who had not had much opportunity to make personal assessments, now watched Abner stroll away with special interest.

The liveryman had evidently also guessed all he had to know because he returned almost at once burdened with two saddles, then he wordlessly and briskly returned for another saddle and the blankets and bridles. For a person whose truculence had been noticeable halfway up the alleyway, he had made a rather complete metamorphosis. He still looked bleak and he watched the outlaws closely, but he was careful to give no offence.

Ladd had a chance to get over beside Joe Reilly when Walt stepped ahead to lend the hostler a hand, and while Abner watched them both as he and Cass stood side-by-side, conversing in near whispers.

Ladd asked if they might have been seen abandoning the jailhouse. Joe's whispered reply was curt. "You can bet on it. They're all around the place. By now they'll be all around this end of town."

"Will they let us leave?"

Reilly put a sardonic look upon his friend and shook his head just once, very emphatically.

Walt swore at a tall black gelding they were rigging out and the gelding stopped fidgeting, but now he rolled his eyes.

Abner was sent up to the front of the barn to look over the town and the northward roadway. To Ladd this seemed like an excellent moment for the townsmen to storm the barn. But it did not happen that way.

Cass, who never once allowed either of his companions to carry the sack with the money pouch inside it, turned toward Harrison, the cowman, with a question. "You know those mountains, too?"

Harrison replied judiciously. "I've hunted 'em a little, and I've rode after lost livestock up in there a few times."

"You'll know whether we can out-sly the damned Apaches, then," replied the outlaw leader. "You walk up ahead with Buckner."

Cass turned his back on the captives again as Abner returned to report that there was no more sign of life now than there had been a couple of hours earlier. "It's plumb unnatural for a town to be this quiet," he warned. "Hell, there's only a couple of range riders up in front of the saloon, and a feller across the road out front working on the wheel of someone's freight rig in front of the blacksmith's place."

Abner, getting no acknowledgment, turned beside Cass to watch the saddling process. He had holstered his Colt for a change.

A man whistled out back in the alleyway, which brought the outlaws around in a blur of drawn weapons and apprehension, but the whistler was making no secret of his advance and in fact the tune he was whistling was a very popular one called "Gerryowen." It was the tune Custer's 7th Cavalry had favored on their long march to oblivion on the Little Big Horn. It was also popular among saloon patrons; scarcely a Saturday night went by in most cow towns that someone with a mouth organ, a banjo, or even a jew's-harp didn't liven up the comradeship and the drinking by playing it.

The outlaws did not come out of their crouches or lower their guns, although, as the whistler approached, it became increasingly evident that he had no intention of trying to sneak up on anyone. Then he rounded the doorway from out back and Ladd recognized Constable Lew Brennan. So also did everyone else including the burly hostler who seemed to be of half a mind to draw encouragement from the appearance of Paso's lawman. Clearly the hostler like most other people in town did not as yet realize the extent of the perfidy of their town constable.

But Brennan did not keep the hostler long in doubt. As he walked forward and as the outlaws were hauling back up out of their fighting stances, Brennan said: "Cass, by God, you deliberately tried to get rid of me so's you fellers could leave town."

Cass shrugged. "If you mean because we didn't figure to take you along . . . that's right, Constable."

"I mean," averred the angry lawman, "you figured to beat me out of that money you owe me. You lied about how much you got down at Piñon so's you wouldn't have to come up with my full percentage. Then you was going to ride out. That's why you sent me to that damned meeting."

Cass said nothing. He gazed at Lew Brennan with completely dispassionate regard, then turned and nodded at Abner. Without any warning Abner drew and fired. Ladd was just as astonished as was Reilly and the hostler, as was the lawman who took that slug hard, high in the body. Ladd glimpsed the expression of pure surprise that flashed for seconds over Brennan's face, then the lawman went down backward, struck wood, and rolled into the center of the runway, dead.

Abner's gunshot acted as a signal. From far up the runway and out across the roadway where that jacked-up freight wagon was parked in front of the blacksmith's shop, four men pushed off a tarp, raised up, shoved rifles over the sideboard, and fired a ragged volley. No one inside the barn was expecting this, but they all reacted the same way by frantically trying to hurl themselves into the nearest shadows.

Abner paused to fire back, face twisted into a murderous expression. The men prone in the wagon bed fired another ragged volley. Abner's gun went off into the overhead air, and from the alleyway out back someone yelled at him. Abner tried to turn and another ragged volley cut him down and rolled him in the dirt.

XVI

Joe Reilly had called the shots when he had told Ladd the outlaws would not be allowed to leave Paso, but now that the fight had started Ladd had a moment to wonder if those townsmen would allow anyone else, including the hostages to survive, either. Bullets came down through the barn from across the front roadway, and out back several men on either side of the big doorless opening also fired up through. The wonder was not that Abner had been riddled to death; the wonder was that everyone else hadn't also been riddled including the terrified big black horse wearing a saddle but no bridle, as it wildly snorted and charged out the back of the barn and beyond town.

Ladd had been careful to go with Joe Reilly when everyone scattered. They crouched inside an empty horse stall, listening to the gunfire. During a brief pause Joe said: "The whole darned town's mobilized. Simon and Doc and I saw to that when you didn't return from the jailhouse. We figured something had gone bad wrong up there. One or two folks around town told us Brennan wasn't considered to be above helping outlaws hide, for a price."

Ladd had no time to comment. The gunfire started up again, but there was nothing he had to tell Joe Reilly about Paso's dishonest lawman. In fact, there would be no point in talking about Brennan to anyone from now on. Paso could bury him and that would be that. There were only two outlaws still alive in the livery barn, but, as Ladd learned to differentiate between gunfire outside the building and gunfire emanating from inside it, he was impressed at the defense Walt and Cass were putting up. Then all the gunfire from outside ended very suddenly and a man's bull-toned voice sang out from the roadway.

"Hey, you boys in the barn, listen to me! You aren't going out of there except you come out hands high or except you come out feet first. We agreed to give you this one chance to surrender. What'll it be?"

The answer was a gunshot in the direction from which that voice had come. It was something done in frank defiance only, since no one could see the man who had spoken. Now, when Ladd and Joe braced for more wild gunfire, only two riflemen took up the fight, one in front, one out back.

Ladd listened and Joe Reilly said: "Don't think for a minute all they got over here is clods. There's a feller works at the general store who was badly wounded in the war who was a full colonel. He's directing things. Right now he's using his sharpshooters. Simon and Doc and I sat in on their war council and this feller took command. Believe me, those outlaws don't stand a single blessed chance."

"If they were smart, they'd give up," Ladd said, but Reilly shook his head.

"Too late."

"You mean that man meant it. They aren't going to let Cass and Walt give up?"

Joe was emphatic. "They said they'd give 'em one chance, and after that they'd bore in until they'd killed every blasted one of them."

Ladd listened to the gunfire. It was more like a duel between two men with rifles or carbines, and two other men with six-guns, and that was exactly what it was. First one side would fire, then the other side would retaliate, but the riflemen seemed repeatedly to change position while the pair of outlaws inside the livery barn remained stationary. What ultimately broke up this duel was someone with a shotgun firing from inside the barn. The noise was not just deafening; it also was followed by the splintering of wood and the loud cursing of a man Ladd thought was Walt.

For a moment only the ear-ringing echoes lingered, then two six-guns blazed away, and this time they were firing at something inside the barn. Again the shotgun went off, first one deafening barrel, then the other deafening barrel. A man cried out, a pair of simultaneous six-guns blazed back, and Ladd joined Joe Reilly in crawling belly down to the doorway of their horse stall to peek around.

That bully day man was lying face down over along the opposite side of the runway, the shotgun still in a grip of one scarred big fist. The townsmen beyond the barn were suddenly silent, listening and trying to guess what had happened. Harrison, the cowman, utilized this moment to sing out: "Cass, you're done for." It was said in his customarily calm and casual tone. "Did you see Walt? He's caught one of those full-bore blasts in the chest. You can read a newspaper through him, and that means you're all that's left. Cass . . . ?"

There was no answer or any more defiant gunfire. Joe screwed up his face. "He's hit sure as hell, and maybe he's even dead," Joe whispered to Ladd. "Which stall was he in?"

Ladd had no idea. When they had all initially scattered in panic, the only person Ladd had kept an eye upon was Reilly.

"Can you see around the door?" Joe asked.

Ladd inched ahead a little, until he saw the dead lawman and Abner, then he squeezed over closer and craned harder until he could also see up past the harness room where the dead day man was lying, still gripping his shotgun, all the way to the front roadway. There was no one to be seen and there was no noise. He pulled back. "Three corpses and that's all," he reported.

Reilly, upon the opposite side of their stall opening, also inched ahead and sought to look out and around in the opposite direction. Without warning someone fired, a long pale splinter of stall door wood took flight, and the door itself was slammed back hard against Reilly, almost stunning him, but instinct made him back-pedal as swiftly as he could. Ladd thought Joe had been hit until the saloon man pointed to the splintered stall door.

A man said—"I know which stall he's in."—and followed this up by firing into the siding of the stall where Joe and Ladd were crouching.

Horse stalls were usually built of planking that would resist the normal abuse animals might give, but they were never built to withstand gunfire. The siding that was protecting Reilly and Buckner stopped a number of slugs and turned aside more slugs, but it was also gradually disintegrating until Ladd decided, if he continued to lie there, he and Joe Reilly were going to be killed, and pulled back as far as he could into a corner, then waited for the gunfire to pause, so that he might make a dash for some other place of concealment.

The lull arrived when Paso's townsmen decided they surely must have obliterated someone inside that shot-up horse stall, but just as Ladd was rising to run, someone in a stall up closer to the front roadway fired twice, very fast, and over among the men in the freight wagon a man cried out in pain. Now, those men in the alleyway saw their mistake. They shifted their sights and began systematically blazing away at the stall where Cass had fired from. Reilly motioned for Ladd to get back down flat again, and in this position they heard someone running toward their stall and were absolutely helpless to do anything about it. They hadn't even heard the man running until he was so close they had no time to jump up and face him.

It was Harrison, the range cowman, and he was clutching that shotgun the day man had died firing. As he sprang inside and saw the pair of men lying prone inside, he swung the shotgun for a moment, then swung it away, and sank to one knee as he said: "I think I can nail him from here."

Before either Joe or Ladd could speak, Harrison knelt in the doorway and raised his shotgun to rest on the door top. After a moment without the exposed shotgun barrel drawing gunfire from the outlaw leader up front, Harrison slowly raised up to snug back the shotgun as though it were a rifle, and aim it.

That was when the six-gun blast came without warning and Harrison went down backward and rolled in agony, his shotgun falling close to Ladd in the straw. Without a moment of reflection Ladd grabbed the weapon and jumped over to the edge of the door, but low enough so that he would come around it from the floor. He looked up as soon as he was exposed. Cass was just lowering himself again. Ladd fired even though he felt certain it was too late.

Wood burst up where Cass had been and a man's clear-toned profanity erupted up there. Ladd hauled back the second hammer and waited. Cass did not make an attempt to fire back, and he did not expose himself, but Ladd had accomplished something the dozen or so men out front had most earnestly hoped for and that none of them had been able to accomplish. Ladd pulled the outlaw leader's full attention away from the roadway, which allowed those men out there to get realigned. One of them suddenly leaned around the doorless front opening and fired on the spur of the moment. The bullet raked the paneling one foot from Ladd. He dived back inside his cell where Joe Reilly was working over the wounded cattleman. Neither Harrison nor Joe glanced up as the gunfire became brisk again.

Ladd waited. He had one more loaded barrel in his scatter-gun so he could not join in any indiscriminate shoot-outs. He waited, listening and estimating and deciding what his chances might be. When there was another lull, he eased to the broken door again, eased around it to peer in the direction of Cass's horse stall, and from out back in the alley a man yelled at him.

"Get the hell out of the way, Buckner!"

Ladd glanced over his shoulder. Simon, the Piñon blacksmith, was down there holding a long-barreled rifle in both hands.

Ladd turned his back on Simon. Up ahead Cass fired into the roadway again. Ladd knew what he would do, finally. He waited until the townsmen had got Cass to fire back at them again, then Ladd stood up and moved swiftly on the balls of his feet. He had about ten or twelve yards to traverse before he could look down into the horse stall which was his objective. He heard someone out back sharply commanding someone else not to shoot. Otherwise, he did not feel especially exposed, although there was no doubt about it, he was not just exposed, he was also unknown to most of the townsmen out there, waiting. He was in the most dangerous situation of his lifetime when he stalked the deadly outlaw leader up in one of those front stalls.

Simon had made certain those townsmen out back would not fire at Ladd. Out front, over in the freight wagon where the wounded man was still groaning, Dr. Orcutt was not just working on the injured man; he was also explaining to the townsmen around him and within hearing distance of his voice who that whisking shadow was, down there in the runway.

Ladd only knew he was close enough to Cass's horse stall to raise his shotgun. He could not risk a snap shot. He had only one blast in the old weapon, and, if he missed with it, or if he wasted it, he was going to pay with his life. He knew it. He had never thought of Cass as any less of a murderer than Abner had been. He began to rise up just outside of Cass's stall. Inside, since no one was firing at him, Cass was down on his knees, reloading. As it turned out, this was the last time he would be able to reload; he had shot out all the extra shells from his shell belt. One way or another, Cass had come to the end of his personal trail.

Ladd kept rising up. When he was able to do it, he lifted the scatter-gun in both hands, then began the final maneuver that would permit him to lift the shotgun over the half wall of the stall. As he did this, the man in there on his knees caught sight of a shadow from the corner of his eyes and with incredible speed slammed closed the gate of his Colt and twisted from the waist, simultaneously tipping up the Colt barrel. Ladd had the shotgun pushed straight ahead when he pulled the trigger. That blast, in such a confined place, sounded like a Howitzer being fired, and the full bore of that scatter-gun charge lifted Cass half to his feet and hurled him violently back into the far wall, then allowed him slowly to fold forward and slide off the wall, dead.

XVII

Enos Orcutt had six wounded individuals, which was somewhat of a surprise to Ladd and Joe Reilly. The only wounded men they were aware of were two in number; one of them was over in the freight wagon out front of the blacksmith's shop, and they had heard that man cry out when Cass had shot him, while the other injured one was that cattleman, Harrison, and he had been less than ten feet from them when he had been hit. Otherwise, though, they'd seen no one get hit and hadn't really thought much about this possibility except when the townsmen had mistakenly opened up and had splintered the front wall of the stall they had been hiding in.

Now that it was over, Ladd walked back to the stall where Joe Reilly was still working over Harrison. Until now Ladd hadn't even seen Harrison's wound, which was through the left shoulder up high and may not have broken any bones. Ladd pitched something into the straw near Joe. It was the sack with the money pouch inside it. Joe looked over, looked up at Ladd, and said: "You get the son-of-a-bitch?"

Ladd nodded. "How's Harrison?"

Reilly looked down. "He needs Enos. You'd better go out there and find him."

"Mind the money," Ladd said, and leaned the scatter-gun aside as he turned to leave the barn. Out front there were several visible armed men for a change. Everyone seemed to realize it was over. Ladd called across to the men around the wagon.

"Is Doctor Orcutt over there?"

He was, and he'd just completed giving instructions to the injured man's brother for the care of that man Cass had wounded in the wagon. He turned and strode across, accompanied by several armed townsmen. When he got close, he looked closely at Ladd before saying: "You hit, by any chance?"

"No. Joe and I made it through all right, but there's a cowman in the stall with Joe who got hit . . . Enos?"

Orcutt paused to say: "Six injured ones counting your cowman, Ladd . . . Cass and Walt and Abner?"

"Dead in there. You'll see them." Ladd felt tired and drawn out. "I'll be at the bathhouse if anyone needs me," he added, and turned to walk away. Enos Orcutt barked at a couple of townsmen who started after Buckner.

"Leave him alone for a while," the doctor said.

The town was beginning to show new signs of life as Ladd approached the jailhouse, then walked right on past it all the way up to the rooming house where he got the key to the bathhouse, plus a towel and a chunk of lye soap from a teen-aged boy who couldn't fathom someone wanting to bathe at a time like this, when three notorious bank robbers were holed up down at the livery barn, fighting it out with the entire town, plus several men from over at Piñon. Ladd listened to all the youth had to say, nodded, and walked out back to the one place in Paso, aside from private dwellings, where a body could get a decent bath. He was also hungry, but that consideration could wait.

By the time he was freshly attired and smelling strongly of lye soap, Paso had assessed the cost of its unexpected, savage fight. There was no undertaker in Paso, but the proprietor of the general store, the only person in town who owned a sawdust-filled icehouse, allowed the dead to be stacked in his icehouse until other dispositions could be arranged for.

There were still people who had difficulty grasping the fact that Constable Lewis Brennan had not only been killed, but had also been in league with outlaws. On the other hand there were enough other people around the Paso countryside who suspected that Brennan had never been a man of purest virtue. As Harrison was to say later, when he was able to be up and around: "Maybe they sometimes start out plumb honest, but after a few years in office . . . providin' they was raised by folks who themselves never could make out the difference between real right and wrong . . . they just sort of slide right down to the renegade level."

Ladd Buckner and his companions from Piñon did not hear Harrison say that because by the time the cowman was able to be up and around, the men from Piñon had been back home for a week or so.

On the ride back, with Joe Reilly in charge of the money sack, it was the taciturn blacksmith who made the most cryptic observation. "Two days wasted, damned near killed a dozen times, got the money that don't belong to none of us, and now we go home to hand it over to folks who'll never understand all we went through to get it back for 'em. Why?"

Dr. Orcutt, looking more raffish than ever in his tipped back dented derby, his torn and rumpled and soiled frock coat, and his unshaven countenance, replied with a twinkle: "Simon, you do things without thinking because you know without thinking you should do them. If any of us had coldly thought this thing through, we wouldn't any of us have struck out like we did. Emotionalism gets people killed every day, but even when they are dead, they are still better men than the ones who react coldly and avoid their responsibilities." Doc glanced at the blacksmith. "How's that for being profound when I need a bath, a shave, and probably protection from the folks in Piñon who'll be mad as hornets about me traipsing off to play lawman?"

Reilly fished in a saddle pocket and brought forth a bottle of brandy. "Got it free in Paso," he said, offering it around. Doc took two swallows and Simon Terry had three swallows, but neither Reilly nor Buckner took a drop.

They were coming down the near side of the pass and could distantly make out roof tops and sun-brightened glass windowpanes even from that distance, when the southbound coach headed for Piñon, after having briefly stopped back in Paso, careered past, stirring dust to high heaven and forcing the men from Piñon to the shoulder of the road where they cursed the driver with considerable feeling.

"He can't wait to get down to Piñon to tell all he knows," growled Dr. Orcutt. "They never get anything right."

Joe Reilly had vindicated himself honorably, had resolved what he would have classified as his civic responsibility, and now was perfectly free to think in other terms. He therefore said: "Lads, when we get back and you've had a little time to clean up and get straight again, drop by the saloon this evening. You'll be deserving all the free likker the boys'll want to pour down you to hear the lurid and true story of all we've gone through in the interests of law 'n' order."

Ladd, remembering that his background had been exposed, pointed to the sack tied to Reilly's saddle horn. "Just you be damned certain you get that pouch back to the folks at the bank. And not tonight. The minute you get back to town."

Joe looked aggrieved. "That was my intention right from the start."

Doc smiled at Simon and the blacksmith did not smile back. He simply looked dead ahead, already thinking of the work he had to do, starting fresh tomorrow.

Promise of Revenge

I

In the moonlight the roadway looked oddly strange. There was no life in it anywhere. Dark shadows lay heavily across store fronts, across roof lines, and along the plank walks beneath wooden overhangs. It dropped from eaves in its many overtones; in some places it was darker and deeper than in other places. In front of the Cowmen's & Drovers' Bank, for instance, the darkness had a cold, bright lining to it, because the moonlight was reflected from a large glass window with golden letters upon it. Everything that lived was shrouded in this black and silver, cold, strange world of absolute silence. West of town where low hills lay there was flat open country for perhaps six miles, then the rise and lift of running land frozen in motion; a man on horseback atop the nearest hill could see the valley as it was.

Beatty was the hub. Emanating outward from Beatty were a dozen pale roads, the spokes. Around the valley, far out, were the hills, silver-tinted now in the pale light. It was a scene to put a man in mind of an immense wagon wheel. The man atop the hill shifted in his saddle. Then he moved again because a pinched nerve in his right hip reminded him of the old wound. He looped the reins, made a cigarette, lit it, and exhaled. The silence was as deep as it would be at the bottom of the sea. He smoked and looked down into the valley and remembered.

There was a fine iron bird bath in Judge Montgomery's front yard behind the gleaming picket fence. There was a swing there, too, where the judge's daughter had been playing the first time he'd seen her. There was the fine gold lettering on the bank window; the substantial brick courthouse that rose majestically where the old plaza had been, and always—except in bad weather—the flag atop its white-painted pole. And the people. The good and orderly people. Of course many of the faces would now be strange; some would have moved on; a few perhaps would have died; but in the main they would be the same people. Judge Montgomery, Banker Elihu Gorman, Moses Beach of the Beatty Mercantile Company, Sheriff Tim Pollard—all the excellent, substantial citizens of Beatty.

The solitary rider's lips drew down at their outward corners. All the fine people of Beatty. He pushed out his cigarette against the saddle horn, took up the reins, and kneed his mount down off the hill, moving slowly and very deliberately as though forcing himself to relive each twisting, hurting part of some deep-seated memory.

The north-south stage road ran on ahead, so bright in the moonlight it seemed to glow. He rode out in plain sight, the only moving, living thing, riding steadily southward toward Beatty. While the world slept, he was fully awake, feeling confident and strong and free. He took a deep, sweet breath. In this world there was only one vice, only one crime, only one sin—failure. You could be anyone you desired to be; you could do anything you wanted to do, but you could not fail, for the good and orderly people of this world respected only success and they despised only failure. Well, sometimes it took a man ten, maybe fifteen years to learn this, but once learned it was not a lesson a bitter man readily forgot. Promise anything, say anything, be anything, only just don't fail!

His horse's hoofs scuffed up pale moonlighted dust; each iron footfall had a separate echo in the stillness of the roadway. The wide, straight roadway narrowed a little as it entered town, but continued to flow southward through Beatty and out as far as the eye could see, southward. He dismounted at the livery barn and tied up at the hitch rail. Then he leaned there, gazing at the town.

At the Royal Antler Saloon, at the Cowmen's & Drovers' Bank, at the Beatty Mercantile Company store front, at the Hereford County Sheriff's Office, at the Queens & Aces Café, at the Beatty Hotel, and the Hereford County Abstract Office—Land Sales Our Specialty. And finally he gazed longest at the square brick courthouse.

Twelve years ago, he thought, a barefoot kid walked north out of this town in the middle of the night. And now he's back. Fine, that's the way it should be. Judge . . . you sleep good tonight, hear? And you, too, Sheriff. And the rest of you good, substantial citizens . . . you well-fed sanctimonious buzzards . . . you all sleep good tonight, you hear? Because Tom Barker is back and from this night on you're not going to sleep so good . . . any of you!

II

"Get up, damn you! Get outen them blankets, you dirty little . . . !"

It was late in the night and his head rang from the first blow. He leaped up—and fell, tangled in the bedding. He rolled away from the arcing boot of his father, wide-awake in mind but still sluggish in body, terribly frightened but wide-awake.

"I'm awake, Paw. I'm up . . ."

The arm had clubbed downward again, striking hard.

"Please, Paw, I'm up. I'm up."

"Yes, you're up, you sneakin' little snake, an' you helped her, didn't you?"

The arm was rising again.

"No, Paw, I didn't help anyone. Honest I didn't."

The arm descended again, and that time the boy's knees went soft. Something warm ran down his cheek from an ear.

"Where is she, damn you?"

"Who, Paw?"

The man's wildness remained but its first force was spent. He stood there in the lean-to, reeling like a tree in a high wind, his beard awry, his face shiny with sweat, and his black eyes burning with an endless cruelty and hatred. "Your maw, that's who. Don't lie to me, damn you. You helped her, didn't you? Who did she go with? Where did they go?"

"Honest, Paw, I don't know."

"Oh, don't you, now!"

The man moved forward, his arm rising. He was a massive person, a freighter by trade. His strength and harshness were famous as far away as Chihuahua. The boy quailed, giving ground, sick in his stomach with fear. One blow felled him, lifted him bodily, and hurled him against the wall, and left him crumpled, white nightshirt spotted with blood.

* * * * *

Later, with the night as quiet as death, the boy had stirred, sat up, seen that his father was gone, and had gone out to the well to wash his face and daub at his torn ear, swollen as large as his fist. And then he had heard the man coming along the road roaring drunk, had run back for his clothes, put them on in panting haste, and had fled into the night without his shoes.

First, he had hidden at Grogan's Livery Barn, but the night hawk had run him off. Later, after sunup, he had begged Moses Beach to let him work for his meals and hide in the store until his father went south with the wagons again. But Beach had also run him off. Then his father had come searching and in terror he had gone to Judge Montgomery, ashamed that Antoinette should see his swollen, purple face, the blood on his clothing, and the terror in his eyes. Portly Judge Montgomery had taken him to Sheriff Tim Pollard and there at the jailhouse, when his father had come in red-eyed and reeling, he had been handed over.

He had never been able to recall accurately what had followed. He remembered being knocked down twice before they had gotten home, but beyond that he knew nothing at all until, after nightfall, he had found himself lying in the yard with his father's drover's whip in the roiled dust beside him, its shot-loaded handle less than ten inches from his head. And that was the night he had left Beatty, sore outside and sick inside, walking barefoot northward.

Then had come the long years between when he had wandered among rough towns and hard men, growing larger, taller, hard-muscled, and as agile as a cat, becoming the deceptively calm-eyed and soft-spoken man he now was. And through those years he had never ceased to cherish the memory of a beautiful woman with dark-red hair, a sad mouth, and gentle blue eyes who had deserted her husband and abandoned her son.

Many a night, with his body turning soft against the hard ground, he had smoked and watched night come on, each silver star a tear, each reddening rampart a wealth of auburn hair, each sighing breeze a smile, letting memory and longing work their sad magic in the one soft spot that remained to him. What had become of her? Who was that man? Of course he had been the one, but it had taken years for the boy to understand this. All he knew, then, before she had left, was that during those long months when his father was away with the wagons, that a man would come to the house, would call for her in a top buggy, would bring her presents from St. Louis or St. Joe.

He had been a middle-size man with a constant, big-toothed smile and a way of looking from beneath his lashes that had been cultivated. And he was a soft-spoken man with a gentle air, and that, too, had been part of his cultivated personality. Did she, even yet, in her new life, think of the little boy back in Beatty? Yes, she would remember him. A mother couldn't ever forget.

He could visualize her very clearly sitting somewhere combing her hair with silver-backed brushes; they had initials engraved on them but he could not make them out, and the room she was in was a fine one. It had flowery paper on the walls and a thick carpet underfoot. It was somewhere in the East, maybe in St. Louis, or maybe even farther East, maybe in Chicago or Cincinnati or New York. In his sadness he had always been glad for her. He had only wished he might have been with her. But he couldn't, although he had never permitted himself to believe she hadn't wanted him with her. It was the man with the false smile; he had not wanted her son to be with her. He had wanted her for himself alone.

Also during those years he had heard of his father. Down along the border and over into New Mexico—even as far south as Chihuahua—there were tales of terrible drunks, savage fights, legends of bitterness, of cruelty, and unrestrained ferocity. They had left him unmoved. He had never doubted that he and his father would one day meet again face to face, but this plausibility had long since ceased to mean anything to him. He had neither pity nor hatred for the man. He thought of him only as a failure, a man who goaded oxen and mule trains, a laborer, a drover who sweated and froze and fought to deliver the goods of others. He remembered the beatings and cursings, but only distantly and vaguely; they might have happened to someone else. He rarely thought of the man at all, and, when he did, it was simply to measure him by the same yardstick he measured all men with—success or failure. Beyond that his father might have been dead—or as vanished as his mother—or as meaningless and distant as all those departed yesterdays. With the exception of the one memory, the past was past and he did not mean for it to influence him in the future, beyond putting to practice the lessons it had taught him.

Now, standing in the paling light of a new day, smoking and watching the town, he could afford a small smile. The lessons he had learned were practical ones. The hand dangling above his gun holstered at his hip, for instance, was very experienced. The dark eyes, beguilingly gentle, were all-seeing. The naturally dark face, further colored by Arizona's fierce sun, hid all emotion behind its smoothness, its blank, almost melancholy expression. Only the square jaw, thin lip line, and molded thrust of chin offered any clue of the inner man Tom Barker had become.

III

Judge Montgomery remembered hearing what had sounded to him like a shot. But he had been busy at the courthouse, and, since no one had mentioned it, he had forgotten about it until, upon arriving home in the warm brightness of a long summer evening, he found Sheriff Tim Pollard on the porch with his daughter. The judge was a stout man with a handsome head and thick gray hair. He looked every inch a judge, or a senator, or perhaps an Indian commissioner from Washington. He was a punctual, orderly person whose long tenure of respectability had covered him with layer after layer of decorum. He disliked spontaneity, had never in his life given a snap judgment, and he abhorred raw emotionalism in any of its myriad forms. Violence, rawness, sensationalism in any form was anathema to him, and, because he was this way, the substantial people of Hereford County had returned him to office at every election in the past twenty years.

Judge Montgomery's own life having been an orderly sequence of dignified advancement under the law, he looked upon any other kind of progress as a form of sordidness. He outwardly respected the people of Hereford County who had won the wilderness from the Indians with guns and scalping knives, but inwardly he disapproved of them strongly. They were crude, savage, dirty people, in his opinion no better than the Indians themselves. Therefore, when he saw Tim Pollard, himself an old Indian fighter, sitting on the porch with Antoinette, his secret antagonism rose up. Besides it was a beautiful evening, he was a little tired, and had been looking forward to relaxing in the soft, silent twilight. He nodded to the sheriff, smiled at Antoinette, touched her shoulder lightly in passing, and sank down upon a chair with a repressed sigh.

"There was a killing in town today, Judge," Pollard said.

Remembering the gunshot sound, Judge Montgomery nodded without speaking. He knew Tim Pollard; the sheriff would tell his story in his own way and in his own good time.

"Charley Ingersoll got it."

Judge Montgomery drew up in his chair. Ingersoll was one of the more prominent settlers. He was an industrious man, a hard worker, violent tempered perhaps, but substantial, and a man with a good bank balance. Anger slowly built up in the judge. "Tim, we've got to do something about those cowboys. I've been telling you for years there's got to be an ordinance against carrying pistols in town."

"It wasn't the cowmen this time, Judge."

"No? Then who?"

Tim Pollard ran the back of one freckled hand under his drooping longhorn mustache; he squinted toward the faraway hills where the sun was fast disappearing. He pushed long legs out in front of him and regarded the scuffed toes of his boots.

"Well?" the judge said impatiently.

"You recollect Tom Barker's kid?"

"His kid?"

"Yeah. Think back, Judge. You recollect how Tom's wife run off one night, and old Tom went around town like a crazy man for a couple days afterward?"

"I recall that," Judge Montgomery said shortly, finding the subject sordid and therefore unpleasant, particularly so in front of his daughter.

"Recollect young Tom . . . the kid . . . hidin' from old Tom and tryin' to get folks to keep the old man away from him?"

"Hmmmmm, vaguely, Tim."

Pollard turned a long, thoughtful gaze on the judge. "He went to you an' you brought him to me."

"Well, what of it?"

"And I turned him over to his old man."

The judge was frowning. "I remember now," he said. "It was back a few years."

Antoinette spoke for the first time. "It was over ten years ago." She was watching her father now. "He ran away that same night."

Sheriff Pollard nodded slowly. "That's right. He run off that night and no one ever heard of him again. Well, Judge . . . he's back. It was young Tom Barker who killed Charley Ingersoll today."

The judge digested this in silence. He could not place the boy's face at all; he remembered only the general details of that earlier sordidness, and, since he had no respect at all for the elder Tom Barker, he found it easy to extend this antipathy to the returned son. "Did you arrest him?" he now asked the sheriff.

"No."

"No? Well, why not, Tim?"

"Charley was beatin' his horse at the emporium hitch rail, Judge. He was usin' a pick handle. Young Barker walked up, knocked Charley down, took up the pick handle, and worked him over a mite with it." Pollard's words fell quietly, slowly into the soft glow of dying day. He was squinting far out again, and obviously his mind was reliving the events of another decade. "Well, Charley commenced to get up. Young Barker stood back. Charley went for his gun under his coat and quicker'n scat young Tom killed him." The sheriff was looking steadily now at Antoinette. "It was a fair fight, Judge. Ingersoll was killed going for his gun."

"Witnesses?" the judge asked mechanically.

"Four."

"I see. And I suppose they were Barker's friends."

"Nope, not a one of 'em knew him."

"Correction, Sheriff," Antoinette said. "One of them did."

Pollard's blank face puckered into the smallest of rueful smiles. "Excuse me, Toni." He shifted his gaze to the judge. "One of 'em recognized him right off as young Tom Barker. She was the only one who did, though."

"She?" Judge Montgomery said, then, with understanding coming, he looked incredulously at his daughter. "You, honey?"

Antoinette nodded.

"But what were you doing . . . why, you might have been hurt?" Judge Montgomery's face reddened. "Tim, confound it, I'm going to insist on a special meeting of the town council. Now, tonight, we're going to pass that no guns ordinance."

Pollard was tugging at his mustache. He said: "It'll be a good thing, all right, Judge. Only I think there's something else ought to be tended to first."

"What? What can possibly be more important . . . ?"

"Young Tom Barker."

Judge Montgomery fixed angry eyes on the sheriff. He had known Tim Pollard many years; the sheriff was a dry and laconic man; he emphasized his opinions with a minimum number of words. "Elaborate, Tim. What about young Barker?"

"Judge, I've seen a heap of gunmen in my time. I don't mean just the fast guns, either . . . I mean the kind of men who use guns to serve their private ends. That's the kind of a killer young Tom Barker is."

"I don't follow you, Tim."

"A killer rides into town, Judge. He shoots someone, collects his five hundred dollars, and rides on to the next town. That's the kind of gunman most of us are familiar with. But in the past few years another kind of gunman has come along. The Wyatt Earp kind. They don't kill just for the five hundred They don't kill for hire at all. They use their guns to get something they particularly want, something like wealth or position. That's the kind of a gunman young Tom Barker is. He's in Beatty for a good reason."

Judge Montgomery settled back in his chair. He, too, turned his gaze outward toward the marching ranks of shadows moving down the distant hills. He said quietly: "I take it you talked to him."

"I did."

"What did he say?"

"Nothing. He offered to surrender his gun. Told me why he shot Charley Ingersoll. That's all."

"Did you ask him why he came back?"

"Yup. He said it wasn't any of my business . . . which it wasn't."

"Then what makes you leery of him, Tim?"

"A feelin' I've got, Judge. Like I said, I've seen a heap of gunmen in my time. Young Tom's not in Beatty to look up any old friends because he's got none here. He's here for a good reason and he aims to stay until he's worked it out."

A long interval of silence descended. Antoinette finally arose. "I'll get you both some lemonade," she said. "Mister Beach got a fresh load of Sonora lemons in today."

After she was gone, the judge settled deeper into his chair, sighed, put both hands palms down on his paunch, and let his eyelids droop. He felt resigned, remote, pleasantly loose. "If Ingersoll's killing was justifiable homicide, Tim," he murmured, "I suppose that's that. But I'm still going to push for the town ordinance against firearms."

"The ordinance will help," Sheriff Pollard replied, bending forward to make a cigarette. "But that doesn't solve the Barker problem. He'll kill again, Judge."

"Who?"

Pollard shrugged. "How would I know? I just know that he will. He's in Beatty for a damned good reason, Judge. The first one of us who gets in his way will get called out."

"Well, what do you suggest? We can't just run him out of town. He has his legal rights."

"I got nothing to suggest. I just wanted you to know that your gun ordinance all of a sudden ain't so important to me any more."

"You're barking up a tree, Tim. The boy has a bad background. He won't stay long in a place as quiet and orderly as Beatty."

Sheriff Pollard lit his cigarette, smoked it a moment in silence, then grunted. As far as he was concerned the conversation was ended, and it had run just about as he had expected it to. Judge Montgomery was a good man for the town, and on the bench, but he'd never, in Pollard's opinion, been much of a man in a lot of other ways.

IV

Under a hot pink brightness Tom Barker stirred in his blankets, raised up, and propped his head on one hand, gazing along the pearl-gray floor of desert, misty and silent, until the land lifted and met the sharp edge of the rising sun. It was after 5:00, daylight was coming, and it would be another scorching summer day. While he watched, the first dazzling rays shot above the distant hills, raced across the desert, and struck with quick brightness the warped roofs of the little town down on the plain that he had left the night before to go up into the hills and camp. Nearby were the graceful willows in a narrow arroyo, dim and gray, still holding the dregs of the night; they lined an unseen stream that tinkled pleasantly in the hush. He yawned, spat, pushed back the blanket, and sat up. Down along the creek fetlock-deep in yellow forage grass his horse stamped and blew its nose.

Tom scrubbed at the creek, hustled twigs for a breakfast fire, and worked silently with the fat, rich aroma of frying side meat rising into the air. He was rocking the iron fry pan gently when a laughing voice drawled behind him, back in the tangled willows.

"If I was a sheriff, you'd never live to eat that, Tom."

Barker made no move. He rocked the pan gently over its arrow points of blue fire, his averted face turning handsome under the influence of a dry small smile. "If you were a sheriff, I'd have roped and tied you when you scuffed that rock with your spur ten minutes ago."

The newcomer straightened up and came out of the willows. He was as tall as Barker but not nearly as broad. An air of litheness preceded him; he walked like an Indian, balancing forward on the balls of his feet. Beneath his hat a tawny lock of sun-rusted dark hair hung upon his forehead. His face was youthful, burned brown, and prematurely lined. He squatted next to Barker, watching the faint gray smoke rise up, then curve away and hang in the arroyo to mingle with the shadowy vestiges of night.

"I'm hungrier'n a bitch wolf," the newcomer said, watching the bacon curl. "You know . . . that's quite a ride in one day and one night, Tom."

"I'll feed you and I'll pay you," Tom replied without looking away from the fry pan, "but damned if I'll sympathize with you, Tex."

A strong, boyish ripple of laughter came from Tex. His eyes crinkled and danced. "That's good enough," he said. "Just feed me first . . . then tell me what this is all about."

Tom divided the side meat into two rations and settled back. "Eat," he said, and for a moment added nothing to it. "I won't tell you why I'm doing this Tex. All I'll tell you is what you're to do."

"Suits me, Tom. Shoot."

"See that little town down there?"

"Yup. Saw it before sunup."

"That's Beatty."

"All right."

"I'm going to make it or break it."

Tex paused to look across the dying fire. He did not speak; he only shrugged, then returned to eating.

"I'm going to be top lash in that town. I'm going to tell the sheriff who to arrest and who to leave alone. I'm going to call a tune and the judge's going to dance to it. I'm going to buy and sell a feller named Moses Beach . . . and you're going to help me do it."

Tex put the fry pan down and wiped his fingers along the seams of his worn trousers. He reached for his tobacco sack, frowned over a cigarette, lit it with a twig from the fire, exhaled mightily, then leaned back and gazed steadily at Tom Barker from fearless, hard blue eyes. "You know I ain't a questioning man, Tom. We've shared too many bedrolls an' cook fires an' roundups an' drunks not to know one another pretty well."

"That's right."

"I'm not a killer, Tom."

Barker scoured the fry pan with dry grass and dust. He worked hard at it, frowning, lips flattened in a bleak line. "I don't need a killer, Tex. All I need is a man who'll do what I say. Any killing's got to be done . . . I'll do it."

"You don't understand me, Tom. I don't want to tie up with a killer, either."

Barker's head came up slowly. "You think I'm a killer, Tex?"

Tex thumbed back his hat; the heavy dark curl spread more fully across his forehead. His face creased slightly. "Tom," he said slowly, "you're plumb capable of becoming a killer. Years back, I figured there was something inside you that was pretty twisted. Like I said, fellers get to know one another pretty well when they pardner up and face all sorts of situations together. Also, like I said, I ain't a questioning man. I always thought the world of you, Tom . . . but I've always known there was something inside you, too . . . I just never questioned what it was or why it was there."

Tom turned away to push the fry pan into a saddlebag. He spoke while his head was averted. His voice sounded deep and gentle when next he spoke. "I killed a man yesterday, Tex. He was beating a horse with a pick handle. There was blood running out of the critter's nose."

Tex nodded understanding and approval, but the speculative expression did not leave his face. "All right. That's no crime. But that ain't what I'm talking about, either, and you know it."

"There'll be no unnecessary killing, Tex."

A space of solemn silence settled around the guttering cook fire. Finally Tex killed his cigarette and regarded its broken, brown form in the bent-flat grass. "All right, Tom. We understand one another. What am I to do?"

Barker reached inside his shirt, brought forth a thick packet of oilskin, unwrapped it gently, and withdrew a $100 bill from the thick sheaf of green paper. "Take this and spend it at the Royal Antler Saloon. Listen to everything that's said. Twice a week we'll meet up here, on Mondays and Fridays."

"Listen for what, Tom?"

"Gossip. Who is buying whose cattle, who is in need of a jag of hay, who's borrowing money at the bank. Stuff like that."

"Just local gossip? Tom, you sure you know what you're doing?"

Barker grinned. "If I don't, the worst thing that'll happen is that we'll ride out of this country like we rode in . . . quietly."

Tex folded the $100 bill thoughtfully. "Must've been a lot of loot on that stage," he said, arising.

Tom's grin lingered. "Maybe there was. Only I didn't get it. I saved that money . . . been saving it for years."

"Uhn-huh. One more thing, Tom. I don't know you?"

"That's right. You're a stranger. You're just riding through. You're resting your horse. You've been on a long drive, been paid off, and aren't in any hurry about hunting up a new job."

"All right," Tex said, gazing along the perimeter of hills, then lowering his eyes suddenly to Beatty. "It's your money and your play. I'll be here come Friday."

* * * * *

Tom did nothing for half an hour after Tex departed. He smoked beside the dead fire, narrowed his eyes against the fierce sun smash, and gazed steadily down at Beatty. Then he caught his horse, saddled and bridled, stepped across the saddle, and swung out across the hills southwesterly so that, when he rode into town shortly before high noon, he came in from the south.

He paid for a room overlooking the town at the Beatty Hotel, one month in advance, then he hired a boy to haul water for a tub in the lean-to bathhouse, and soaked. Afterward, freshly dressed, his thick hair shiny with oil and his ivory-butted gun lashed down and moving rhythmically with each step, he went to the Royal Antler, took a wall table, and called for a drink. There he sat, low and loose with his back to the wall, feeling the full run of confidence; he had waited a long time; now he was back. One slip, one error, could spoil it all. He would make no mistakes; his impatience was under an iron leash. This chance would never in his lifetime come again. And yet, in spite of the hot willfulness in his mind, this sitting here was a form of release, too. It was a nearing of the end of the trail. It was the kind of release a man like Tom Barker had to have. The years had built up too much inside of him. Some way, all of this was going to come out fiercely, in a drunk, a fight, or a kiss.

The second whiskey made him hungry. He moved to the food table, spooned chili into a bowl, slapped a fat slice of Sonora onion between two dark slabs of bread, and took the meal back to his table. For a man who had been hungry for days on end many times in his life, food was both a reward and a luxury. It was a deep comfort to be eating, freshly bathed and dressed, in Beatty's finest saloon, listening to the ebb and flow of talk, the sharp slap of booted feet and the soft ring of spurs. His presence here was in a sense a personal triumph and he savored it.

Later, smoking a cigar, studying the range men, the townsmen, travelers, and drifters, drawing in the smoke with keen relish, he considered the room with thoughtful complacency. This was one of those rare times in a man's life when the little things that meant so much gave him his greatest moments: cold spring water on a scorching day; the powerful softening of his body against the earth after a punishing ride; the biting flavor of a cigar after months of abstinence; returning to the town that had ignored a boy's breaking heart, knowing this time the town would never forget him. These were the simple, gratifying things of life, things that went down deep into a man. But none of them were free. A man earned them by sweat and hunger, by privation and fatigue, so in the end that was why they were good.

He saw the tall, loose body come through the door, hesitate, cross his blank dark stare with its moving blue glance, then proceed to the bar and lean there, elbows extended, long legs knee-sprung in total relaxation, and he smiled to himself. Tex Earle was a fine actor, as good perhaps as Wilkes Booth himself, and now there was no further need for him to linger. He arose, left a coin on the table, and crossed the room to pass out into the warm night beyond.

Beatty was drenched in blackness. It dripped on him from roof tops and curdled the orange glow from windows. It was a formless substance that smothered everything except movement, and, because it did, he did not see the rangy silhouette even after he had passed it by. Then a voice, softly commanding, struck him in the back.

"Barker. Just a minute."

He recognized the voice even as he turned. He remembered it from his last day in Beatty as a youth. The yellow-stained light of a saloon window ran sickly across the older man's path as he approached, and for a moment Tom could not see above it.

"It's Pollard, Barker. Tim Pollard." The sheriff stepped across the yellow dust and peered ahead. His raw-boned appearance was accentuated by the night. When next he spoke, his voice was crowded with thoughtfulness. "Figured we might talk a little."

Tom remained motionless and silent, separating the man from the night.

"I got a notion about yesterday's killing," Pollard said.

"Have you?"

"Yeah. I figure you could have kicked the gun out of Ingersoll's hand. Or maybe knocked him out with that pick handle. I don't figure you had to kill him."

"Didn't I?"

"No. I've disarmed a lot of men, Barker. When you're standing less than six feet from 'em, it's no chore."

"Then why did I kill him?"

Pollard slumped, resting all his weight on one leg. Before replying he ran a hand under his heavy mustache. "Because you wanted to."

"I didn't know the man."

"You didn't have to, Barker. You were cocked and primed to kill someone. Ingersoll gave you a plumb fine excuse."

"You make it sound like murder, Sheriff."

"I wish I could prove it was, Barker."

"Why? You scarcely remember me."

"Well," Pollard said slowly, picking his words, "you got no reason to like this town. I understand that. Sometimes a feller gets something like that fixed in his head and packs it around with him for years. Sometimes he gets a chance to come back and cut a swathe. Sort of make the town get down on its knees to him. I think that's what's wrong with you. Why else would you come back here? You got no friends here. Your folks . . . well, I reckon you understand about them."

Barker's voice turned husky. "No, Sheriff," he said, "tell me about them."

But Tim Pollard recognized the signs and simply wagged his head. "I can't say it the way it should be said, so I'd best not say it at all. But you understand me all right, Barker."

Tom ground his heels down into the dust of the plank walk. "You talk too much, old man," he said coldly. "Talk too much and do too little. You're not the only one in Beatty who's been eating too regularly for too many years."

"So?"

Tom Barker's jaw snapped closed. He continued to regard the sheriff a moment longer, then turned on his heel and went along the plank walk as far as the hotel. There, he turned in without a backward glance.

Sheriff Pollard made a cigarette, lit it, leaning against a post, and smoked in thoughtful silence until a short, ugly man came up beside him and stopped.

"Beautiful night, Tim."

Pollard grunted. "Moses, us old-timers've had it pretty good in the valley for a long time, haven't we?"

Moses Beach looked up with a scowl. "Sure. What of it? We settled this damned country, didn't we? We made 'er what she is, didn't we? Then we're entitled to a reward, aren't we?"

"Maybe," the sheriff answered, gazing up the darkened road. "But maybe we've taken too much for granted these past ten or twelve years, Moses."

"What the hell are you talkin' about?"

"That killin' yesterday . . . and the feller who did it."

"Young Barker? Is he still around? I thought he'd hightail it when you let him go."

"I never had him, an' he didn't hightail it."

Beach puffed a moment on his cigar, following the direction of Pollard's gaze. "Too bad he had to pick Ingersoll," he said finally. "Charlie was a good account."

The sheriff made a mirthless smile. "He was also a human bein', Moses. That's what I mean about us old-timers havin' things too easy these past years." He threw down his cigarette and stamped it hard. "Beatty's due for a jolt, I think."

"What d'you mean . . . a jolt?"

Pollard straightened up. "Just what I said . . . a jolt. Good night, Moses."

Beach's small eyes regarded the sheriff's retreating back until it disappeared into the night, then he turned and struck off in the opposite direction.

V

Tom Barker had been three weeks in Beatty before he made a move, and of course by the end of that time everyone knew who he was. Mostly they addressed him as Mr. Barker. What the cowmen and merchants and townsmen did not know was that Tom Barker knew as much about them as they knew about themselves. No one had as yet associated the blue-eyed Texan who hung out at the Royal Antler Saloon with the black-eyed man who, rumor said, had had a drunk for a father and whose mother had run off with another man years before. Folks had, after the fashion of people, weighed and measured Tom Barker, had decided he was a gunman, and accorded him all the respect that appellation inspired, but socially they had nothing to do with him. Still, after three weeks of obvious inactivity even Sheriff Pollard was beginning to have doubts about his earlier suspicions. It did not seem reasonable that a man like dark Tom Barker would sit around day after day, if he had anything sinister in mind, or if he had anything better to do.

Then, when Tom finally struck, no one at first associated the action with Mr. Barker who spent his time between the Royal Antler Saloon and the Beatty Hotel, and had never once set his foot inside Beatty's bank, where rancher Gerald Finnerty and banker Elihu Gorman faced one another across Gorman's desk.

"The receipt," Finnerty was saying, enjoying Gorman's discomfort very much, even smiling openly at it, "the receipt, Elihu."

"That's a lot of money," the banker murmured, his gaze fixed to the pile of bills on his desk. "Couldn't you use it to better advantage restocking or expanding, Gerald?"

"I could," Finnerty assented. "Only I'd rather have my note back. The receipt, please, Elihu."

"Where did you get it, Gerald?" the banker asked, making no motion to take up his pen.

Finnerty colored; his eyes turned hard as flint. "Well, now," he said coldly, "I don't figure that's any of your business . . . where I come by that money."

Gorman picked up his pen and began to write. Beyond the glassed-in cubicle of his office there was the subdued sound of talk, the sigh of movement, the swish of clothing. Inside the cubicle there was only the scratching of Gorman's pen upon the paper. When he put the pen aside, Gerald Finnerty reached forward, took up the paper, and scrutinized it. Then he folded it very carefully and put it into his pocket, and the smile returned to his face.

"One thing more. When the note's receipted at the courthouse, mail it to me."

"Yes, of course."

Gorman pushed himself upright again. He looked physically uncomfortable and his voice sounded weak. "If you extended the loan . . . which the bank'd be glad to do for you . . . then you could buy out the Miller place and really expand."

"I can buy out the Miller place anyway," Finnerty said shortly, taking up his hat and turning toward the door. "In fact, I took a cash option on it day before yesterday."

Elihu Gorman remained standing for several minutes after Finnerty left, then he went as far as the door and called to a clerk. "Go get Mister Beach," he ordered, closed the door, returned to his chair, and sat down to wait.

When Moses Beach came into Gorman's office, he looked annoyed. It was early in the day and most people, wishing to avoid the heat, did their shopping early. "What is it?" he demanded shortly.

"Finnerty was just in here. He paid off his note." Gorman nodded toward the crumpled money on his desk.

Beach moved closer. “In full?”

“In full and I gave him a receipt. I had to.”

Beach stood a moment, then retreated to a chair and dropped down. “How?” he asked as the annoyance vanished from his face. “He had his back to the wall.”

“I don’t know how.”

“What d’you mean . . . you don’t know?”

The banker’s face darkened; his voice got sharp. “What difference does it make how he got the money, dammit. There it is. His loan is paid off. We can’t make the deal with Houston. And . . . we’re committed to pay off that thirty percent money we borrowed for three months, which we figured to buy the Finnerty place from the bank with after it’d foreclosed.”

“I want to know where he got that money,” Beach said, his face gone white beneath lowered brows. “Maybe he stole it, robbed a stage or something.”

Gorman’s irritation increased. There was perspiration on his forehead and upper lip. “You fool, Moses,” he snapped. “The money’s not important right now. What if he did steal it? We’ve still got to honor the note.”

Beach made an agitated gesture toward the frosted glass partition. “You want the whole world to know?” he demanded. “Lower your voice.”

Gorman subsided, threw himself back into his chair, and remained silent.

“How do we get out of this, now?” the storekeeper asked.

“We don’t.”

“There’s got to be a way, Elihu.”

“Sure, we pay off like we agreed to do . . . in three months at thirty percent interest.”

“No!”

“Yes! We’ve been building up the value of the Finnerty place to Evan Houston for a year now. We even justified our own borrowing by making that loan on the false appraisal.”

"Damn it, I know all that."

"Sure you do. You also know Houston is ready to buy, too, and that the bank was set to foreclose this month, and on the strength of that . . . and my position here . . . you and I borrowed forty thousand to redeem the place from the bank. Now, Moses, you take your copy of that loan paper to Phoenix and ask any lawyer down there how you get out of repaying . . . and he'll tell you that you don't get out of it, that you repay."

Beach wiped his face with a sleeve and continued to stare at Gorman. "There's got to be a way, Elihu," he said huskily.

"I don't know what it is. While I was waiting for you, I did some thinking."

"Go on."

"Suppose Houston goes to Finnerty now?"

"Well, what if he does?"

"Finnerty'll sell to him."

Beach's eyes widened with comprehension. "After we've built Houston up on the value and Finnerty'll get the profit . . . ?"

"That's right."

After a moment of agonized silence Moses Beach got to his feet and crossed to the door. "I got to get back," he husked. "I'll see you tonight, Elihu. We got to think of something . . . something . . ."

Gorman also arose. "When you gamble big," he intoned, "you win big or you lose big. All right. I'll be here at the bank after closing time."

Moses Beach stopped on the plank walk in front of the bank, gulping big lungfuls of insufficient oxygen. It was difficult to breathe. When people passed, some nodding, some speaking, he ignored them. Riders and buggies and battered ranch wagons ground through the roadway's dust; he scarcely saw them. Opposite him in the shade of the Royal Antler's overhang, two talking men caught and retained his attention. One of them was broadly smiling. Moses recognized him instantly as cowman

Gerald Finnerty. The other man, hawk-like in profile, dark and thoughtful-looking, was Tom Barker. Very gradually suspicion began to form in Moses Beach's mind.

Barker and Finnerty passed from sight through the saloon doorway. They were going to have a drink together, going to celebrate. Beach's eyes turned glassy; a haziness obscured things. He put out a hand, grasped an upright, and steadied himself. How? How had Barker found out? Why did he give Finnerty the money? What was he doing? What was he up to?

When the dizziness momentarily lessened, Moses crossed the road. Gorman had said it didn't matter where the money had come from; the important thing was that Finnerty had redeemed his note. Moses grimaced. The important thing wasn't Finnerty or his note at all; it was the $40,000 repayable within ninety days at thirty percent interest.

As the day wore on, Beach's trouble getting enough oxygen increased and he went home at 3:30 in the afternoon. At 6:00, while Elihu Gorman was consulting his watch impatiently, Dr. Albigence Spence was informing Moses Beach's wife that her husband had suffered a severe stroke and would be bedridden for weeks, and might even be permanently paralyzed.

At 6:30 Dr. Spence left the Beach residence, went to the Royal Antler for his nightcap, met Judge Montgomery there on his way home from the courthouse, and told him what had happened. The judge was aghast; so was the lanky blue-eyed cowboy lounging beside him at the bar.

"But he's not an old man," the judge said, looking down upon the medical man's less majestic height. "He's no older than you or me, Al."

Dr. Spence drank off his sour mash and nodded for another. "Since when's age got anything to do with a stroke?" he asked absently, watching the bartender's hands.

"Well, I don't know, but . . ."

"You're pale as a ghost, Judge. Have a refill on me."

The judge had his second drink; color returned to his face; his voice firmed up. "What caused it?" he asked.

Dr. Spence turned irritable. "How the hell would I know? All I know is that he had it."

"Will he recover all right?"

"Who knows? He'll never be the same again, I can tell you that. My guess is that there's damage to his brain. How much damage, or to what extent he'll recover from it, I have no idea. Only time can answer that."

The doctor was turning away. Judge Montgomery put out a hand. "What did he say?"

"Nothing. They don't talk, Judge. Cerebral hemorrhages don't ordinarily occur or continue to occur during consciousness. He's unconscious. In fact, he may not even know anything's happened to him for several days."

The doctor started forward again, then stopped as a tall, erect man, looking disgruntled and testy, came up, nodded, and motioned for a drink.

"'Evening, Judge. 'Evening, Doctor."

Spence bobbed his head. "Just came from Moses's place, Elihu. He's had a stroke."

The tall man stiffened; his hand, extended for the shot glass, grew still on the bar top. "A stroke?"

"Yes." Spence looked from Judge Montgomery to the banker. His voice sounded dry now. "You'd better drink that. I don't want any more patients tonight."

Elihu Gorman drank and set the glass down. "Is he dead?"

"No, he's alive. But he's not out of the woods by a damned sight."

"I need another drink," Gorman said, and abruptly turned his back on the room, bending forward over the bar.

Dr. Spence frowned, nodded to the judge, and left. The lanky cowboy beside Montgomery had both elbows on the bar. He was nursing an amber glass of ale in both hands and looking steadily into the backbar mirror. Visible to him against the north wall, lounging there with a bottle, a glass, and a bowl of chili was Tom Barker. From time to time the dark man would gaze at the banker and at the judge, then he would sip his whiskey. The lighting was poor except in the center of the room and Barker's face was obscure. The Texan drank his ale a little at a time. He was wondering how much revenge Tom wanted from this little town.

VI

Moses Beach regained consciousness the day following his stroke, but Albigence Spence's prognosis had been correct; there was brain damage. There was also a partial paralysis that prevented Beach from using his hands, arms, or vocal cords. He lay like a vegetable in his bed, alive and physically functioning, but in all other respects quite dead. Dr. Spence called often; it was an interesting case. He had no great feeling for Beach, he had known him too long for that, but it was an interesting case. One rarely found real medical challenges on the frontier. What particularly intrigued Spence was the extent of brain damage, and when, if Beach recovered, he would be normal again. Spence rather doubted it. Another thing that interested him was the odd attitude of Elihu Gorman since Beach's stroke. Gorman was drinking more lately and he was so preoccupied most of the time that he scarcely recognized lifelong acquaintances.

Dr. Spence knew, as did everyone else around Beatty, that Beach and Gorman were allies in any number of financial ventures, that they held whip hands over most of the cowmen and some of the merchants. He could easily surmise, then, that Beach's stroke affected in some way their financial partnership and Gorman was worried over it. The extent of Gorman's anxiety was plain in his actions. Dr. Spence found this amusing because he held Elihu Gorman in as scornful a light as he did Moses Beach. In fact, it cheered him, which was a vast improvement because his normal disposition was cynical and generally brusque.

Two other men were affected by Beach's illness. Tom Barker met Tex Earle at the creek overlooking Beatty on a blistering Friday afternoon. They smoked and talked and sat cross-legged in the shade, Indian-like, through intervals of long silence, each busy with his thoughts. Tex whittled a twig with long, smooth sweeps of his Barlow knife and puffed desultorily upon a cigarette dangling from his lips. "You know who owns half the livery barn, don't you?" he said.

Barker shook his head. "No. Who?"

"The judge."

"And . . . ?"

"And the barn gets its hay and grain from Finnerty. Has for years."

Tom's dark face hosted a faint smile. "Fine. The price of hay and grain just went up."

Tex continued to whittle. "They'll get it somewhere else."

"Where?"

"I don't know."

"Find out."

Tex regarded his stick through squinted eyes. "You'll run out of money, Tom. You can't buy every cowman in the valley."

"No, but I can option all their hay and grain."

"Huh?"

"Pay 'em a little money to tie up their crops for, say, sixty days. If I don't pay the rest, they keep my money. If I do pay 'em the rest . . . the grain and hay are mine."

"Oh, that's what's called an option, eh?"

"Yeah."

Tex lowered his head; shavings fell in long pale curls under his knife. "But it's still a losing proposition. You're still going to lose your money."

Tom made a cigarette and lit it before he replied. "Maybe," he conceded. "And maybe not. Finnerty's making up a drive of fat two-year-olds for the San Carlos Agency. He's going to pay me off as soon as he gets back. Fifteen percent interest on my money." Tom exhaled and fixed his gaze upon the town below them. "That fifteen percent'll amount to nine months' wages as a rider, Tex." He paused. "I'm beginning to understand how men make money without working for it."

Earle threw the twig away, snapped his knife closed, and pocketed it. "Yeah," he said dryly, getting to his feet. "But they earn it, Tom. Take that storekeeper lying in bed down there and turning purple in the face trying to tell folks things."

Barker's head twisted. "What do you mean?"

"That cantankerous old sawbones. He gets a couple drinks behind his belt and shoots off his mouth like an old squaw. He was telling the sheriff last night that Beach's rational now, and acts like he's about to bust trying to talk."

Barker considered this. It required no vast deductive power to guess what Beach was upset about. Someway, perhaps through Finnerty although the cowman had been sworn to secrecy, Beach knew who had put up the redemption money. He was apparently trying to tell who it was, which meant that Gorman didn't yet know. If Beach did know and Gorman didn't know, then . . .

Tom got quickly to his feet. Tex covertly eyed him, saw the sharpness of his expression, the hooded knife-edged glitter of his eyes, and let a noiseless sigh pass his lips. He was moving toward his horse when he said: "All you want to know is where else Montgomery'll get the hay?"

"For now, yes."

"See you Monday, then," Tex said, gathering his reins and vaulting into the saddle. "Tom?"

"Yeah?"

"You going to the dance?"

"What dance?"

"Volunteer firemen's dance at the Methodist Church Sunday evening."

Barker started to speak and stopped. He was balancing something in his mind. He shrugged finally and said: "I might at that, Tex. You supposed to fetch a girl along?"

"If you want to, but it ain't the law hereabouts. Me, I'm taking Miss Eloise from the Royal Antler."

"I might see you there."

Tex laughed and the boyishness returned to his face. In a light voice he said: "If you're there, you'll see me all right." Then he rode away.

Tom did not mount immediately, and, when he did, he made the same circuitous ride he ordinarily did after one of their meetings, and loped into Beatty from the south with afternoon shadows running along before him.

At the hotel Sheriff Tim Pollard pushed himself up out of a chair when Tom entered and stopped him on the stairs with a mild greeting.

"'Evening, Mister Barker."

"Sheriff."

"If you're not too busy, I'd like to have a little talk with you."

"All right," Tom replied. "Talk."

Sheriff Pollard considered this. From the corner of his eye he saw the desk clerk straining to hear. "Might be better in private," he mumbled.

Tom led the way to his upstairs room, kicked a chair forward for Pollard, and crossed to the window, turned and stood with his back to the dying light, legs spread wide and impatience shading his face. "Talk," he said again.

Pollard did not start right away. He studied the powerful shoulders, thick legs, and finally bent his serene gaze upon the handsome, forceful face. "I guess you can take care of yourself, all right," he speculated. "Leastways you got the look of a man who can."

Tom stood in silence, waiting.

"Charley Ingersoll's brother is comin' for you."

"Is that a fact?" Tom said coldly.

Pollard's eyes narrowed the slightest bit. "It's a fact," he repeated quietly. "Y'know, Barker, you're sure not goin' out of your way to make friends in Beatty."

Tom rocked forward on his toes. "There's a Methodist minister in town, isn't there?"

Pollard nodded, looking a little puzzled.

"Then let him do the preaching, Sheriff."

Pollard flushed and stood up. The deceptive drowsiness was gone now and his voice was hard. "We don't like troublemakers here, Barker."

"But you got no law against a man protecting himself."

"An ordinary man . . . no. A gunfighter . . . yes. We got laws here."

"Sundown laws, Sheriff?"

"That's right. A gunfighter'll get till sundown to leave town."

"I'm not a gunfighter, though."

Sheriff Pollard went to the door, opened it, and stood half in, half out, of the room. "I'm checkin' on that right now, Barker. If I can prove that you are, you'll leave Beatty. We don't want any more killings here."

Pollard was moving to close the door when Tom's voice stopped him. "One thing you forgot, Sheriff. A man isn't as easy to push around as a kid."

Pollard closed the door and went along the hall and down the stairs with a deep frown. Back in the room Barker remained stiff and straight. His jaws cut hard lines against his cheeks. He turned slowly and gazed down into the roadway. Puddling shadows were thickening there; there was the acrid scent of dust in the air. Across the road lamplight showed from the bank. Slowly bunched muscles slackened and Tom moved toward the door.

* * * * *

Elihu Gorman was standing beside his desk with one hand braced against the cubicle's flimsy wall, shoving his full weight against it, feeling a heedless kind of fury and frustration. He did not at once hear the knocking, nor did he immediately heed it after he heard it. The knocking grew more insistent. Gorman dropped the arm, pulled himself up, and went out through the empty building and flung back the panel. There were caustic words on his tongue and pointless anger in his eyes, but the big, powerfully-built dark man standing there, evil-looking in the orange light, held him silent.

"My name is Barker," the big man said. "I'd like a few words with you."

"The bank is closed!"

Barker's stare hardened; Gorman braced into it.

"I won't take much of your time and you may find it profitable to listen."

Elihu stepped begrudgingly aside. Tom entered and watched the banker lock the door, straighten up, and march to his office.

From behind his desk Gorman nodded curtly, indicating a chair. Barker did not sit down. He said: "I've got forty thousand dollars I want to put out at small interest on long-term loans."

Gorman's stiffness slowly departed. He sank down behind the desk. The sharpness left his voice; it became deep and pleasant. "How long, Mister Barker?"

"A year, two years."

"You want this money to work for you . . . is that it?"

"That's it."

"Well," Elihu said, and smiled. "Three percent interest?"

"I had three percent in mind, yes."

"Would you consider putting it all out in one loan at three percent on, say, a two-year basis?"

"I had in mind several small loans."

"Oh, well, of course it's your money, but I can tell you frankly . . . in confidence . . . that I have a place for forty thousand on a two-year plan, and I honestly believe I can get you four percent. It's gilt-edged, Mister Barker."

Tom's brow furrowed. "Four percent sounds good," he said.

"It's as good as gold, Mister Barker."

"Well secured?"

"The bank itself will guarantee it."

Tom's expression of concentration deepened. After a moment he said: "I'll sleep on it."

Elihu arose, held the door for Tom, and escorted him to the roadway entrance. "I'll set it up for you," he said, thrusting his hand out. "All the data will be assembled by eleven o'clock."

"I won't be able to make it until later. About three in the afternoon."

Elihu's teeth flashed; he pumped Tom's hand in a close grip. "At three o'clock." He smiled. "Good night."

Tom crossed to the Royal Antler, exchanged glances with Tex, had two quick jolts of Old Hennessy, and departed. At the livery stable he engaged the night hawk in casual conversation, rented a horse, and rode out. It was then slightly after 8:00 p.m. He did not return until after midnight, and again he engaged the hostler in conversation. He finally went to the hotel and retired at 1:45 in the morning.

Saturday the sun rose bitterly yellow and heat poured over the land in dancing waves. Few riders were abroad. Tom did not meet a soul until the afternoon was well along and he was returning to Beatty. Then he crossed trails with Sheriff Pollard and a young deputy named Jack Havestraw. Enormous crescents of sweat darkened the younger man's shirt but Tim Pollard was only slightly flush-faced and red necked. He reined in beside Tom with curiosity bright in his eyes.

"Poor time o' day to be ridin'," he said probingly. Tom let the words sink into dead silence.

They rode perhaps two miles before Pollard tried again. "Lots of cow country hereabouts. Thinkin' about going into the cattle business?"

Tom swung his head, fixed Sheriff Pollard with a steady gaze, and said: "I guess you didn't turn up anything."

Pollard shifted slightly in the saddle. The amiability left his voice and he sighed. "I haven't yet but I'm not through, either. Listen, Barker, I usually bend over backward to get along with folks. You're expectin' me to break my back."

"You don't even have to bend for me, Sheriff. Just keep out of my way."

Tom booted the livery horse into a slow lope and rode away. Pollard's deputy looked angry. "Who is he, anyway? Sure disagreeable."

Tim Pollard watched the diminishing figure swerve toward town. "It isn't who he is that bothers me. I know all about that. It's what he's up to that keeps me awake nights."

"Say," young Havestraw said in a rising tone, "isn't that the feller who shot Charley Ingersoll?"

"It is."

"Humph! When Clint finds him, your troubles'll be over."

Tim shook his head with hard emphasis. "Don't you go an' bet any money on that," he growled. "Them as saw him outdraw Charley told me they'd never seen a man so fast with his gun." The sheriff spat aside. "Clint Ingersoll's goin' to get himself killed and you mark my words on that."

Far ahead, Tom hauled up finally and twisted to watch the sheriff and his deputy straggling their way slowly across the shimmering distance. He smiled and his face did not entirely lose its expression of satisfaction until he swung down at the livery stable, handed the reins to the day man, and bent forward to beat dust from his clothing. He took out his watch, gazed at its face, and crossed to the hotel. It was then 3:00. Elihu Gorman would be waiting. Let him wait.

Tom called for the water boy, gave him a quarter, and lay back in a cool, refreshing bath. Later, while he was dressing, he gave the same lad another quarter to go to the bank and tell Elihu Gorman that Mr. Barker had been detained and could not see him until after 5:00. When the youth departed, Tom winked at his reflection in the mirror and descended to the lobby. The clerk smiled wide approval; there was no denying it, Tom Barker was a fine figure of a man. Everything he wore was dark. The only contrasting relief about him was the ivory grip of his sidearm.

He was sitting in the dark corner of the Royal Antler where he always sat, legs outthrust, shoulders slumped, gazing at the blunt ends of his fingers feeling clean and loose and satisfied, when the night hawk from the livery stable shuffled up. Without a word passing between them, Tom counted out $20 and handed them over. The hostler faced toward the bar with his thirst showing.

A tousle-headed cowboy facing Barker's corner from his place at the poker table saw this transaction over the edge of his cards. His eyes followed the hostler to the bar, watched him thump down a coin, and call for a bottle, then swung palely back to the slouched figure in the shadows. His boyish face was wooden but deep in his eyes lay something difficult to define, a guarded expression of strange, cold portent.

VII

Tom saw Elihu Gorman after 6:00 p.m. The banker's grip was weak, his palm clammy, when they shook. His face, too, seemed paler than it had the night before. Tom took a chair and sank down. He said: "Sorry I had to be late but word gets around in Beatty. I've had more cowmen wanting me to buy them out or back them, than you can shake a stick at." He studied Gorman; the wait had been hard on him, which is the way Tom had wanted it to be. "I'll tell you," he continued, cutting across the banker's opening words, "I've just about decided to hang and rattle a day or two over this. There might be other ways to invest that forty thousand."

"Yes, but . . ."

"You see, I know the cattle business, Gorman, and I don't know this loaning business."

"But, Mister Barker, I told you . . . the loan will be guaranteed by the bank."

"I know," Tom said, getting to his feet. There was finality in his voice. "Just the same I'm going to hang and rattle until Monday or Tuesday. Thanks for your time and effort, Gorman."

Elihu did not arise from his desk. Tom let himself out of the bank and stood a moment on the plank walk, tasting the fullness of triumph. Northerly from the bank, in the smoky light of carriage lamps made fast to either side of the livery stable opening, three men were grouped in earnest conversation. He recognized one of them as Judge Montgomery. A second figure was the day hostler. The third man, with his back to Tom, was unrecognizable. He watched them a moment, then crossed to the hotel and went to his room.

Noise rose mutedly up from the roadway—the jingle of spurs, the stamp of boots and the hooting call of happy men. Tom blew down the lamp chimney, plunged his room into darkness, then stood by the window, looking down. Within a week Beatty would know whether he was top lash in the valley or a whipped cur riding out with his tail tucked under him. He smoked a cigarette. If he had to ride out, all right, but at least four men would not forget him as long as they lived: Judge Montgomery, Elihu Gorman, Moses Beach, and that old fogy, Sheriff Tim Pollard. He retired on that thought.

* * * * *

Sunday dawned with a blaze of saffron glory. Sunlight stole down the far hillsides, raced across the range, and burst upon Beatty with a soft brilliance that turned quickly to yellow, breathless heat. Tom awakened to the tolling of a church bell. He stared at the ceiling; he could close his eyes and hear that same bell tolling him out of bed as a boy. He and his mother had often gone to that church; since those days he had not once been inside a church. He swung out of bed, dressed, and went to the Queens & Aces Café for breakfast. There, unexpectedly, he met Tex and a high-breasted, long-legged girl, bold of eye and with a wide, full mouth that promised a generosity of spirit to match its size and heaviness. He nodded; the girl was from the Royal Antler; he'd often seen her there. But this meeting was different. In this setting she didn't look the same. No, he decided, it wasn't the setting, it was her attire. She had a subdued, well-cut dress with a primly high neckline; her hair was brushed severely back and in a bun at the nape of her neck. He squinted at Tex, at the buttoned suit coat, the peg-top pants, and yellow shoes—not boots. Tex's pale eyes avoided him and a slow stain mounted into his boyish face. My God, Tom thought, they're going to church. Those two are going to church!

"Yes, Mister Barker?"

"Coffee, fried meat, and potatoes."

He drummed on the counter, keeping cadence with the tolling bell. The girl threw him a wide smile. "I didn't know you ate, too," she said, laughing. "All I've ever seen you do is drink."

He continued to drum on the counter, gazing straight ahead at a garish curtain made hideous by enormous cabbage roses. From the corner of his eye he saw Tex nudge her and get uncomfortably to his feet. When they passed through the door, Tom twisted for another look. Miss Eloise—she had a way of walking . . .

"Your coffee, Mister Barker."

He faced around and lifted the cup. When the cook returned with his platter of food, Tom said: "Mike, you go to the firemen's dances at the church house?"

"Yes, every year, Mister Barker. I wouldn't miss one."

"Why wouldn't you?"

"Everybody's there . . . all the pretty gals, the boys from the ranches, music, food. No, sir, I wouldn't miss one of them dances for the world."

Tom finished eating and left the café. He ran head-on into Judge Montgomery's daughter. If the choice had been his, he would have avoided the meeting; since he could not, he touched his hat and started past.

"Tom?"

It stopped him still. When they had been very young, she had called him that. He turned back, sweeping off his hat. "Yes'm."

"Are you going to church?"

"No'm."

Beneath her brows was the inquiring line of frank gray eyes. She had a beautiful, composed mouth; the lips lay together without pressure. He could see in them her flare of temper; she could charm a man or chill him to the marrow. She was slightly taller than the average woman, and maturity had given her a handsome figure, slightly full at breast and hip, and a face with both strong and pleasant contours. Her skin was creamy ordinarily, he could see, but now it was flushed by the steady-rising heat.

"Why not?"

A quick flash showed in his eyes, then died instantly; he forced a smile. "It's been so long I've forgotten how to act in a church, Toni."

Her smile came, long and soft. "Tom, you're the only one who ever called me Toni. Even yet . . . I'm Antoinette or Tonette. Except for Tim Pollard, of course."

He stood silently before her, courteous but impassive and distant. She regarded him levelly through an interval of silence. "Why . . . Tom?"

"Why . . . what?"

"Why did you come back?"

"You'll be late for prayer meeting, Toni."

Again the silence settled between them. She started to move, to turn away, then she called his name again, and he waited. "You'll be at the dance tonight?" she inquired.

"Yes'm. I reckon so."

"Should I save you a dance?"

Sweat broke out on his face and he could feel the color mounting there in waves. He wanted to hasten away but instead he said gravely: "I'd like that, Toni."

She smiled then, and left him.

He thought of his room but restlessness drove him to the Royal Antler. Even with a bottle and glass and the morning hush of a saloon on Sunday, the restlessness did not leave. "Roy," he called to the bartender, who was the only other man in the room, "did you know Charley Ingersoll?"

"I knew him, Mister Barker."

"Do you know his brother?"

"Yes."

The barman leaned over the counter, looking round eyed at dark Tom Barker. In all these weeks this was the first time Tom had addressed him other than to call for a bottle. Also, Roy had heard the gossip and had as much curiosity as the next man, even though, in his trade, he had to work harder to conceal it than most men did.

"You've heard the talk . . . that he's going to hunt me up one of these days."

"I've heard it, Mister Barker."

Tom drained his glass before speaking again. "What's holding him back, Roy?"

"Nothin', I expect, Mister Barker. He'll come." Roy threw a long glance outward toward the shimmering road. "Clint's a freighter. He don't often get home."

"Well, I don't particularly want to kill him."

"I expect you're goin' to have to, though."

The bell ceased its tolling. Deep silence settled over the town. In the far distance a dog's barking rose keenly in the heat. Tom turned his back on the bar and gazed steadily out the window; beyond Beatty lay the pure flare of open range; beyond the range was a blue blur of rising hills, cowed now by midsummer's heat. Like all desert lands this was a country that went down deep into a man, remained there, a part of him, so long as he lived and breathed. It was for Tom Barker a solid part of memory, a segment of his life stream. He twisted, refilled his glass, and held it untouched in one fist, caught in the grip of memory.

He remembered her as a sweet child gripping the seat of a wagon watching him with solemn admiration. He recalled her, too, sitting beside him while a black Arizona night closed down around them, thick and mysterious, and only their tiny yellow-pointed campfire burning bravely while they pretended he was an Apache buck and she was his squaw. But his most vivid memory of her was the morning he went to her father full of a great and desperate fear, pleading for help. He could never forget how she had looked at him then, nor could he forget how her father had listened gravely, then had taken him to the sheriff to be rid of the squalor and sordidness he represented.

Four mounted men trotted into sight from the south, their horses pushing up gray gouts of dust as far as the Royal Antler hitch rail. There, the riders swung down, tied up, and started purposefully forward. Tom watched them briefly and put down his glass, arose, flung a coin upon the table, and walked out. He didn't want to hear laughter right then.

There has never been a man so wholly alone as the one who waits outside a church. Tom smoked a cigarette, leaning upon a store front with soft singing coming to him across the empty roadway. He thought of Moses Beach; how he was lying there, guarding Tom's secret unwillingly, and there was quite suddenly no flavor to the thought. But a hard man with a lifelong ambition to amount to something in the town that had turned him out could not easily change back to the boy he had once been. Willful energy lived in him; it showed in the uncompromising blackness of his eyes and in the set lines of his jaw and lips, and while, on the one hand he took no satisfaction from Beach's plight, on the other he could not, and would not, turn back.

The church was emptying. Women in bonnets and men in stiff collars and carefully greased shoes made their uncomfortable way through the heat. Judge Montgomery walked sedately beside Antoinette, and for just a moment black eyes and gray ones met in a distant clash and an electric shock traveled to Tom over the intervening distance. Then she was talking to a young man with glossy blond hair and did not again look in Tom's direction.

He threw down the cigarette and moved off toward the hotel. Behind him, coming out of the crowd, Tex and Miss Eloise paced evenly forward on the plank walk. They both saw his back moving away from them and each let a long glance linger on him. Miss Eloise said: "He's a strange person, isn't he?"

Tex was slow in replying. "He wasn't always that way, though, ma'am."

Liquid violet eyes lifted swiftly. "Oh? Do you know him?"

"Yes'm."

"But you didn't speak to him at the café."

"He wants it that way."

Miss Eloise's nose wrinkled. "You mean he doesn't want his friends to recognize him here in Beatty? Why, is he an outlaw?" Her eyes widened noticeably.

"No'm. That's just the way he wants it."

"Oh." Miss Eloise searched the empty plank walk for Tom Barker's figure but it had disappeared into the hotel. "Tex, will he be at the dance tonight?"

"I reckon he will. Leastwise he said he might show up."

"Well, would you care if I danced with him?"

Tex lowered his eyes to her face. "No'm, I wouldn't care. Only I'll give you odds he won't ask you to dance."

Miss Eloise's round eyes were momentarily lost behind a slow, feline blink. "What kind of odds, honey?" she asked silkily.

Tex looked rueful. He said: "I just remembered something. I ain't going to bet with you."

"Aren't going to bet with me."

"All right . . . aren't. It's the same thing anyway."

"Tex . . . ?"

"Yes'm."

"Why's everyone scairt of him? Is he truly a gunman?"

"He ain't no gunman, and if anyone's scairt of him, I expect they got a reason to be. He was born and partly raised up in this town."

"I didn't know that."

"Well, he was. And he's got a grudge against it, too."

"Against the town? You mean against the whole town?"

"Yes'm."

"I declare, I never heard of such a thing before."

Tex turned thoughtful. "Listen to me," he said quickly. "Don't you breathe a word of what I've told you to a living soul. You understand?"

"Don't worry, I won't. Cross my heart."

Tex's boyish face resumed its normal open expression. "Shall I meet you at the dance or fetch you from the Royal Antler?"

"From the Royal Antler, silly. I'm not going to pay my own way into that dance."

Tex smiled, then he laughed. "That'd be something, wouldn't it . . . you paying your own way to a dance?"

VIII

When darkness came down, the mystery of the night closed in. Tom was still in his room when he heard the musicians start playing. He examined himself in the mirror as best he could—it was not a very large piece of glass—then crossed to the window and stood a moment, watching couples strolling toward the plank pavilion beside the church. There was an elusive feeling of excitement in him that would not be pinned down, hard as he tried to catch it in words. He saw Tex enter the Royal Antler and reappear shortly with Miss Eloise on his arm. He smiled flintily; if Tex wasn't careful, he was going to find himself with a ring in his nose. Well, no matter how good a cowboy a man was, he would not be young forever, and in the end perhaps it was better to have a woman and children and a piece of land, a place to rest your head when the storms came. He shrugged and started for the door. It would not be hard to tame Tex Earle; he'd always had the seeds of domesticity in him anyway.

It was a fluid crowd that eddied around him as he approached the pavilion. The music was loud and lively. Laden tables groaned under the weight of food and four huge punch bowls stood brimming. A dozen young men were clustered around one particular bowl and their mischievous grins told the story of a smuggled bottle that had been emptied into the punch there. He caught a glimpse of Antoinette whirling past on her father's arm, and he thought, in that brief moment, that her searching gaze had come to rest with something like relief when she saw him. Tex and Miss Eloise pranced by and Roy the bartender, hair neatly plastered, face set woodenly to endure discomfort, glided past. Even Elihu Gorman was dancing, a sturdy woman near his own age in his arms.

When a quiet voice drawled at his side, he turned to see Sheriff Pollard slouching there, fierce mustache waxed and set, faded eyes crinkled in a tolerant smile. "You got a gun under that coat, Mister Barker?"

"Yes. Is it against the law to have one here?"

"Nope."

"Then why did you ask?"

"Because Clint Ingersoll's wagons were seen southeast of town this afternoon." Pollard continued to regard the dancers. "He'll likely show up here tonight."

Tom was jostled from behind; he moved closer to the sheriff to permit several laughing couples to squeeze past. "I can't stop him from coming here," he said.

"No," Pollard conceded, "you can't. Would you . . . if you could?"

"Yes."

"Why? You worried?"

"No."

"Mebbe you should be. They say Clint's fair to middlin' fast with a handgun."

"That's not fast enough," Tom replied, and edged away through the crowd.

Sheriff Pollard watched the broad retreating back, and, when Jack Havestraw came up, he turned and said: "Y'know, it's hard to like a man that don't like you . . . but it isn't always hard to respect 'em."

The youthful deputy looked around at the crowd. "Who?" he asked, not seeing Tom.

"Barker. I was just talkin' to him. I don't think he wants to use that gun so bad, after all."

"Oh. Did you get the answers back on him yet?"

"Nope. And likely when I do, I'll already know all I want to know about him. I got a feelin' about that."

The sheriff moved off in the same direction Tom had taken. People called his name, jostled him, and offered him drinks. It made him feel good, as a lawman, to be liked rather than disliked. Once, he caught a fleeting glimpse of Tom Barker talking to a high-breasted girl. It was Miss Eloise and the flashing smile she wore suggested that perhaps it wasn't altogether a coincidence that, at that precise moment, the dance caller held up his fiddle for the crowd's attention and bellowed: "Ladies' choice, gents. Ladies' choice."

There was more than challenge in the violet eyes in front of Tom Barker; there was interest and curiosity, and perhaps flirtation as well. He took her arm and went forward; the music commenced, louder and wilder it seemed to him, and they whirled away. He had not danced in years and her closeness troubled him. He felt the rhythm of her body and was conscious of the clean smell of her hair. She held her dazzling smile and gazed directly into his eyes.

"You are a good dancer, Mister Barker," Eloise said, then, before he spoke, she rushed on: "Can I call you Tom?"

His discomfort increased: "Yes'm, you can."

"And you call me Eloise."

He inclined his head slightly. She was dancing very close to him and he could feel the ripple of flesh and muscle. He also knew many eyes watched them and winced from the thought of Antoinette.

The dance finally ended. Tom escorted Miss Eloise to the sidelines and made a quick exit. He did not see Tex push through and claim Eloise for the next dance, and so he missed the pale light in Earle's eyes that crystallized into hardness as Eloise talked.

Tom was nearing the outer fringe of people when a chirping voice hailed him. "Nice dance, ain't it, Mister Barker?" He looked around and down. It was Mike from the Queens & Aces. He nodded, and pushed past.

There was a scent of dust in the air and shadows twisted and turned where the lanterns hung. On the side wall of the church gigantic figures jerked and plunged, their shadowy distortions trailing off into deep murk. A restless bubble of talk quivered on the air; people continued to arrive; laughter, flashing eyes, and flushed faces moved forward in a strong blur.

"Tom?"

He was making a cigarette. His hands grew still as he twisted. She was smiling up at him, but there was something in her gray eyes that only partly smiled.

"You dance very well."

He finished the cigarette, lit it, and blew out a gust of smoke. "So do you," he said.

She came closer and leaned upon a bone-gray old cottonwood log that had long ago been shored up as a bench. "Do you recognize very many of them?" she asked.

He shook his head, watching people pass. "No, not very many, Toni. Only a very few. I guess twelve years is a long time on the frontier."

"It is. It's a long time anywhere."

"Would you care to dance?"

"If you want to."

He looked at her. "But you'd rather not."

"I'd rather walk," she replied.

They inched their way clear of the throng and she took his arm. He was aware of her nearness, of the swaying of their bodies along the plank walk through the deserted town.

"Do you remember the time you made me climb into the church bell tower with you?"

"Yes, I remember. You were scairt to death."

She smiled, keeping step with him. "And the night we both got tanned because we were an Apache warrior and his squaw and stayed out after sundown?"

He smiled.

"Why, Tom?"

He made no immediate reply, but he knew what she meant. It took a moment to bring himself back from the past, though, and with the rush through time came also his defenses.

They continued to walk along, neither breaking the silence until finally he said: "For a lot of reasons, Toni."

"Wise reasons?"

He sought for words and failed to find the right ones, and through his thoughts her words came again.

"Revenge? To show Beatty you are as good as it is?"

He stopped and swung her around. "I wouldn't have to be very good for that, Toni." His gaze was brittle. "To show Beatty I'm better than it is."

"Then," she said gravely, "you shouldn't have come back, Tom."

He dropped his arms. The quarter moon lay its soft silver light across her face. He saw its stillness, its beauty and strength. He also saw the deep and unknown things in her eyes and averted his face. She took his arm and gently propelled him forward again.

"I think there is something in this world that can destroy men more surely than bullets, Tom. Hate. It would break my heart if that happened to you. When we were children, you were my ideal, my hero." She paused; then: "But there's not much left in you from those days."

"How do you know?"

"Do you remember what Abraham Lincoln said about men's faces?"

"No."

"He said that every man is responsible for what shows in his face after he is thirty."

"And what you see in mine you don't like."

"I didn't say that, Tom. It isn't so easy to destroy your gods. What I said was . . . hate can ruin you."

"I don't hate, Toni. I don't hate Beatty or the men here who . . ."

"Are you sure of that, Tom?"

"I'm sure."

"Then what is it you feel toward them?"

"Contempt, I guess."

"But they're good men, Tom. Listen to me, I've known them all much longer than you have."

"But you were not the son of a drunk freighter or a woman who ran off with another man. You were Judge Montgomery's kid, Toni."

"Let me finish," she said. "I've known them longer than you have. They are human, Tom. They make mistakes. Their judgments are not always good. But they are as good and honest as any men are, anywhere, and it's wrong for you to scorn them for their errors." Her grip on his arm tightened. "How can you sit in judgment on them, Tom?"

"Why shouldn't I?"

Her step slowed, then halted altogether. She looked up at him, searched his eyes and his features, then she looked away and they continued to walk.

She said, in a thoroughly impersonal manner: "You've changed more than I'd guessed, Tom." She said it as though it were a contingency that no longer mattered; there was a dullness in her voice and her hand fell away from his arm.

He walked along with angry, troubled thoughts. They had been very close once, but that was long ago. It was far away; it was in another life; he had long since become hard and dedicated and he could not possibly change after one stroll in the moonlight.

"I should have known, when you killed Charley Ingersoll." His lips drew out in a flat line. He might have spoken but her words cut across his marshaling thoughts. "I should have seen then that you do sit in judgment over people. Only I didn't think of that, then. I only thought . . . Tom is back. Life will be like it was."

"Toni, they sat in judgment on me, or have you forgotten that?"

"And so," she intoned in the same lifeless voice, "that gives you the right to sit in judgment on them." She looked at the buildings around them and slowed to a halt. "Let's go back, Tom."

The walk back was made mostly in silence and none of the earlier buoyancy remained in their steps. Neither of them was aware of the blond man following them through the soft summer night, his face tense and angry, his light eyes fixed with strong hatred upon Tom's broad back.

People began to pass them; a few were elderly couples but more were young girls leaning on the arms of happy youths. There was a sprinkling of lean cowboys from the ranches walking proudly beside town girls. Near the stone water trough Tom took Toni's arm and steered her into the bland darkness of an ancient cottonwood tree. Strains of music carried easily this far and overhead, through a filigree of dusty leaves, the high, brilliant stars and the capsized moon rode serenely in a cobalt heaven.

"You'd ask me to give up all the plans I've made for the last twelve years, wouldn't you, Toni?"

She shook her head slightly, slowly. "No, Tom, I wouldn't ask you to give up anything. That isn't something others can ask of you. It's something you've got to ask of yourself."

He made a cigarette. She heard the full sweep of breath in his chest. He moved a short distance off and sank down on the lip of the old water trough. He sat with cigarette smoke eddying up around his face, with his elbows on his knees, and with his lips set in a hard, tough line.

She turned her head, gazing at him. Each curve of his body registered in her mind. She looked for, but did not find, the boy she had once known. Now, in his place, she saw only the signs of a strong man's reticence, his certain confidence, his tempered hardness, and the full sweep of his passion, which would be as hot as fire in anger—or in love.

"I think we'd better go back," she said. "Dad will be wondering about me."

He got off the stonework but went forward only as far as the tree, where she was leaning. He seemed to want to say something, but the held-back expression in his face told her, whatever it was, he would not say it. The stillness went on like that, full of unexpressed and puzzling emotions. Then he groped for her hand and held it tightly in his grip, too lost within the tiny sphere of his own absorption to notice a vague shadow fade into a doorway, watching them, nor see another shadow stop suddenly over by the Royal Antler, then slide forward, moving in behind the first shadow.

He released her hand and she pushed forward off the tree. Suddenly, looking up, she saw only the moving blur of his face, the full sweep of his shoulders against the night. He looked very sad and very solemn, and his dark eyes were blacker than a well's depths. Both his hands came up, dropped upon her shoulders, and pulled her in. Her head was tilted; one hand came up to rest against his chest with gentleness, and he kissed her with soft, long pressure, with a painful hunger that seared into her mind. When he released her, she clung to his arm for a moment, then without a word they started forward out of the semidarkness, pacing slowly together back toward the sound of music.

"Toni?"

Yes."

"Should I apologize?"

"No, Tom."

They were on the fringe of the crowd now; people nodded and smiled and shouldered them this way and that way. He touched her, stopping, wide-legged, bracing into the stream of humanity, seeing nothing but the directness of her gaze.

"When we were kids . . ." he began.

"That's gone now," she said swiftly. "That's all over, Tom. It might never have been at all." She freed her arm and cast him a final look. "That's what the kiss was for. Memories, Tom. It was a salute to something that was very sweet, very innocent, and wonderful. Good night, Tom."

IX

He walked through the crowd, low in spirit, and did not at once hear the voice at his side.

"Tom . . . you said it would be all right for me to call you that."

He looked into Eloise's violet eyes and made a mechanical smile.

"Folks are still dancing, Tom."

He stopped, looking over her head. "Where's Tex?"

"He went to the saloon for a minute. He'll be coming up soon. About that dance . . ."

He didn't feel like dancing, but he took her arm and pushed forward, and they danced. Once, near the pavilion's edge, he glimpsed Judge Montgomery in heated conversation with two men, then other dancing couples cut across the line of vision and he lost them. Finally the musicians ended their sweaty labors with a crashing finale and Tom led Miss Eloise to the sidelines and left her.

The crowd was not quite as thick as before. Now, there was standing and sitting room. There was also a noisy drunk being forcibly escorted away from the area by Tim Pollard on one side and young Jack Havestraw on the other side. Men smiled broadly and their girls giggled.

"Enjoying yourself, Mister Barker?"

It was Judge Montgomery, and, although his words had been affable enough, there was a hot, wrathful glitter to his eyes.

Tom nodded, waiting.

"Can I have a few words with you?"

"Certainly."

They walked beyond the milling crowd and Judge Montgomery turned finally, lamplight showing his face to be pale and agitated.

"I understand you are in the hay and grain business," he said, faint acid in his tone.

Tom felt for his tobacco sack and began manufacturing a cigarette. "I am."

"I also understand that you bribed my former night man at the barn to tell you how soon I'd be needing feed."

Tom kept his eyes on the cigarette. Part of his bribe had been for keeping this information from the judge. He felt both mean and outraged, and he made no reply at all.

"I can guess your purpose, Mister Barker."

"Can you, Judge?"

"Quite easily, in fact."

Tom lit the cigarette and looked steadily into the older man's face over its burning tip. "Did you bring me out here to call me names, Judge?"

Montgomery's jowls rippled, his eyes burned with a fierce light, but he controlled his voice. "No, Mister Barker. I asked you out here to sell me some hay and grain."

"How much do you want?"

"Twenty tons of hay and ten tons of grain. What is your price?"

"Eleven dollars for the hay and . . ."

"Eleven dollars! Hell! I've never paid more than three dollars a ton in my life!"

"Judge, you asked my price and I told you. You don't have to buy from me."

"Barker, this is robbery," choked Montgomery. "Highway robbery. You'll not get away with it! I know what you've done . . . taking options."

Tom shrugged. "Ride it out," he said evenly. "If you know about the options, you also know they're only for sixty days. Just ride it out for sixty days, Judge, and maybe you'll get the hay for three dollars again." Tom exhaled slowly. "And again . . . maybe you won't, too. I may exercise those options."

"You won't and you know it, Barker."

"I don't know it," Tom replied. "I'm arranging right now to haul that hay to San Carlos. If Uncle Sam takes it, Judge, he'll take every blade of it."

Judge Montgomery was breathing heavily. He plunged fisted hands into his trouser pockets and said: "I could have hay hauled in."

Tom's eyes lit up with cold humor. "I looked into that before I took those options, Judge. It'd cost fifteen dollars a ton to load your loft through freighters. My price is only eleven a ton."

"Barker . . ."

"Listen, Judge, you're out of hay and grain. You can't operate a livery barn without them. Your profits are good. You make more money from that barn than you do on the bench. Eleven dollars a ton isn't going to put you out of business. I think you'd better pay it."

"I'll see you in hell first!"

Tom turned on his heel and walked back toward the pavilion.

Judge Montgomery remained stiff and outraged on the far fringe of the crowd. He had never been a profane man or he would have sworn savagely at that precise moment.

Tom came upon the sheriff, mopping his face with a large blue bandanna. He smiled at him. "Hot night for escorting rambunctious drunks," he allowed. Pollard stuffed the bandanna in a hip pocket and nodded.

"Hot for other things, too," he said. "I just heard about your hay deals." He squinted at Tom and wagged his head. "You know, if you was working steady at making enemies in Beatty, you couldn't do it no better'n you are now. I worry about you, boy."

"You don't have to, Sheriff. As for the hay deals . . . isn't that how businessmen get ahead?"

Pollard's squint remained. "It's legal, if that's what you're drivin' at, but it's sure gettin' folks down on you."

"Are they down on Beach and Gorman and the judge? Are they down on you, Sheriff, for doing what you have to do to make a living?"

Pollard rolled his eyes. "Why is it," he cried, "that sharpers always got logic on their side when they're cornered?"

"I'm not cornered, Sheriff. Far from it. I've got money to invest and I aim to make money with it." Tom dropped the cigarette and ground it underfoot. "If you think I'm cornered, you see where I am in another month."

He was moving away, toward the roadway, when Sheriff Pollard said: "Dead. That's what you'll be in another month, Barker. Dead and buried."

Tom continued on his way. He walked south nearly as far as the stone water trough, then angled through the dusty roadway toward the hotel. The far side of the road was drowned in shadows and darkness; he did not discern slow movement along a northerly store front, but behind him, rigid beside the old cottonwood tree, another detached figure caught the gliding outline and shifted to face it.

"You, there! Barker!"

It was a soft, sharp call. It rode down the night to Tom with unmistakable meaning. He stopped still, then began to turn very slowly. The silhouette back by the cottonwood tree moved swiftly northward until lost in the night, then cut rapidly across to Tom's side of the roadway and came down behind the emerging blond man who was walking flat-footedly toward Tom, right arm bent slightly and fingers crabbed.

"You see me now, Barker?"

Tom turned a little more, brushing back the right side of his coat as he did so. "I see you," he said, finding much in the other man's outline to remind him of dead Charley Ingersoll.

"I never yet shot a man in the back, Barker, but I could've blown you in two a dozen times tonight."

Tom waited for the man to step off the plank walk into the dust; when he finally did, still walking purposefully forward, the same kind of blond hair was visible, the same flat features and brutish expression that Charley Ingersoll had had.

"You know who I am, Barker?"

"I can guess."

"Let's hear your guess."

"You're Clint Ingersoll."

The blond man halted fifty feet away and tilted back his head. Moonlight softened the harshness of his face and hid his eyes in sunken shadows. "You're dead right. I'm Clint Ingersoll. Did you figure I'd be scared to face you?"

"No," Tom replied levelly, catching a flicker of movement twenty feet behind Ingersoll, along the front of the Queens & Aces Café, and incorrectly thinking it was either Tim Pollard or some confederate of Ingersoll's.

"But you sweated a little, waitin', didn't you?"

Tom said no again, in the same quiet way, and added: "I was hopin' you wouldn't think you had to do this."

"You was hopin' I'd forget you murdered my brother?"

"I didn't murder him. He drew on me. What did you expect me to do . . . stand there and get shot?"

"That's what's goin' to happen to you now, Barker. You're goin' to stand there an' get shot."

Tom saw the distant shadow behind Ingersoll move out clearly and straighten up out of a crouch. He saw the cocked gun lift to bear and heard a voice he recognized say: "Ingersoll, you make a move toward that gun and you'll be dead before you get it out."

The blond man turned to stone. Not a face muscle moved. Then, very slowly, his lips curled in a twist of contempt and he said: "If you wasn't scared, Barker, why'd you hire a bodyguard?"

Tom moved forward into the road. He watched Tex ease Ingersoll's gun out and throw it down. "I have no bodyguard, Ingersoll. He happens to be a friend of mine."

Tex spoke from behind the disarmed freighter. "He's been shagging you all night, Tom. I've been watching him."

"Good thing for him you was," Ingersoll growled.

Tex's hard laughter was short. "You damned muleskinner, Tom Barker'd kill you with his left hand. You'll maybe never know it, feller, but I saved your bacon tonight."

"Give me back my gun and let's see about that!"

Tex swore and started to push the gun forward. Tom stopped him with a word, then he went still closer and gazed into Clint Ingersoll's face. There was hate and unreasoning fury there. Tom sighed, bobbed his head toward a dogtrot between two buildings, and started forward. Tex prodded his prisoner along. They emerged into a back lot where broken pottery lay like bones in the moonlight. Tom removed his coat and gun belt and faced Ingersoll. He was standing relaxed and resigned and was unprepared when Ingersoll dug his heels into the ground and hurled himself forward, driving Tom back, low and hard, until his shoulders struck wood and his ears rang from impact. He was wise enough, however, to lie limply in the freighter's grip until he had one arm free, then he sledged downward with the full power of his arm and Ingersoll's knees sprung inward and his grip softened.

Tom spun sideways and got free. Ingersoll was shaking his head. A sullen purple bruise was fleshing up behind his ear. He cursed and rushed forward a second time, head low, arms extended. Tom moved forward instead of backward and threw a crashing fist that made Ingersoll stumble. Before the blond man could recover he had him by the shoulders, slammed him against a building, and, when Ingersoll bounced off, he swung his body weight in behind his right fist and buried a granite-hard set of knuckles in Ingersoll's belly. The freighter's breath whooshed out and his mouth hung far open. Tom hit him again, and again, then he stepped back and Ingersoll slumped at the shoulders, bent in the middle, broke over at the knees, and went down into the refuse to lie crumpled and without movement.

Tom moved away, toward his coat and shell belt. He was sucking hot night air into the bottoms of his lungs when Tex moved quickly forward to hold his coat.

"He looked tougher'n that," Tex said, helping Tom shrug into the coat. "Hell, I think I could've taken him, myself."

Tom grinned, breathing deeply. "There he is, if you want to try."

Tex bent a long look on the unconscious man. "Why didn't you just kill him?" he asked.

"You sure got a short memory," Tom said, drawing upright again, shifting his holstered gun to its normal position. "There you sat, up there by that damned creek, preaching me a sermon about being a potential gunman . . ."

"This was different," Tex protested. "He was all set to draw on you."

"Well, why didn't you let him, then?"

Tex rubbed his jaw and scowled perplexedly. "Damned if I know," he said. Then his face brightened. "Wait, I'll get some water and douse him. When he comes around . . ."

"Go bed down," Tom said dryly. "I don't want to shoot the simpleton any more'n I wanted to dance with Miss Eloise."

Tex's shoulders pulled up straight. He faced Tom.

"An' that's another thing," he said heatedly. "She told . . ."

"Tex, do me a favor, will you? Marry her or whatever you got in mind. Right now I'm tired. I don't want to fight with anybody." Tom cocked his head. "We've run together a long time, haven't we?"

"Yes."

"Did you ever see me try to cut in on another man's woman?"

"No, I guess not."

"Then for gosh sakes go bed down, will you, and just remember one thing. I'll be waiting for you up by the creek tomorrow."

Tex prodded Ingersoll with his toe. "What about him? Tom, maybe you don't want no war, but he does. After this licking he'll want one worse than ever."

Tom considered Clint Ingersoll's inert figure. Tex was probably right; they would meet again. Maybe not. You could never tell about other people. He shrugged. "If he comes around again, I guess next time I'll kill him, Tex."

They parted then, Tex heading for the livery stable loft and Tom bound for his hotel room.

X

He and Tex relaxed in the shade along the creek on Monday. These weekly rendezvous were the bright spot in his life now. Here, he could fully relax. This morning, the out-of-character sensitivity he'd sensed in Tex lately was entirely gone, too, and that cheered him a little. He gazed at his friend of many campfires and spoke in a voice as dry as wind rattling cornhusks.

"It wasn't altogether Miss Eloise, was it?"

"What d'you mean, Tom?"

"Cut it out," Tom said shortly. "Fool anyone under the sun . . . but me. I've known you too long."

Tex was smoothing the dust in front of him with a stick. "No," he admitted. "It wasn't just Eloise. I expect it wasn't Eloise at all, Tom." He etched a Texas brand into the smoothed dirt with methodical detail. "I was getting kind of sick of this thing, to tell you the truth." He threw the stick aside. "Y'know, when that ugly little storekeeper got took down sick, I got to remembering something an old Indian once told me. If you think evil about someone, they get sick. That ain't my way of fighting, Tom. If I got a grudge, why I take up my gun and go out 'n' settle it. What you've been doing sort of . . . well, it sort of makes me ashamed. It don't seem manly, somehow."

Tom tugged his hat forward to shade his eyes. "Listen, Tex, you can't call out a judge or a storekeeper or a sheriff. They won't fight you. So, you meet them on their own ground. That's the only way you can beat them. That's all I'm trying to do."

"I reckon," Tex said resignedly. He let off a big sigh. "But I still think it's better to come right out in the open when you got fight talk to make."

"I did that last night with Ingersoll."

"I know, Tom. I thought about that last night in bed. But this other stuff, well, if that's the way it's got to be, all right, go ahead. I'll string along, but it's not my way at all."

Tom smoked a cigarette. They sat in silence for a while, then Tom said: "I'm in a helluva fix. I broke Beach and I've got the only man in town who can bail him out eating out of my hand."

"Who's that?"

"The banker."

"What's the fix, then?"

"The judge."

"Hell, Tom, you got the hay an' he's hurtin' for some. You got him, too."

Tom continued to gaze at nothing. "You don't understand. It's his daughter . . ."

"I understand all right," Tex said carelessly. "I saw you kiss her under the cottonwood, Tom." Tex twisted on the ground. "I don't approve of hitting a man through his girl . . . but like I said, I'll string along. For a little while longer anyway."

"I wasn't hitting at Judge Montgomery through Toni."

Tex looked disbelieving. "No? Then what were you doing?"

Tom pushed his legs out, crossed them at the ankles, and stared at his toes. "I . . . I'm not sure what I was doing. But I don't want to do it again, I can tell you that."

Tex picked up a blade of grass and began chewing it. He stared steadily at Tom and several minutes later he threw back his head and roared with laughter.

Tom straightened up. "What's so damned funny?"

"Nothing," Tex said, choking on his mirth. "I just felt like baying at the moon."

"Well, don't do it so loudly, you idiot. Someone'll hear and come looking."

Tex subsided. He chewed a while longer on the grass, then he moved as though to arise. "Tom, I ain't smart like you. I never was. I recognized that six, eight years back. But there's sure Lord some things I can see that you sure as hell can't see. I can tell you that for gospel truth."

"What can't I see?"

Tex stood up and dusted his trousers off. "Never mind," he said. "The sky'll fall on you one of these days . . . then you'll see." He squinted at the sun. "About time to be getting back. Finnerty wants me to make the drive to San Carlos with him. What about it?"

"It won't take more'n two weeks, will it?"

"Less than that, Tom."

"Then go ahead. I won't need you for a while anyway."

"Couple more things."

"Shoot."

"You ain't aiming to humble that old sheriff, are you?"

"Yes."

"Dammit, Tom, he's an old man."

"He owes me something, Tex."

Earle's pale eyes clouded over, but he said no more on the subject of Tim Pollard. Instead, he spat out the grass and said: "How long you think you can go on bluffing on a busted flush? I know how much money you've spent lately . . . on all that there hay and what-not. You ain't got but a couple hundred dollars left, Tom."

"I know that and you know it," Tom conceded. "But no one else does." He arose and stretched. "Now comes the big one, Tex."

"What do you mean?"

"When you get back from San Carlos, you'll find out. I'll either be spoon-feeding that damned town and its crop of righteous fat-backs, or I'll be saddling up to ride on. One or the other."

"I got my ideas about which," Tex opined, and went to his horse, caught up the reins, and mounted. "Just wait for me to get back is all. I'd sort of like to be in on the finish of this thing, since I got roped in on the beginning."

"I'll wait. And, Tex . . . while you're at San Carlos, find out what the Army's paying for hay, will you?"

"Sure. Adiós, Tom."

"Adiós."

He rode back the usual way, entering Beatty from the south, and the first person he saw was Tim Pollard's young deputy. Havestraw threw him a reserved nod and called out: "Elihu Gorman's looking for you!"

Tom said—"Thanks."—and dismounted at the livery stable. The hostler who faced him was a new man, nearly as large as Tom was, and disagreeable-looking. "You Mister Barker?" he asked, studying Tom's features as though to identify them from a description. Tom nodded, holding out the reins. "You ain't welcome here," the hostler said, pocketing his hands and leaving Tom standing there with the reins outstretched. "Boss' orders."

Tom continued to regard the man through a moment of blossoming antagonism, then he turned abruptly and crossed to the hotel hitch rail. As he was mounting the stairs to his room, he spoke over his shoulder to the clerk. "Have someone find a place for my horse. Not the livery barn. Understand?"

"Yes, Mister Barker."

Tom was unlocking his door when a man's deep voice greeted him from behind. He turned. Elihu Gorman was arising from a ladder-back chair. Tom pushed open the door and motioned for the banker to precede him inside. The encounter at the livery barn had left him feeling angry. He closed the door, watched the way Gorman folded over onto a chair, and flung his hat on the dresser.

"I have all the data on that loan for you," the banker said with false briskness.

"I told you, I'd think about it."

Tom crossed to the window and began making a cigarette. Gorman watched his every move with anxious eyes. "This thing can't wait," he said. "It's the best investment in the area. Someone else will come along."

"Let them," Tom said, lighting up. He shot a slow glance at Gorman's face, noted its paleness, its poorly concealed agitation. He had been keeping track of the weeks; Beach and Gorman didn't have much time left.

Gorman was starting to speak again when a quick rap echoed from the door. Tom called out: "Who is it?"

"The desk clerk, Mister Barker. Doctor Spence is downstairs looking for Mister Gorman."

Gorman looked annoyed but he arose. "Mister Barker . . . ?"

"I'll give you a definite answer by the end of the week," Tom said. "And meanwhile, to start our association off, I want to see how good your bank's judgment is."

"Sir? I don't exactly follow you?"

Tom removed his wallet, extracted a thick sheaf of papers, and held them out. "Take them," he growled, and, when Gorman extended his hand, Tom said: "Arrange a five-thousand-dollar loan on those options for me. Put the money in an account for me. I won't be needing it, but it'll establish our relationship."

Gorman was gazing at the papers. "Hay and grain options?" he said, his voice rising.

"That's right," Tom answered, crossing to the door and holding it open. "I'll be over to see you within the next few days."

After Gorman left, Tom stood thoughtfully frowning for a moment, then scooped up his hat, and left the hotel with long strides.

It was mid-afternoon. Except for the coolness of the Royal Antler and one or two other such places in Beatty, there was little relief to be found from the punishing heat. Tom took his usual table at the Royal Antler and nodded silently as Roy brought forth a bottle and glass.

"Seen you at the dance," Roy said quietly, letting his eyes cut quickly across Barker's dark and brooding face. "Seen you later, too."

Something about the way Roy said "later" made Tom look up.

"Behind the café, I mean. You and your friend and Clint Ingersoll."

Tom poured a drink, offered the glass to Roy who declined, and tossed the liquor off neat. "You've got pretty good eyesight," said Tom in a tone as quiet as the one the bartender had used. "Where were you?"

"In the outhouse behind the saloon here." Roy straightened up. "That was quite a battle, Mister Barker. Wish I'd seen the start of it, though."

"That was the start of it."

Roy shook his head. "I mean when you two first met. Y'see, I know Clint pretty well. He'd use his gun before he'd use his fists. I'd have liked to have seen you disarm him."

"It wasn't me who did that, Roy."

"Oh? Tex, then. Well, you two're quite a pair, Mister Barker."

"Are we?"

"Yep." Roy lowered his voice. "A feller in my job's got nothin' much to do during slack times but watch people."

"Meaning?"

"Hell's bells, Mister Barker. I spotted you and Tex tradin' looks three weeks back."

Tom poured a second drink but did not lift the glass. "You told anyone else about this, Roy?" he asked.

"Naw. Ain't any of my business, really."

Tom continued to regard the glass of whiskey. Roy probably had not told anyone else; barmen were notoriously close-mouthed. Still, what one man had noticed, others might also have noticed. He suddenly felt no desire for more liquor.

"Maybe we'd ought to keep it like that," he said, arising.

Roy smiled. He raised one hand and touched the graying hair over his ear.

"See that there gray," he said. "A man in my job don't live that long unless he learns damned early to button his lip."

Tom nodded and started to move past.

"Mister Barker?"

"Yeah?"

"Clint's still around."

"Making fight talk is he, Roy?"

"Not that I know of, but just the same you'll want to grow an eye in the back of your head."

Tom gazed steadily at the bartender. "He didn't strike me as a bushwhacker, Roy."

The barman shrugged. "Who knows what a man'll do? You beat him fair with your hands, Mister Barker, and he's heard the talk by now of how you handle a gun. Them things're usually enough to make a man do a little figurin' . . . if he's plumb set on killin' somebody."

Tom fished a $20 gold piece out of his pocket and put it in the bartender's hand. "Thanks, I'll take your advice," he said, moving off toward the door.

Outside, the plank walk was nearly deserted and heat waves arose in dancing ranks from the roadway. Tom was walking north, past a bench in front of Beach's store, when Sheriff Tim Pollard came through the doorway and met him.

Tom nodded. The sheriff's eyes pinched down suddenly and he caught Tom's arm. "Set on the bench with me a minute," he said. "I know somethin' that might interest you."

Tom sat. Pollard fished for his pocket knife, opened it, and began leisurely to pare his fingernails. "You seen Doc Spence today?" he asked.

"No."

"Seen Gorman, the banker?"

"A couple of hours ago. Why, what of it?"

"Well, a real strange thing happened this mornin'. Doc Spence calls it a medical miracle."

"Then it surely must be," Tom said dryly.

The sheriff chuckled. "I take it you don't much cotton to Doc Spence."

Tom put both hands palms down on the bench. "Is that what you stopped me for . . . to talk about Spence?"

"No. Everything in good time, boy. Just relax."

Tom's glance sharpened. The old devil knew something; there was no mistaking that look on his face. Tom settled back and stifled an impatient curse.

Pollard clicked the knife closed and turned to gaze at Tom. "Moses Beach got his voice back this morning."

XI

In the stifling silence of his room Tom sprawled on the bed thinking. Moses Beach knew, somehow, that he had given Finnerty the money to redeem his note at the bank. The proof that he knew was in the way he had sent immediately for Elihu Gorman when he could talk. To warn Gorman about him. What would Gorman's reaction be? He would of course refuse to loan money on the options, for one thing, and he might even suspect that Tom had met Evan Houston and had learned from the cowman that Gorman had offered Houston Finnerty's ranch before the bank had been in a position to foreclose. He gazed fixedly at the ceiling. Well, let Gorman think what he wished; it did not change anything. Gorman and Beach still had less than ten days to repay their loan and the thirty percent interest. Tom's lips curled. Beach would have another stroke. He smiled more broadly and leaped up, went to the window, and gazed down at the road.

The shadows were moving in. There was a faint and acrid breeze blowing in from the range. Far out the hills squatted in faded patience awaiting dusk, and surcease from the blinding sun rays and moonlight. Somewhere, beyond town, a bull roared and mules whinnied. There was a freight outfit camped there somewhere. He thought immediately of Clint Ingersoll. What a fool he'd been; he should have killed him. Why hadn't he?

He crossed to the washstand, mopped at his face, combed his hair, and hunched into his coat. He hadn't, he told himself, because of Tex. He hadn't wanted to lose the respect he'd kept these past years. No, that wasn't altogether the reason, either.

Antoinette Montgomery was mixed up in it some way. Kissing her under the cottonwood tree had done something to him that night, had somehow softened the resolve in him.

He moved to the door, opened it, and passed through. Tex had been only partly right when he had told Ingersoll he had saved his bacon. Toni had been responsible, also, for Ingersoll's remaining alive.

The lobby was empty when he passed through and halted briefly in the swift-falling dusk beyond. Summer night air was good, he thought, drawing his lungs full of it. He was moving, turning south on the plank walk, when the shot came. He heard it clearly for the fleetingest part of a second before the hammer blow knocked him forward to his knees, pushing his breath out in a loud grunt. His mind said to go flat and roll, to get away from there. He went fully down and scrabbled through the roadway's dust, automatically drawing and cocking his gun as he did so.

There was no immediate sense of pain, only breathlessness. It was not a new sensation; he'd had it once before, when he'd fought a wild Mexican in Wichita. The result of that battle still bothered him occasionally, a sliver of deeply embedded lead in his right hip. There was a frothy mist forming before him. He strained to see through it. It widened, deepened, turned crimson. He shook his head irritably, struggling to find the peril lying beyond. Dimly men's voices came, raised in excitement. His head began to roll forward. He fought to hold it up; it went slowly downward despite his heroic efforts; then a wonderful feeling of pleasant drowsiness came.

"It's Barker, Sheriff. He's shot, by God."

Pollard came up and stopped, looking down. "Uhn-huh," he conceded. "Damned if he isn't. Jack, fetch Doc Spence. Couple you other boys give me a hand packin' him to his room upstairs."

"Nasty-lookin' wound," someone said, with much more interest than sympathy. "Wonder who done it?"

Pollard was grunting under Tom's weight. He twisted an upward look at the crowd. "Any one of you could've done it. I expect there's probably a pretty fair price on his hide by now." He straightened up with an effort. "Come on, dammit, lift, don't drag."

"He's heavier'n a horse-mule, Sheriff," said a man in grunting protest.

"Well, what'd you expect? Feller's got as much money as he has, eats good an' eats regular."

Eleven men trouped up the hotel stairway to Tom's room. Sheriff Pollard stopped all but those carrying Tom with a scowl at the door. "Go on," he rasped. "Go wet your fangs."

They put Tom on his bed. Pollard dismissed the remaining two men and closed the door behind them. Then he removed Tom's gun, hat, and coat, opened his shirt, and bent forward, squinting at the hole in his chest. "My, my," he said aloud, but softly. "That bushwhacker was a fair to middlin' shot at that, what with there bein' shadows an' all. He only missed by about six inches."

Dr. Spence entered, methodically removed his derby, pursed his lips, and advanced upon the bed. The sheriff moved back.

"Right through the lights," he said.

"I got eyes, Tim."

"Humph!"

"Get the clerk to send up some hot water."

Sheriff Pollard went to the door, opened it, and bawled out for hot water. He closed the door and went back over to watch the doctor work.

"Went clean through him, Tim."

"I know."

Spence straightened up. "Who did it?"

"Dunno. He was a fair shot, though, wouldn't you say?"

Dr. Spence's neck swelled. "No I wouldn't say," he snapped. "When the day arrives that people look on shooting more as a crime than a test of marksmanship, this country'll be a lot better off."

"Uhn-huh. The judge's been talkin' about an ordinance against firearms in town."

"Fat lot of good that'll do, what with the high-powered rifles they make nowadays. Dammit, what's holding up that water anyway?"

"I'll go see, Doc. You just simmer down."

Spence tossed aside his coat, rolled up his sleeves, and bent over the unconscious man. Pollard returned with the water, a clean basin, and several old towels. "Everybody's talkin' about it, Doc," he said, drawing forward a table and filling the basin.

"They have to talk about something, don't they?"

"What I meant was, I got to leave you for a while."

"Why?"

"Trouble. It isn't that folks care about Barker gettin' shot. They just don't approve of bushwhacking."

"Who're they after? Dammit, light the lamp, Tim."

Sheriff Pollard put the lamp on the table and canted the mantle so the doctor could see. "Clint Ingersoll. How's that?"

"Fine."

"Adiós, Doc."

Spence grunted. When he was alone, he worked faster. Finally he drew back, examined his handiwork, went to his coat, withdrew a pony of bourbon, drank deeply, and coughed. "There, Mister Mysterious Barker, you'll probably live . . . only I'm not sure you ought to, after what you did to Moses."

Tom spoke in a quiet tone and Spence's eyes popped wide open. "What did I do to Moses, Doc?"

Spence pushed the bottle into his coat quickly and cleared his throat. "Mustn't talk yet," he admonished. "You got a bad thing there."

"What'd I do to Beach?"

"Well, he had a stroke, didn't he?"

"You think I'm a magician, Doc?"

"Mister Barker, I was there when he came around and started talking. I know what you did. He told me."

"And that's what caused his stroke?"

"I would say it was, yes."

"Then he's got only himself to blame, Spence. He's the one who wanted to bust Gerald Finnerty so bad he got greedy. It wasn't me. I just came along in time to help a hard-working man keep what's his."

Dr. Spence had fully recovered from the shock of hearing a man he had thought totally unconscious speak to him. "No more talking," he ordered. "That ball pierced your lung. You've got to lie perfectly still and be absolutely quiet for at least a month."

"A month. You're crazy, Doc."

"Am I? Then go ahead and get up, and bleed to death internally. It's your life. Damned if I care what you do with it."

Spence was donning his coat when Tom said: "Who did it?"

"Tim Pollard said a bushwhacker."

"Of course it was a bushwhacker," the man on the bed said impatiently. "If he'd been out in the open, I'd have seen him. But who was he?"

"Don't know yet." Spence picked up his hat, his bag, and crossed to the door. "I'll look at you a little later. Lie still and be quiet."

Tom waited until the door closed, then explored the bandaging with his right hand. He felt slightly feverish but aside from that there was no sensation of illness or shock, not even a headache.

Daylight waned beyond the window. By turning his head to the left he could see the darkening sky. Below him, Beatty was turning quiet; it was the supper hour. A soft knock echoed from the door.

"Come in," he said softly, and raised his head.

"Tom! We just heard."

She floated across the room. Lamplight made her large eyes smoky in the shadows; it reflected off a rapid pulse in the V of her throat.

"You shouldn't have come here," he said, feeling more than uncomfortable, feeling strangely guilty of something.

She drew up a chair, sat down, and took his hand in both hers. "If I didn't come, Tom, who would?"

He heard the reproach and steeled himself to ignore it.

"Didn't you have any warning?"

"None," he said shortly, looking out the window at the sky.

"But you think you know who did it, don't you?"

His eyes swiveled to her face. "I think I know all right, Toni. Want me to tick 'em off for you? Pollard, Clint Ingersoll, the judge, Elihu Gorman . . ."

"How can you say that!" She let go of his hand.

He watched redness fill her cheeks and under other circumstances he might have smiled. "They're the ones who'd like to have done it, Toni. But a couple of them haven't got the guts."

She was staring into his eyes with her back rigid and her mouth thinned out by disapproval. Suddenly she said: "I shouldn't have come."

"That's right . . . you shouldn't have. But since you did come, tell me something. Does the judge want his twenty tons of hay at eleven dollars yet?"

She had control of herself now, but the smokiness remained in her eyes. He thought he saw a sob tear at her throat and looked quickly away.

"Tom, please . . ."

"You'd best go, Toni."

"I'm not ready to go yet. Look at me, Tom." His head did not move on the pillow; his dark stare was stonily fixed on the brightening stars beyond the window. "Tom . . . ?"

"Listen to me, Toni. Last night you practically called me . . ."

"That was last night. You're hurt now."

"Nothing's changed. I'll be up and around again in a few days." He faced her with a quick turn of his head. "Toni, I can't change. I came here for a purpose. I'm going to stay until I do it. Do you understand me?"

"I understood you last night, Tom. I know what you're here to do. Ruin Mister Beach and drive the judge out of the livery business. And there'll be others, too, won't there?"

"Yes."

She drew back in the chair. Her body softened and settled lower. After a time she said: "Is it completely useless to try and reason with you, Tom? Are you that far gone?"

"I think so, yes."

She got up suddenly, stood there gazing down at the bed. "Can I get you anything?"

"Yes. Please hand me my gun." When she had complied, he said—"Thank you."—without looking up at her.

"Shall I send up something to eat, Tom?"

"I'm not hungry, thanks."

"Tom . . . ?"

"Good night, Toni."

"No," she said in a voice that had to be swift to be steady, "not good night. Good bye!"

The pain started then. He could feel it spiraling upward and locked his jaws against it. It pulsed in cadence to her steps as long as he could distinguish them, and continued in the same way when he no longer could.

The hours passed. Dr. Spence came and went; they exchanged no more than ten words. Spence was gruff and Tom was silent. Down below in the road he heard riders jingling past, their light, carefree voices raised in merriment. Nostalgia touched him; it had been good to ride into a town like that, full of laughter and thirst and sticky with sweat. Then he heard booted feet slamming up the stairs two at a time, ringing spurs mingling in their echo. The door burst open and Tex stood framed in the opening, eyes wide with disbelief.

"Hell, Tom. We just heard . . . out at the ranch. You going to make it?"

"I'll make it. When're you and Finnerty taking that drive out?"

"Finnerty, pardner, not me. You need a nursemaid."

"Like hell I do."

"Well, now," Tex said, straddling the chair Toni had vacated and grinning from ear to ear. "Like hell you don't. But do or don't, you got one. Want to jump up and whip me so's I'll go away?" When Tom glared in deep silence, Tex's grin threatened to tear his face. "Just what I thought. Can't do it, can you?"

XII

Tom earned Albigence Spence's eternal disapproval by walking down to the Queens & Aces Café nine days after he had been shot, and eating a steak breakfast. But his arrival at the Royal Antler Saloon to some extent ameliorated Spence's dire prophecies; there, he was greeted with broad smiles and congratulations by men he knew only by sight. He bought a round of drinks, sat for a while at the wall table, then crossed the road to Pollard's office.

"You know who did it, Sheriff?" he asked.

Pollard eyed him laconically and said: "Nope. There's more'n one would like to see you dead. I don't know which one to start with."

"Ingersoll?"

"I talked to him. I don't figure Clint's a good enough actor to fool me. He swore he didn't do it. He also said he wished he had . . . only he didn't shoot from hiding."

"I believe that," Tom agreed.

"He also told me about your fight."

"Well?"

"Nothing. Just proves I'm right. I said Clint wasn't a bushwhacker. I told the crowd that the night you got shot. I was right about another thing, too."

"I'm listening."

"You aren't out to kill anyone for the hell of it."

Tom turned toward the door. "You're getting wiser by the minute, Sheriff."

"Just a second!" Pollard called. "You've been out of circulation a few days. I've been learnin' things about you in that time."

"Go on," said Tom, leaning on the door.

"You got Moses. You about got the judge. Elihu Gorman wasn't around when you was a kid here in Beatty, but you've got him eatin' out of your hand, too. That leaves only me." Pollard's steady faded stare lingered on the younger man. "When you goin' to call me out, boy?"

"Would you come?" Tom countered.

The sheriff considered this through an interval of silence. Then he drew up in his chair. "I reckon I would. I wouldn't want to, not over anything as silly as what's eatin' you, Tom, but I would if I had to."

"I'll let you know," Barker said, and walked back out into the sunlight.

He was heading for the bank when Dr. Spence came floating across the road from the Royal Antler. He was moving with the immense and solid dignity of a drunken man who was concentrating very hard on walking erect and straight. "Ah, Barker," he intoned with greater irony than Tom would have thought anyone in his condition capable of, "the damned walking dead, eh?"

Tom would have moved past but only the infirmity of his prolonged siege with a bed was bothering him now—weak legs.

"You are a fool," Spence said, squinting upward. "A fool and a hero, eh? Not afraid. No, sir, you are not afraid he will return for another try . . . and that's why you are a fool. Of course he will try again. He didn't get caught, did he?" The doctor's squint spread over his entire screwed-up face. "A fool, a hero, a rugged physical specimen, but more than any of those things, you are a fine hater." Spence swiped at his damp forehead. "Do you know what a hater is, Barker? No? Well, I'll tell you. It's a man without reason. No reasoning animal hates as deeply and for as long a time as you have. No reasoning animal . . . but you aren't a reasoning animal, are you? You're a cold, merciless, unreasoning hater."

"You're drunk," Tom said coldly.

Spence absorbed this philosophically. "Of course I'm drunk. Why shouldn't I be? I studied nine years to become a great surgeon and I've spent thirty years in this infernal country digging bullets out of people. I've wasted an entire human lifetime, digging bullets out of carcasses so damned ignorant . . . most of 'em . . . that they couldn't even write their own names. Of course I'm drunk." The doctor looked around for something to lean against or sit upon, found nothing, and faced Tom again, weaving a little from side to side. "You want me to unbosom myself, as they say in the theater?"

"No."

"Well, I'm going to anyway, my boy. I'm going to anyway." He drew in a big breath and exhaled it slowly. He squared his shoulders and threw back his head. "I'm going to tell you something you don't know, big man. I'm going to watch you shrink down to my size."

Tom's legs felt better; he started past. Dr. Spence reached out and caught him in a tight grip.

"Just a minute, Barker. I'm going to tell you this if it's the last damned thing I ever do."

"Take your hand off my arm, Doctor, or it just might be the last thing you ever do."

"Ho!" Spence hooted. "You'd shoot me, would you?" But he removed his hand. Then his face smoothed out and his eyes burned with a strange and sardonic light. "You recollect the night your mother left this damned town, Barker?"

Tom made no reply. His mouth turned slowly flat and dangerous-looking.

"I see you remember all right," Spence said, grinning. "Know what I think? That's mostly what's eating at your innards. Well, let me tell you something about that . . ."

"Doc!"

Sheriff Pollard's voice cracked like a whip. Dr. Spence started, turned his head to watch the lawman come up, then, without another word, he started away from Tom. Just before he turned down an alley, he halted, looked back, drew himself up, and squared his shoulders, then passed from sight between two buildings. Tom's throat felt as though it was full of ashes.

"He gets kind of windy every once in a while," Pollard remarked, stopping to face Tom, his voice back to normal. "Too bad. I expect that's why he hangs on here 'stead of going back East where the money is."

Tom's black stare was unwavering and knife-sharp. "Why'd you shut him up like that?" he demanded.

"Pshaw, boy, he was makin' a spectacle of himself, bein' drunk an' disorderly."

"It was more than that, Sheriff."

Pollard's inscrutably squinted eyes remained mild. "Naw," he protested. "What else could it have been?"

"Whatever he was on the verge of telling me."

Pollard shook his head without speaking, and Tom, studying his face, came to the slow realization that Tim Pollard would never tell anything he did not want to tell. He turned abruptly away and resumed his way toward the bank.

Elihu Gorman was not in. There was another man waiting to see him; it was Judge Montgomery and he looked annoyed. When he saw Tom enter the building, he snapped at a clerk: "Tell him I want to see him this evening."

Tom watched the judge depart, then collared the same clerk. "Gorman in?"

"No, sir. He went out into the country. I don't think he'll be back until pretty late."

"Tell him Tom Barker wants to see him."

"Yes, sir."

Once more on the plank walk, Tom met Tex. They spoke together briefly, and Tex was starting away, toward the livery stable, when three unkempt men came out of a saddle and boot shop nearby. Tex swung wide to avoid a collision and noticed only that they were freighters. He would normally have forgotten them but one made a grunt at sight of Tom and sang out unpleasantly: "The big man himself."

Tex turned. He could see Tom's face over the head of the shortest, thickest of the freighters. It was white to the eyes.

"Come ridin' out o' nowhere," the freighter went on. "Come ridin' into Beatty plumb loaded down with money. Goin' t'be top lash. Hah!"

The tallest of the three freighters was Clinton Ingersoll. He stood slouched now, one hand hanging free, the other hand hooked in his shell belt. He was smiling with naked hatred in each line of his face. But it was neither Clint nor the other young freighter who spoke; it was the grizzled older man between them. "Top lash o' Beatty . . ."

Tom started to turn away. Six feet behind the freighters Tex was rooted to the ground. He had never before seen dark Tom Barker walk away from a fight, and it was very clear the freighters were enjoying his discomfort immensely. It was also clear to Tex that their intention was to force a fight.

"Hey, big man," the grizzled freighter said. "Where you goin'?"

Tom made no answer, but continued to move off.

Clint Ingersoll spoke one word then: "Bastard."

Tex's eyes sprang wide. Tom was turning; the whiteness of his face let that one word sink into dead silence.

"Go ahead," Ingersoll said, his meaning very clear.

Tex flexed his gun hand while the stillness ran on. The freighters in front of him, concentrating their full attention upon Tom, were oblivious to the danger in their rear. Tom was not going to fight. Tex could see that. He was not even going to speak. Tex's mouth went dry with distaste; anger burned in him. He said very thinly: "Turn around, Ingersoll. I'll oblige you."

The grizzled freighter's shoulders stiffened but he made no move. The other, younger man, licked his lips, the light of battle dying in his eyes. Clint turned slowly.

"Any time," Tex said, and, when Ingersoll made no move, his lips curled in scorn. "Big talk, Ingersoll. Big talk when you figured it'd be three to one. Go ahead, make your play."

Ingersoll stood erect, his jaw hard-set and grim. He was not a fast-thinking man and this situation was something he could not cope with—a fast gun behind him, another fast gun in front of him. If he got one, he could not hope to get the other one. He licked his lips, the decision forced upon him. "I got no fight with you," he said.

"Well, now," Tex replied sardonically, seeing it plain in Ingersoll's face that he was not going to go for his gun. "That's where you're wrong. I'm a mite partial to that name you called Tom Barker. I just naturally figure to fight whenever I hear it, Ingersoll."

"I wasn't talkin' to you, feller."

"Don't mean nothin', Ingersoll. Like I said, I'm just plain partial to that word."

"I won't draw," Ingersoll said hoarsely.

"Why then I expect I'll just kill you anyway . . . you yellow swine!"

Tom was moving forward; he stopped close to Clint Ingersoll, his hand moved down and up, and Ingersoll's gun thudded across the plank walk into the roadway. Tex straightened up very slowly, face reddening. He looked squarely at Tom, saying nothing. Now the other two freighters turned to look at Tex, and Tom disarmed them the same way.

"No fight, Tex. Come on."

The freighters continued to stare at Tex as though imprinting his features upon their memories. The older man was a vicious and dissolute looking person. Tex had seen murder in men's eyes before and he recognized it now.

"Better give 'em back their guns, Tom," he said past stiff lips. "I ain't like you. I ain't goin' to give 'em a second chance to kill me."

Tom prodded the freighters. "Go on," he said. "Move off and don't stop."

Ingersoll led out, imminent peril sharpening his perception. The other two men followed him in stony silence. Tom watched them go along the walk as far as the Mexican café on the west side of the road and turn in there, then he finally relaxed.

Tex, round eyes speculative, lingered a moment waiting for the distance between them to be broken. When it was not, when it became hard to bear, he struck out for the Queens & Aces Café without a backward glance. He knew Tom was still standing there by the boot and saddle shop, looking into the glittering daylight.

"Excuse me."

Tex's head jerked up. "Ma'am," he said harshly, avoiding a collision, but still moving.

"Sir . . . ?"

He stopped, focused his eyes with an effort and touched his hat unconsciously. It was the handsome girl he'd seen Tom walk away from the dance with. The girl Tom'd kissed in the shadows of the old cottonwood tree. The judge's daughter.

"I saw what happened over there," she said, looking squarely into his face.

"Did you, ma'am?"

"You're a friend of Tom Barker's." She saw the shadow cloud his vision. "I think I know what you're thinking."

He was icily polite. "Do you, ma'am?"

"You're thinking he lost his nerve, that he was afraid to fight them."

Tex remained silent, looking down into her face with his bleak expression.

"But there is something you don't know. Something that was happening over there that goes back many years."

Much of the hostility left him; he slouched; he even smiled slightly at her. His condescension annoyed her; he saw that, too, in the smoky flare of her glance. "Ma'am," he said quietly, "a feller calls you a name like that, you fight. It don't matter what else there is, you fight."

She turned ironic. "Do you indeed? Would you have killed all three of them?"

"The odds don't mean nothing, ma'am. You fight, that's all there is to it."

"Even," she said slowly, "if one of those men is your father?"

XIII

Tom was lying on his bed staring at the ceiling when Elihu Gorman knocked on the door. He called for him to enter and sat up.

"Good evening," the banker said.

Tom nodded, ran a hand through his hair, and motioned for the banker to be seated.

"You wanted to see me?"

"Yeah. Where you been all day, Gorman?"

Elihu would have resented Tom's question and tone if he had dared to, but he did not; he had just come from a bitter visit with Judge Montgomery. "Out in the country," he replied.

"Looking for hay?"

"What?"

"Looking for hay for the judge?"

"Well," Gorman said a little breathlessly, "why would I be doing that, Mister Barker?"

Tom leaned back, gazed briefly out at the settling night, then turned a worn and tired expression toward the banker. "Because you need his friendship, Gorman, that's why."

"Of course his friendship is valuable," the banker retorted with some heat. "He's one of our more substantial citizens, Mister Barker."

"So you were out looking for hay for him."

Gorman reddened. "See here, Mister Barker . . ."

Tom made a tired gesture. "Cut it out, Gorman. You got forty thousand dollars from the judge to buy Finnerty's mortgage from the bank. You engineered Finnerty's foreclosure. You had it all set up to resell Finnerty's place to Evan Houston, the biggest cowman in these parts."

Elihu's working face was pale; his eyes were round and fearful.

"And you've got to get the judge to go along with you because you can't repay the loan and interest on time." Tom took out his tobacco sack, considered it a moment, then returned it to his pocket. Although he felt fine, his lung was not yet healed. As he went on speaking, though, the longing for a smoke persisted.

"That's the secured loan you talked to me about. You figured if you could get forty thousand from me for two years at low interest, the worst that would happen would be that you and Moses could pay it off. On the other hand, if anything happened to Gerald Finnerty in those two years, you could still get his ranch, sell it to Houston, make your big profit, and still come out smelling like roses." Tom's expression hardened. His steady stare remained on the banker's face. "If anything happens to Finnerty, Gorman, you're not going to be around to make any big deal with Houston."

"Barker . . ."

"Shut up and listen."

Gorman subsided. He was sitting very erect in the chair.

"Did you get the hay?"

No answer.

"Did you get the hay?"

"No," Gorman breathed softly, "no, I did not."

"Couldn't scare anyone into selling?"

"I didn't try to scare them, Barker."

"Of course you didn't," said Tom dourly. "The local banker drives up. Any cowman who has ever borrowed money from you or thinks he might have to someday begins to sweat. You didn't have to scare them, did you?"

Gorman was thinking. His face gradually resumed its normal expression. He cleared his throat and spread both hands out toward Tom. "Barker, you want to make money and so do I. I'll tell you how it can be done. Big money, Barker."

"I'm listening."

"You have Finnerty's note."

"Go on."

"You can use it as leverage to get his ranch."

"And?"

"I've got Evan Houston all ready to buy the Finnerty place at seventy-five thousand dollars cash." Gorman leaned back, watching Tom's face. He could tell nothing from the blank expression, nor from the unwavering dark eyes. The silence ran on; Gorman began to squirm on his chair. "Well?"

"I'll tell you a better way to get out from under your trouble, Gorman. Get a bill of sale to Moses Beach's store and use it as collateral for borrowing more money."

"How would that help?"

"It wouldn't help you, Gorman, but it'd sure help me." Tom straightened up on the bed. "I want Beach's scalp, Gorman. I also want Judge Montgomery's scalp. The only thing I've got against you is that you're on their side of the fence. You can break Beach with a note on his store."

"But . . ."

"Listen, Gorman, you keep on crossing me for those two and you're going to wind up pretty badly used up." The banker started to arise. Tom stopped him with a gesture. "I spotted you for a worse crook than a stage robber the first time we met. What you just suggested I do to Gerald Finnerty clinches it for me. Now, I'm going to give you a choice of leaving Beatty on the next stage or of getting called out the next time we meet."

Gorman sprang to his feet, eyes blazing. "You're a fool and an idiot, Barker. Moses Beach told me all about you."

"That shouldn't have taken him long," Tom replied dryly, also arising. "All that he remembers was that he wouldn't help a little kid because it might've interfered with his storekeeping." Tom reached out and tapped Gorman on the chest with his finger. The banker backed quickly away, not from the finger but from the strange, black light in the big man's eyes. "Gorman, you're a pretty good shot for a banker. I owe you something for that and I believe in paying my debts."

"What are you talking about?"

Tom's hand dropped to his side. "This bandage I got under my shirt."

"You're crazy, Barker."

"Gorman, the judge wouldn't have done it. Moses Beach couldn't have done it. Sheriff Pollard came up from the south of town a minute after I went down, but the bullet that hit me came from around a building to the north. That leaves you."

"It does not. It leaves Clint Ingersoll."

Tom shook his head. "I've met Ingersoll twice. Both times he could've bushwhacked me easy. He didn't. He isn't the bushwhacking kind. You are, Gorman. Now tell me why you tried it?"

The banker retreated as far as the door and put a hand behind him. Tom crossed the room swiftly toward him. Gorman ducked away, breathing heavily. Tom stopped suddenly, his right arm swinging, hovering above the gun he wore. Gorman bleated: "I'm unarmed, Barker!"

"You won't be when the sheriff finds you."

"Barker, hell . . ."

"Why, Gorman?"

"It was Moses's idea."

"I'll bet."

"I swear it, Barker. He said you'd ruined us by backing Finnerty, that you wouldn't stop there, and that you had to be put out of the way."

Tom walked to the chair Gorman had vacated and sank down. He did not look at the banker. "Get out, Gorman. Get out and remember what I told you. Be on the evening stage out of Beatty or I'm going to kill you."

The banker left.

Tom got up finally, crossed to the window, and looked out at the night. It was hot out; there was not the slightest hint of a breeze. His room was like a furnace. Below the window two men were talking. One he recognized as Tim Pollard; the other man was deep in shadow and murkily silhouetted. The longing for a smoke came back stronger than ever. He reached for his coat, shrugged into it, and left the room. He went out into the night, moved along the walk, sniffing the air and reaching with his eyes for movement. Pollard was still across the road, sitting now, on a bench outside the jailhouse, whittling a stick that shone dimly white in the gloom. He looked up when Tom approached, his knife hanging in the air, then he resumed his whittling. Tom sat, pushed his legs out, and sighed.

"Hot," Pollard opined.

Tom ignored it. Around him Beatty lay in soft shadow, gentled by it.

"Your pardner's over at the Royal Antler."

Fishing, Tom thought. The old devil's heard about Tex and me and now he's curious.

"Guess he gave you a bad start today. Him an' your paw."

Like an old Indian squaw, always seemingly indifferent, disinterested, and lazing around, but missing nothing, Tom watched two riders enter town from the west in a tight lope side-by-side, swerve in at the Royal Antler, and swing down.

"He come in with that latest train of wagons, Tom. If I'd've known, I'd've told you."

Busybody, Tom thought. Why would he have told me my father had returned to Beatty? What business was it of his? "You trying to soften me up, Sheriff?" he asked finally. "Because if you are, save it."

Shavings fell, pale and curled and pine-scented. "I reckon you don't know me so well, after all," Pollard retorted quietly. "I'm not the blarneyin' kind. Never have been." Shavings continued to peel off and tumble to the ground. "And maybe I don't know you so well, either."

"Meaning?"

The knife snapped closed, went into a Levi's pocket, and Tim Pollard stood up. "Care to walk a piece with me?" he asked.

Tom cocked his head back. "To where?"

"Just walk. Not far, boy. Exercise'll do you good."

Tom stood and considered the craggy old face, then they moved off together. For a while Sheriff Pollard contented himself with saying nothing. Finally he opened up again. "Doc Spence left town last night."

Tom felt surprise rise in him. He went back over his last meeting with the medical man. "Why?" he asked.

"Just up and left. Didn't even come by and tell me s'long."

"If he's gone, maybe you won't mind telling me why you shut him up the other night, Sheriff."

Pollard evidently had given this much thought, for now he had a ready answer. "Some things a feller knows that don't come easy to say, boy."

"Then you did shut him up?"

"We both know that," the sheriff said simply.

They came to the end of the plank walk. Beyond, stretching inkily to invisible bald hills, lay the northward plains.

"Are you going to tell me, or aren't you?" Tom demanded.

Pollard teetered on the walkway, gazing outward. "I'd rather not, Tom. It won't do no good to tell you." He stepped down off the last plank into the dust and turned westerly. "Come along. It isn't much farther."

"What isn't?"

But Tim Pollard trudged along in total silence, shoulders bowed forward and eyes fixed on something neither of them could see, but which they both knew lay just beyond town within its rusting, sagging iron fence. Beatty's cemetery.

When the sheriff stopped, put out a hand and closed his fingers around an iron paling, Tom also halted. He had that peculiar taste of ashes in his throat again. Something darkly, instinctively knowing was working in his mind.

"Ever been here before, Tom?"

"When I was a kid, yes."

"Lots of folks buried here. Lately, when I've followed the hearse out here, I've had the feelin' I know more of these folks than the ones back in town." Pollard twisted to gaze at him. "When a feller gets to feeling that way, I expect he's about at the end of his rope. He's gettin' pretty damned old."

Tom's eyes were accustomed to the darkness. Beyond the iron fence he could discern headstones and, occasionally, forlorn little tins with dead flowers in them. "Does this have something to do with what you don't want to tell me?" he asked.

The lawman nodded. "Yes, and like I said . . . there's things better left unsaid." He straightened up a little, gazing at the dry, flinty earth. "You still bent on knowing, Tom?"

"I am."

Sheriff Pollard's eyes went to one stone and remained there. He seemed to be selecting words. "That grave yonder, boy, the one with the little pillow-like stone, you see it?"

"I see it." Tom's voice had sunk to a whisper. The thing in his mind was taking on form, substance, solidity; it was becoming a premonition with shape and meaning. "I see it, Sheriff."

"That's your mother, son. She's restin' there."

"That's what Spence was going to tell me?"

"That's part of it, Tom."

"Then why did you shut him up?"

Sheriff Pollard put both hands out, curled them around cold iron, and leaned a little forward. "What's the use, Tom? She's gone. You recollect her one way. That's the way you should always remember her, son."

"Tell me the rest of it."

"All right," Tim Pollard said gently. "She come back to Beatty the year after you run off. She was sick, Tom, had lung fever. Doc did everything he could for her . . ."

"Doc Spence?"

"Yes. This is the part it'd've been better left unsaid, Tom. Doc was in love with your maw. He kept her at his house for a year an' your paw never knew . . ."

"Then she died?"

"Then she died, and he buried her here." The lawman narrowed his eyes. "There's only her first name on that stone. Doc didn't want your paw to know, naturally."

"Why did she come back, Sheriff?"

"To get you and take you away. But you was gone and no one ever heard of you again until the day you come ridin' in a couple months back, Tom."

"And . . . the man she ran off with?"

But the sheriff straightened up and dusted off his palms. "Doc never asked and she never said. What's the difference?"

"There's no difference, I guess."

"No. Your mother was a fine woman, Tom. Don't you ever doubt it or forget it." The lawman was turning away.

"One more thing," Tom said to him. "Did you know Doc Spence was hiding her?"

"I knew. Doc and I were sort of close. There's another thing too, Tom. Your paw made her life hell on earth. That doesn't give you no call to hunt him down . . . and believe me, boy, she wouldn't have wanted you to do that. I know."

"How do you know?"

"She an' Doc an' me used to sit on his back porch that last summer, in the evenings, and sort of talk."

"I see." Tom also turned away from the iron fence. "Now tell me the end of it. Why did Spence leave Beatty?"

Sheriff Pollard shrugged as they strolled back toward town. "Who knows why folks do things? Maybe it was seein' you. Maybe you opened an old wound in him. Maybe he just couldn't stand Beatty any more. All I know for certain is what the stage driver told me. He bought a ticket to Saint Joe, Missouri."

XIV

Tom did not sleep in his hotel room that night. He took two blankets, got his horse, and rode up into the hills. He spread one blanket on the dry forage grass by the little creek where he and Tex often met, lay down, and draped the upper blanket over his body. The last echoes of movement died around him, the moon-shot blackness and the deep hush of late night closed down, and mystery trembled in the windless night while he breathed an incensed air. Overhead, glittering in their purple setting, an immense diadem of diamonds shone down. To the motionless man whose black eyes were dull but sleepless, they seemed to turn soft, like a woman's tears.

It was a long night and it held no surcease for him. He did not sleep until shortly before the east was streaked with pale pink, and even then he slept so lightly that the sound of a horse's shod hoof striking stone brought him fully awake.

"Howdy, Tom," Tex said, dismounting. "Figured you might be up here." He flung down saddlebags and began grubbing for twigs. When he had built the tiny, pointed range-man's cooking fire, he rummaged through the saddlebags for his dented, black coffee pan, filled it with water, then sat back watching flames lick and curl beneath it.

"This isn't Monday," Tom said gruffly, sitting upright.

"It ain't Friday, either," Tex said imperturbably, pouring ground coffee sparingly into the water and wrinkling his nose. "Nothing on this earth smells as good as cooking coffee. Too bad it doesn't taste as good as it smells."

Tex sat back, made a cigarette, smoked a moment with obvious pleasure, then brought forth three cups that he swabbed out carefully with grass switches, and lined up one beside the other. Tom watched this briefly, then got up, went down to the creek, washed, combed his hair, and came stamping back. He dropped down, crossed his legs, and regarded the three tin cups. "You going to drink two at a time?" he asked grumpily.

Tex smoked a moment longer before he replied. "Nope, we got company."

The dark eyes raised swiftly. "Who?"

"More'n one."

"Who, damn you?"

"Better mind your language," Tex said, unruffled, then raised his voice. "Coffee's on, ladies."

Tom turned. They emerged from the willows south of where he'd washed, side-by-side—Miss Eloise and Toni Montgomery. He felt like swearing, or jumping up and leaving, or even striking Tex. Instead, he sat there watching Toni move toward him. She was wearing a split riding skirt and a very white blouse. Her hair was caught up at the base of her neck and held in place by a small blue ribbon. She looked fresh and cool and lovely. The rising heat of the new day seemed not to affect her and its reflection from her blouse was painful to his eyes. Eloise smiled into his face, her violet gaze dancing, but Toni only nodded and passed him, stopping beside Tex who held up a cup.

"Thank you, Tex."

The words jarred Tom out of his silence. He took the cup Tex offered and hunkered, not looking in Toni's direction at all.

Eloise sat down and looked quickly at the others. Of them all she was the least affected by undercurrents. "Any sugar?" she asked sweetly of Tex.

"Never use the stuff," Tex said, darted a look at Tom, and stubbed out his cigarette. "Sit down, Miss Toni." She sat. Tex drew in a big breath. "Tom," he said, speaking clearly and as though he had rehearsed what he was saying, "Finnerty's back. Came in about dawn on the stage."

"Yeah?"

"Yeah. He's got your loan money, too."

"All right. I'll look him up when I go back to town."

"Something else," Tex said. "That banker left town last night."

"Did he now?"

Toni squirmed. Tom sensed rather than saw it. "My father has taken over the bank, Tom," she informed him. "Temporarily, until someone else can be appointed to Elihu Gorman's position."

Tom blew into the steam arising from his cup. "That's fine. The best man in town for the job."

"I'm glad you think so."

"No question about it."

"Tom . . . ?"

"Yes'm."

"Dammit, look up when I'm talking to you."

The profanity startled all of them. Tex looked at her with his lower lip hanging. Eloise was round-eyed, and Tom's head sprang up.

"That's better," said Antoinette, her voice going soft and rich again. "There is a forty thousand dollar note at the bank with your signature on it."

Tom was crouched like a stone image staring at her. He put aside the cup of coffee very slowly. "What do you mean?"

"The judge found it this morning."

"I never gave any such note, Toni."

"Of course you didn't. That's what Tex said when I told him. That's why we three are up here this morning." Some of her spirit showed in the gray eyes. "Otherwise I wouldn't be here at all . . . regardless of what Tex or Tim Pollard said."

"What did they say?" he demanded.

"It doesn't matter. What matters is that your signature is on that note to the bank."

"Are you telling me I owe the bank in Beatty forty thousand dollars, Toni?"

She nodded.

Tom looked at Tex and spoke a name: "Gorman?" Tex nodded. Tom stood up. "I see. That's paying me back."

"Huh?"

"Nothing."

"Where are you going?"

"After him."

"Wait." Tex was on his feet. "You won't get a mile down the road. Not unless you listen first."

"Why not?"

Toni and Eloise also got to their feet. "Because my father and Tim Pollard have posses out looking for you, Tom," Toni said.

This was something he hadn't considered. Now he said: "Are you saying that Gorman actually took forty thousand dollars of the bank's money and left that note he'd forged?"

"Yes. And the judge believes you're fleeing with the money."

"No, I don't believe he really thinks that, Toni. I think your father sees his chance for hitting back and he's doing it this way."

She flushed scarlet and for a moment he thought her wrath was going to break out. He was bracing into it when she regained control and spoke in an icy voice: "He'd have reason to believe that, the way you've acted since you've returned, Tom. But Eloise and Tex and I think we can prove to him it was Gorman and not you who took the money."

"How?" he demanded.

Tex fished a paper and pencil from a pocket and shoved them at Tom. "Write your name on there like you always write it."

"Why?"

"Consarn it! So's we can take it back to the judge and make him compare it with the signature on the note. That's why."

Tom wrote his name and returned the paper and pencil. He was nodding. "Sure, and here's something else, too," He gave them the creased note he and Gerald Finnerty had signed. "Give him that, too. It also has my signature on it and it's dated over a month back."

Tex was putting the papers into his pocket when Tom caught his horse and bent to saddling it. As he led the animal forward, he beckoned to Tex. "Fetch your horse. You're going with me. Give the notes to Miss Toni."

Tex obeyed. While he was moving toward his horse to secure the saddlebags and check the cinch, Eloise walked toward him, leaving Toni and Tom Barker facing one another across the smoldering fire. She made a fluttery motion with her hands. "The thing that will save you is that you haven't signed anything back in town."

"Oh?"

"He couldn't have known what your signature looked like, Tom."

He looked grimly at her. "That's not the only thing that's going to save me. Gorman's going to help, too."

"What if you don't find him, Tom?"

He mounted and gazed down from the saddle. "I'll find him. I'll find him and fetch him back."

"Tom . . . ?"

"Yes'm."

"Can I ask a favor of you?"

"I owe you that much, Toni."

"Let me tell Gerald Finnerty it's all right to sell twenty tons of hay to my father."

He lingered a moment to look into her face, then he shook his head negatively, spun his horse, and rode off. Tex, mounted and looking on, stifled a curse and shook a fist at Tom's retreating back. "Ma'am," he said to Toni, "this'll likely take some riding. You just hang and rattle. I'll have his harness shook out, talked out, or kicked out, by the time we get back. You go ahead and tell Finnerty it's all right to bring in that hay."

But Toni was standing as though she hadn't heard, watching Tom lope northward toward the far lift and fall of a side hill.

Tex caught Tom on the downward side of the hill and slowed beside him. He made no mention of what was uppermost in his mind, but said instead: "He's got a long start on us."

Tom made no answer. He jogged along, gazing ahead at the unfolding plains coming up the hill to meet them, the sun-dried floor, the faint gray of banks where winter's deluges had scored the shifting earth, the faint showings of shadows under brush and rocks, and farther out like a flung-down old snake the roadway leading north.

"Of course, since he's traveling on coaches, we'll make faster time."

"And if he went south instead of north?" Tom asked dryly.

But Tex knew as well as did Tom that the night stage out of Beatty only went one way—north. He looped the reins and began manufacturing a cigarette. "You're sure hep for arguments today, aren't you?"

No reply. The road shimmered and writhed and the heat increased. There was no depth to the distance, only a pale, bright yellowness.

"If I had your conscience, I'd feel meaner'n poison, too," Tex opined, inhaling and exhaling. "Funny how some fellers are, Tom. Mean inside and not really very mean-looking on the outside." He inspected the cigarette, knocked off gray ash with his little finger, and took up the reins again in his left hand. "And when they really got no reason to be, too."

"Why don't you shut up?"

Tex became silent.

They rode as hard as they dared in that glaring and waterless expanse, saving their horses when they could, taking time when it was safe to do so, and at sunset the village of Mirage appeared dead ahead. They refilled their canteens, had their horses washed down, grained, and watered, then struck out again, riding through the hot but pleasant night side-by-side.

"Feller at the stage station said it was him, all right," Tex reported. "Said we'd catch 'em if we stayed with it all night, more'n likely."

They stayed with it all night, riding more swiftly as the coolness increased, confident in both their hearts they would catch Elihu Gorman, but beyond that thinking differently. Tex thought Tom would probably kill him. He didn't think he should because the absconding banker was the only one who could clear him before Judge Montgomery. But on the other hand—they were riding the turn-outs in the high north country, and, if he killed the banker, they could just keep on riding, get clear of all this dirt and deceit and discomfort. Tex was a simple, laughing man; his vision extended no farther than the next drive, the next hunt, the next ride into strange country.

"Tom?"

"Yeah."

"That was a lousy thing you done to that girl."

Silence.

"You know, she sweated bullets trying to talk her paw into holding off the posses. And you wouldn't even let her have twenty tons of watery old grass hay."

"It's not her, it's her paw."

"You didn't say that, you just shook your head."

Silence.

"Tom?"

"Now what?"

"I'm splitting off when we find Gorman. I'm heading back for the high country."

The sun was sending up its pink feelers when they saw the little town huddled against a red-stone hill less than three miles ahead. Sharp new light on wooden fronts and low adobe houses stood out, mingling with shadows. "He'd better be here," Tom said, touching cracked lips with his tongue.

"If he ain't, he rented a horse and went on alone," said Tex. "That stationmaster at Mirage said they lay over here until the southbound morning stage comes in."

They were riding down the empty, dust-layered roadway when Tom pointed. "There's the coach."

"Yep. He'll be asleep at the station probably."

As they dismounted in the still and fragrant coolness, Tom looked across his saddle leather. "Tex? You didn't mean that back there, did you?"

Tex kept his head averted, hitched up his shell belt, and patted his horse. "Damned critter's tucked up like a gutted snowbird," he said, ignoring the question. "Well, let's roust him out."

XV

Tex thought the look on Elihu Gorman's face, when they found him bedded down at the adobe stage station and Tom shook him awake, was almost worth the grueling twenty-hour ride, and, if his stomach hadn't been flap-empty and hung up on his backbone, he might even have smiled. As it was, he simply reached down, grasped Gorman's shoulder, and jerked him upright off the cot, and, when Gorman fumbled under his coat, Tex slapped his wrist hard and the little under-and-over .41 Derringer fell to the earthen floor with scarcely a sound.

Three other sleeping men in the room did not stir. Tex propelled the banker out into the soft dawn light and let go of him when he heard Tom cock his pistol. Gorman's head jerked at the little snippet of mechanical sound; his eyes widened and grew very round; they fixed a watery stare on Tom Barker as Tex moved aside. "No," he croaked. "Wait a minute, Barker . . . I'll return it."

"Where is it?"

The banker worked frantic fingers at his clothing, reached under his shirt, and drew out the money belt and let it fall. Tex retrieved the belt, hefted it, and made a silent whistle with his lips. "Didn't know paper money had so much weight."

Tom eased off the hammer and holstered his gun. "You're a vengeful cuss, aren't you?" he said to Gorman. "Why weren't you satisfied just to take the money?"

Before the banker could respond, Tex cut in with: "Yeah. I got a notion if you'd just taken the money, Tom would've let you go. He don't like Beatty anyway. But feller, when you stuck his name on that note, you invited us to run you down." Tex wagged his head. "That wasn't very smart, Gorman."

"Take half the money and let me go," the banker offered. Then, seeing the mirthless smile on Tex Earle's face, he said: "Take it all. Just let me go."

"You're going, all right," Tom said dryly. "But south, not north."

Gorman shuffled his feet. His sleepy, puffy face turned tense and his eyes moved wetly.

Tom shook his head gently. "Don't try it, Gorman. You wouldn't get fifty feet."

A rumpled-looking man came to the doorway of one of the adobe huts, scratched an ample belly with both hands, made a circuit of the inside of his mouth with his tongue, and spat, squinted long at the rising sun, then, hearing voices, turned and stared, mouth dropping open and bleary eyes widening. He jumped back out of sight and reappeared a moment later with a cocked riot gun in both hands.

"Here!" he called out boomingly. "What'n hell's going on over there?"

Tom eyed the shotgun and the stubbly face above it. "Nothing that concerns you," he retorted. "We're just taking a bank robber back to Beatty."

Acting quickly Elihu called out: "That's a lie! These two just took my money belt."

Tex, still holding the belt, looked from it to the man with the shotgun. "Hey," he protested, "point that damned thing some other direction, mister. They got a habit of going off."

The shotgun made a tight, short arc. It's holder snarled: "Drop them guns you two, and make no mistake, this thing'll cut you in two at that distance." As Tom and Tex were moving to comply, the stage company hostler raised his voice: "Sam! Oh, Sam! Come out here!"

A second man appeared in the doorway. He was holding a griddle-cake turner in one hand and he was scowling darkly, as though early morning interruptions upset him. "What is it?"

"Looks like there's robbery goin' on here, Sam."

The man called Sam looked, and lowered his hand with the turner in it. His scowl deepened. "What the hell you fellers doin'?" he demanded gruffly.

"They're robbing me," Elihu Gorman repeated. "They came in with drawn guns, got me out of bed, and brought me out here 'n' took my money belt. Dammit, you can see what they've done, can't you?"

"I can see," Sam said, walking forward, still holding his griddle-cake turner. "Gimme that belt," he ordered Tex. The belt sailed through the air. Sam caught it with his free hand, opened one of the pockets, and peered in. His eyes popped wide open. He dropped the turner and opened several other compartments of the belt. Each time his eyes reflected astonishment. He was still holding the belt when Tom said: "There's forty thousand dollars in that belt, mister. Every dollar of it was stolen from the Beatty bank by this man here. He was the town banker until night before last."

"Y'mean he cleaned out his own bank?"

"That's right."

"That is a lie!" stormed Elihu Gorman. "These men got me out of . . ."

"Shut up," Sam snarled, looking from Tom to Tex and back to Gorman. "Joe, come up here." The man with the shotgun came warily forward. "Gimme that thing," Sam said, taking the shotgun. "Here, squat down there and count this money."

For a moment Gorman's frown reflected perplexity, then his face cleared and he opened his mouth to speak. The man called Sam waved the riot gun. "I said shut up, mister. I meant it. Every time someone interrupts, Joe's goin' to have to start all over again. He can't cipher so good."

"You count it then," Tom said.

Sam's disgruntled look deepened. "An' you keep quiet, too, mister. Besides, I can't cipher at all, an' that's worse'n what little Joe knows about it."

They stood there in the freshening daylight, watching the paunchy man squatting in the dust of the empty roadway counting money with knitted brows and moving lips. Somewhere behind the stage station someone was dragging chain harness with a musical sound. Someone else was forking hay, too, Tom knew, because several horses whinnied in unison and blew their noses. Finally the paunchy man folded the money back into the belt, stood up, and gazed at them all. "Heap of money in here, Sam," he said with awe in his voice.

"Well, dammit, how much money?"

"Forty thousand dollars."

Sam lowered the shotgun. "Mister," he said to Gorman, "where'd you get that money?"

Gorman had his answer ready. "I just sold a ranch," he said in a strong and convincing voice. "I'm going north to locate in Utah."

Sam's gaze studied Gorman through a silent moment, then his attention shifted to Tom. "You say he stole it?"

"I do. He was the banker at Beatty until night before last. He stole the money and . . ."

"Are you the law in Beatty, mister?"

"No, the law's Sheriff Tim Pollard."

Sam nodded. "That's right. I know Pollard. How come he ain't with you?"

"He's out with another posse."

Sam took the money belt from Joe, handed over the shotgun, and turned his back on them, walking toward the stage station. "Fetch 'em along," he growled at Joe. "Breakfast time."

They entered the station and met the startled look of three freshly washed male passengers who were just sitting down at the plank table. Sam was busy at a wood stove in one corner of the room. Those vertical lines between his eyes had not disappeared; he was deep in thought. Elihu Gorman protested loudly at being forced to eat at the same table with the outlaws who had just tried to steal his money. Sam, stacking griddle cakes on a thick crockery platter, started for the table. "Mister," he said dourly, "even outlaws got to eat. Why don't you just shut up and fill your gut?" Gorman subsided.

The three strangers at the table ate furtively, from time to time eyeing Joe, who remained by the door, his shotgun covering them all. They were nearly through breakfast when he sang out: "Northbound's comin'. You fellers got ten minutes 'fore fresh horses are hitched to the southbound."

One of the bystanders at the table raised his head. "I'm goin' north, not south, dammit."

Sam, seating himself at the table, looked up. "Be half hour before the northbound's ready to pull out. Driver's got to eat an' horses got to be changed. Southbound's already hitched up." He looked at his plate. "Half hour ain't long, pardner. Have a smoke and relax."

They all heard the southbound stage rocket up amid a rattle of loose tugs and shod hoofs, and brake to a long halt. Sam continued to eat imperturbably but Joe fidgeted at the door. Voices rose and the scent of dust rode the still air. A burly, whiskered man burst past the door, saw Joe, and stopped stockstill, mouth open but wordless. He was a leathery-visaged man of indeterminate years with bright blue eyes. "What the hell," he breathed finally. "Joe! What you doin'?"

"Been an attempted robbery here," Sam said dryly without looking up from his plate. "The dude here says these two with their hats on robbed him."

The driver circled the table so as not to get between the shotgun and the table, and said: "I'll be damned. Ain't it kind o' early in the day for that kind of stuff?"

"Your griddle cakes are in the oven," Sam said, chewing thoughtfully. "Coffee's in the pot."

The driver removed his hat, shoved gloves into it, and put the hat upon the table. He looked at the seated men a moment, then headed for the stove. Sam said: "No passengers, George?"

From the oven the driver mumbled a negative answer before heading for the table with a plate in his hands. "Joe," he said, looking backward, "be a mite careful with that thing, will you?"

From the doorway Joe smiled.

Tom stood up. Tex cast a swift glance at Joe, and, seeing no movement, also arose. Farther down the table the stationmaster sighed, pushed back his plate, drained off the last of his coffee, and pushed himself upright. "You ready to roll?" he asked Elihu Gorman.

"But I'm going north," the banker protested.

"You're goin' south," Sam said firmly. "Hell, ridin' stages this time of day is right pleasant, mister. You shouldn't mind a little delay."

"I just came from the south. I'm Utah bound, I told . . ."

"Mister," Sam cut in, "there's just one way to find out who is a liar here, and that's to send the herd of you back to Beatty. Folks down there'll know who's a thief and who ain't. Now get up an' let's be movin'. Can't hold the stage up. Hard enough keepin' to schedules as it is."

Gorman marshaled arguments but they fell on stony ground. The stationmaster took the shotgun and drove Tom, Tex, and Gorman out to the waiting coach. There, he put the shotgun aside, sucked his teeth a moment, and said: "Mister, you said you was a rancher?"

"That's right. I sold out down south and I'm going . . ."

"Yeah, I recollect all that." Sam regarded Elihu with an unblinking stare. "Joe, go fetch them guns over there in the road." When the guns were brought forward, Sam took them both, hefted them, and frowned. “You boys ready to go back?” he asked Tom and Tex.

Tom nodded. “We are. Give the guns to the driver. He can hand them over to Sheriff Pollard at Beatty.”

Sam shook his head. “Naw. Why bother the driver with ’em?” He held both guns out, butts forward. When Tom hesitated, he shoved the gun into his hand. “Go ahead, mister, take it.”

Tex accepted his gun and holstered it, but Tom stared straight into the stationmaster’s eyes. “Are you thinking there might be a reward on us?” he asked. “And maybe we might be worth more dead than alive?”

Sam’s expression looked pained. “There’s the shotgun, against that wheel yonder. I couldn’t reach it before you threw down on me, pardner.”

Tom still made no move to take the gun. “Why are you doing this?” he demanded.

The stationmaster bent forward from the waist, dropped the pistol into Tom’s holster, then reached for one of Elihu Gorman’s hands and held it out palm upward. “You ever seen a rancher with hands as soft and pink as these?” He dropped the hand and shoved the money belt into Tex’s hand. “Ever see a rancher’s face as white as his?” he asked. Tom slowly smiled and turned toward the coach. “Maybe you can’t cipher,” he told the stationmaster, “but you can sure read people.”

XVI

Elihu Gorman rode in a sulky slouch until Beatty appeared far ahead on the downgrade, then he drew up on the seat, his face turning pale, and, although Tom, who was closely watching him, thought he was going to speak, he said nothing.

The sun was riding high overhead, lemon-yellow and blindingly bright. Beatty was drowsing; horses at hitch rails stood hip-shot, eyes drooping and lower lips hanging slackly. Except for a number of idle men sitting in the shade along the plank walks there was no movement as the stage drew down to a halt and Tom stepped out. Gorman was next to get down, and Tex came last. Across the road in front of the hotel a man called sharply to someone. At the livery barn Mike Grogan recognized Tom, and stared, rooted to the ground. Another man who recognized all three stage passengers scuttled into the bank.

Tom took Gorman's arm and started south toward the sheriff's office. Tex, walking behind them, was triumphantly smiling.

Deputy Havestraw was in but Tim Pollard was still out with a posse. Havestraw was embarrassed and uncertain until Judge Montgomery burst in with a following of curious townsmen. "Lock that man up!" the judge thundered, jutting his face toward Elihu. "He robbed the bank."

Havestraw moved, finally, putting Elihu in a cell and padlocking him there. Tex leaned against the wall making a cigarette and feeling good, even smiling into Montgomery's white, angry face.

Tom considered the judge's expression without speaking, then turned his back on him, crossed to an iron stove where a coffee pot sat, and filled a tin cup. He drank with his back to the room.

Judge Montgomery was uncomfortable. He had something to say but Tom's back made it hard to speak. Eventually he turned on his heel and left the office.

There was a buzz of voices in the room. When Tom had emptied the cup, he faced around. Jack Havestraw had the money belt and was counting the bills on Tim Pollard's desk; he did it reverently, and, when he finished, he looked up into the still faces clustered around the desk. "Forty thousand dollars," he breathed softly. "Exactly what was stolen."

Tom caught Tex's eye and started for the door. Tex followed him out into the shimmering heat and across the road to the Royal Antler Saloon. Roy the bartender's impassivity slipped; his mouth dropped open.

"You fellers back?" he asked pointlessly.

"Sour mash," Tom said. "Two of 'em."

"Sheriff's lookin' for you," Roy confided, squinting around the nearly empty room.

Tex beamed a big smile. "Yeah, we just come from his jailhouse."

"Old Montgomery's bayin' at the moon for your hides, too."

Tom drank and nodded for a refill. "Hot out," he said. Roy filled both glasses the second time, leaned on the bar, and studied the two sun-darkened faces. "What the hell's goin' on around here, anyway?" he asked plaintively.

"We just brought the bank robber back," Tex said. "Elihu Gorman. He's locked up at Pollard's jail."

"No." Roy was dumbfounded. "Elihu Gorman?"

Tom twisted from the waist and gazed around the room. There were a dozen men lounging at the tables. Four of them were engaged in a desultory poker game. Hurrying boot steps thudded along the plank walk beyond the doors and a man entered. He stopped, squinting into the shaded room, then headed for the bar with a broad grin. It was Gerald Finnerty. "Hey!" he said, putting both hands on the counter and leaning toward Tom. "I just heard. You two been pretty busy."

Tom nodded to Roy for a third drink. Finnerty reached for the glass as he spoke. "Montgomery was just tellin' me." The drink went down; Finnerty blew out a breath and his eyes watered slightly. "He was pleased as punch, didn't even haggle over the hay price like he used to do."

Tom gradually drew up against the bar. "The hay price?"

"Sure, for that twenty tons I had the boys bring in for him."

Tex choked on his third drink and dabbed at his eyes. Roy solicitously got him a glass of water. "Trail dust'll do that to a feller," Roy murmured. "Drink this here water."

"Finnerty, did you sell the judge twenty tons of hay?"

The rancher's smile dwindled; the light died slowly in his eyes. "Sure. You sent word it'd be all right, Tom."

"I did? Who told you that?"

"Miss Antoinette."

Everyone's attention was briefly diverted by a cry of joy from the doorway to the card room. It was Miss Eloise who had just caught sight of Tex and was rushing toward him, arms outflung.

Tom took Finnerty's arm and guided him farther along the bar. "Miss Antoinette told you I'd said it was all right to sell her paw twenty tons of hay?" he asked.

"She sure did, Tom. The afternoon everyone was out lookin' for you 'n' Tex."

Tom let go of the cowman's arm. He called for Roy to bring two more drinks, downed his in one gulp, and headed for the door. Behind him, Tex was seeking unsuccessfully to break out of the iron embrace of Miss Eloise.

The bank was nearly empty when Tom entered it. A smiling clerk informed him that the judge had gone home for his midday meal and would not return probably until late in the afternoon. As Tom listened, he detected the sound of slow-riding horsemen coming into Beatty from the north. He went outside and watched as Sheriff Pollard and five dust-encrusted horsemen plodded through the hot sunlight. When Tim saw Tom standing in front of the bank, he drew up, staring. Finally he dismounted, flung his reins to one of the posse men, and walked stiffly forward into the shade of the overhang. His mustache was limply drooping and his shoulders sagged. "Hotter'n the hubs of hell," he said tiredly. "Well, what're you doin' back here?"

"Brought Gorman and the money back."

Pollard turned this over in his mind. "Gorman, eh? I ain't surprised. Just the same I wished you'd've let me know."

"You wouldn't have believed it."

Pollard's forehead wrinkled. "I think I would have," he replied. "Where is he now?"

"In your lock-up with Havestraw."

"I see, and you look like a bomb goin' somewhere to explode. What's the matter now?"

"Montgomery."

"Over hay?" Pollard asked shrewdly.

"Yes. He got twenty tons under false pretences."

Pollard's eyes crinkled nearly closed. He studied Tom's angry face for a moment before speaking. "Now look-a-here, Tom, you're workin' mighty hard at makin' a mountain out of a molehill."

"I didn't say he could have that hay."

"All right. You didn't say he could have it. Before you go stirrin' up trouble, you 'n' the judge better set down and powwow. I've known him a heap longer'n you have and Phil Montgomery don't pull underhanded stuff. If he got that hay, he thought he was gettin' it legally."

"Like he jumped to the conclusion I robbed his bank?"

"That wasn't no conclusion, boy. He showed me a note you'd signed."

Tom rocked up on the balls of his feet. "You've been out of town quite a while, haven't you? Better go ask Gorman who wrote that note . . . and who forged my name to it."

"I will, Tom, I will. But meantime, you hang an' rattle until I get some time an' I'll look into this hay-stealin' business."

The sheriff removed his hat, mopped his forehead, and replaced the hat. Down the roadway, in front of his office, men were moving among their tired horses. He groaned. "They'll be wantin' their posse pay. I'd better go. Remember what I said, Tom. Set tight for a while."

Tom went to his room at the hotel, called for the water boy, and soaked in a blissfully cool bath for nearly an hour. When he reentered the room for fresh clothing, he found Tex sitting there, feet cocked on the sill, gazing out the window. He spoke a short greeting and began to dress.

"Finnerty had your money with him," Tex said, without looking around.

"I'll see him."

"About that hay, Tom."

"No lectures, Tex. I just got one from Pollard."

"This ain't no lecture. I told Miss Toni it was all right for her to have Finnerty fetch it to the barn."

"You what?"

Tex still did not look around. His hat was pushed back and his pale eyes roamed the far distance. "Just before I left her and Eloise at the creek, I told her it was all right."

Tom went to the dresser and began combing his hair. His face was red with smoldering wrath. "Why, Tex? You knew I didn't want him to have that hay."

"Well, like I told her, I figured I could soften you up before we got back."

Tom put the comb down and leaned upon the dresser, gazing at himself in the mirror. He finally finished dressing and started for the door. Without seeing him, Tex knew he was leaving. "Where you going now?" His voice asked from the window.

"To see Montgomery."

"Whoa," Tex said, dropping his feet and standing up. "Before you do that, let's say our good byes."

Tom had the doorknob in his fist. He said nothing until Tex turned to face him. He searched Earle's face, saw the resolution there, and lowered his brows. "Over twenty tons of hay, Tex?"

"You know better'n that, Tom. I told you I was leaving when we got Gorman."

"But you didn't leave."

Tex shrugged. "Figured I'd see he got delivered is all."

"If I forget about the damned hay?"

Tex shook his head. "I just told you, Tom, it ain't the damned hay. I told you a month back it was you. It still is." Tex started to cross the room slowly. "Anyway, they'll be working the cattle in the high country pretty quick now and there'll be lots of work."

Tom hadn't believed this argument when Tex had used it before. He knew his partner too well, had heard him curse the thin, cold air of the high country too many times. He leaned upon the door. "Wait a week and I'll go with you, Tex."

Earle stopped, his eyes lighting up. "You don't mean that, do you?"

Tom meant it. He had done much thinking of late, particularly on the ride back with Gorman his prisoner. Although he had triumphed in some ways in his feud with the town, none of the victories had been as he had planned, nor had they left him feeling proud. In fact, he felt somewhat ashamed of himself. He hadn't, of course, been directly responsible for Moses Beach's stroke, but he suspected that he had contributed to it. He hadn't forced Gorman to rob the bank, either, but he had certainly helped to drive him to it. He hadn't yet broken the judge, but he had made Tex do something shameful in his effort to hurt Montgomery, and perhaps that was even worse than making the judge kneel.

There were, he had thought on the drive back with Gorman, some undertakings that you simply could not make appear decent—like a stand-up fight—no matter how hard you tried. It had been a slow-arriving and bitter realization, and yet the proof was all around him. At this very moment it was in Tex Earle's face, in his poorly concealed disapproval, in his pale, boyish eyes, and finally it was in Tex's wish to leave Beatty and its memories behind.

"Yeah, I mean it, Tex. We'll leave . . ."

They descended the stairs side-by-side and went out into the lengthening afternoon bound for the Royal Antler. There, they had a solemn drink together, then Tex went in search of Eloise to tell her the news. There, too, Gerald Finnerty came upon Tom again and gravely placed a big roll of soiled bills on the bar top; around the money was a limp strand of buckskin holding it together.

"Count it," Finnerty said. "It's all there. You got my note on you?"

"Montgomery's got it at the bank. I'll get it for you."

"No hurry," the cowman said, beckoning to the barman. "Tom, you ever think about settlin' down around here?"

Tom accepted the drink, inclined his head toward Finnerty, and downed it. "No," he said with a shade more emphasis than was necessary.

"Well, you know I got that option on the place adjoinin' me, and it's a real fine parcel of land. It'll run easy five thousand head year around."

"You need that for expansion," Tom said, turning his empty glass in its own little puddle of dampness. "Besides, I . . ."

"Naw, I don't want to expand. What I want is a good neighbor there who'll run cattle with me. You know, sort of work roundups with me."

Tom was going to speak when a man's voice raised in surprise and anger interrupted him. He and Finnerty turned in time to see Tex's hat sail across the room as though possessed of wings. Beyond Earle's tall back Miss Eloise was aiming another blow. "Run out on me, will you?" she screeched at the swiftly ducking Texan. "Sweet talk me, then run out as soon as . . . !"

"I'll go get your note," Tom said to Finnerty with a quick, hard smile, and hastened out of the saloon.

XVII

He walked through the lengthening shadows toward the bank. A low breeze was freshening the air and people were again abroad now that the day's heat was mostly past. He saw Deputy Havestraw talking to a cowboy in front of Moses Beach's store and, through the weaving press of pedestrians, caught a glimpse of Toni Montgomery. He left the plank walk, stepped out into the roadway, and heat rose up around him from the dust.

At the bank a clerk led him to Elihu Gorman's office. There, Judge Montgomery with spectacles pushed up onto his forehead was gazing at a stack of papers on the desk. The judge glanced up and nodded. Tom returned the nod, waited until the clerk was gone, and spoke. "I want the note Gorman forged my name to," he said.

Without a word Judge Montgomery held up a paper. Tom took it, folded it, and stuffed it into a pocket. "About that hay," he said. "It was brought to you by mistake."

"Mistake?" the Judge said, puzzled. "What mistake, Mister Barker?"

"Your daughter and a friend of mine misunderstood me when I said you were to have no hay."

"Are you inferring that my daughter is a liar, Mister Barker?"

"You heard what I said, Judge. I didn't call anyone a liar. I said you got that hay by mistake."

Judge Montgomery continued to gaze at Tom even after an uncomfortable silence settled between them. Then he got slowly to his feet. "Doesn't it appear a little ridiculous to you, Mister

Barker, to carry a grudge for nearly fifteen years?" He made a deprecatory gesture. "After all, I didn't willingly hurt you."

Tom said dryly: "You've seen horses with broken legs get shot, haven't you?"

"Certainly."

"I doubt if a horse ever breaks his leg on purpose, Judge."

"That's ridiculous, Barker."

"Almost as ridiculous as turning a little kid over to his father when you knew damned well he'd get a beating."

"I didn't know," Judge Montgomery said, coloring. "I had no idea at all."

Tom looked coldly down into the red face. "Then, why didn't you ask Sheriff Pollard," he demanded, "when you took that little kid to the sheriff's office?" He stopped at the door, opened it, and said: "You can either pay me fifty dollars a ton for that damned hay, or you can return it."

"Fifty dollars! Hell, Barker . . ."

"I know. You'll see me in hell first."

Tom returned to the street, read the note Gorman had forged, tore it into tiny pieces, and consigned it to the gently rustling wind.

"There's an ordinance against clutterin' the roadways," Sheriff Pollard said, coming up and stopping. "You been to see the judge?"

"Yes."

"He reward you for fetchin' back Gorman?"

"No."

"Hmmmm. That's odd. Oh, well, it don't matter to a man of your means, does it?" Pollard waved at a group of riders swinging past, sun-bronzed, lean men riding horses that all carried one iron. "Just run Clint Ingersoll and some of his freighter friends back to their camp. Drunk," the sheriff said with mild disgust. "Drunk in the middle of the day." He caught Tom's glance and held it. "Clint said they were goin' to pull out tomorrow, heading for Mirage and points north."

Tom understood what Tim Pollard was telling him. He was grateful for the way the sheriff was doing it. He looked across the road, where sunset was splashing a dozen shades of red over wooden false fronts. "Things'll settle down then," he said, remembering suddenly that he'd forgotten to get Finnerty's note from the judge.

Pollard smiled. "If they get too quiet, I'll get lazy."

"Buy you a drink," Tom said, facing straight ahead.

The sheriff started past. "Maybe later, Tom. I never drink before supper."

Tom watched him move on, then crossed toward the Queens & Aces Café. He was almost to the door when Toni Montgomery stopped him. He touched his hat.

"Tom, can you spare me a few minutes?"

"I can always spare you a few minutes, Toni. You know that without asking."

"Then walk with me."

They went south along the plank walk until the boards ran out, and they continued along through the day's late and softening shadows that faded at last into the merging sky, until Toni stopped and swung to face him.

"You're leaving Beatty, aren't you, Tom?"

For a second he was surprised, then he said: "Eloise told you, didn't she?"

"Yes. Did you know that she is in love with Tex?"

It was on the tip of his tongue to say he didn't know saloon girls loved. Instead though, he looked beyond her hair to the changing lights of the far horizon and shrugged. "She could do much worse, Toni."

"She has already done worse. That's what she told me a few hours ago. She's been married before."

His eyes returned to her face, then fled outward again. Stark and naked in the lowering evening stood a gnarled tree. He remembered it from his youth—Beatty's hang tree. More than one horse thief and outlaw had writhed his last precious moments from its limbs. "You picked a hell of a place to stop," he said suddenly, and took her hand guiding her along through the twilight toward town. "The judge'll be waiting for his supper."

She went willingly for only a hundred yards, then stopped and drew away from him. "Why are you going, Tom?"

"I think you know," he answered.

"But I'd rather have you tell me."

"Why? So you can crow?"

Her head moved slightly from side to side. "You know me better than that."

He drew in a big breath. "No one likes to be wrong, Toni. Maybe I like it least of all, because I've wasted a lot of years waiting to come down here and be top lash."

"Is going back where you came from going to be any better?"

He looked into her gray, wide, and liquid eyes. "I don't believe I like having you look inside me, Toni. Anyway, you might see something you don't want to see."

"What is it, Tom? What's back there where you came from? A girl?"

He smiled. "No girl, Toni, just a lot of big mountains with snow the year around, high meadows, and ice-cold creeks. Pines and fir trees and open range. Just more cattle country."

She was silently gazing at the crooked rim of the northeastern skyline, nearly obscured now by darkness, lost in the depths of her thoughts. "Tex told Eloise about the hay," she said gently.

Anger stirred in him. "Damn that hay anyway," he cursed. "He can have it . . . have all of it as far as I'm concerned."

She watched his face twist, then smooth out again when he caught her watching him.

"You tell him that for me," he growled.

"Tom? Don't you realize he could have it anyway? You haven't kept track of time. Your options expired while you were chasing Elihu Gorman."

This sobered him. He began to trace back the spun-out summer days in his memory. Then he squinted down at her. "Why didn't he say that today, when I was in the bank?"

"Probably for the same reason Sheriff Pollard hasn't told you that Clint Ingersoll killed your father while you and Tex were gone. They don't want to add to your troubles."

He stared at her. "Ingersoll killed him?"

"Yes, Tom."

He was surprised that all he felt was mild astonishment. There was no sense of loss, no sense of pain or remorse, no desire for vengeance. "How, Toni?"

"Several men were drinking out at the freighter's camp. No one knows exactly how it happened, just that it was a gunfight and that your father was killed."

She touched his arm, looking up into his eyes. He was looking blankly past her, waiting patiently for the swiftly flowing childhood scenes to pass. Then his expression altered; he looked at her hand, felt its pressure, and was warmed by its message. Whatever was there in the night lay in both of them. He put up his other hand, covered her fingers, and continued on more slowly toward the orange-yellow lights of Beatty.

"Did you ever hear the story of my mother, Toni?"

Her reply was simple and grave. "Yes, once, a number of years back, I eavesdropped when Sheriff Pollard and the judge were talking on the porch. I afterward cried myself to sleep."

He remembered something with a start, something that appeared quite suddenly out of his memory and that, until that moment, he had not recollected at all. A little glass on the grave beside the headstone with withered forget-me-nots in it. He strode along, holding her hand and saying nothing.

Antoinette looked sideways at his profile in the pale night. There was a reserve about him, a hardness that was not altogether the product of bitter environment; for a space of seconds she was afraid of him. Then she recalled the way other men looked upon him and thought how illuminating one man's judgment of another man was. Women were not good judges of men; they saw only what was pleasing to look upon, only what was handsome or smiling or laughing—or gentle. Men did not see these virtues, or, seeing them, did not include them in their weighing and measuring. Her father and Tim Pollard, for example, had reason to dislike Tom Barker—and yet neither of them really did dislike him. And Gerald Finnerty, and Roy the bartender, who had judged so many men, and Tex Earle. Even, she thought, Clint Ingersoll, who wanted to kill him—even him. He respected Tom or he would have shot him down before this, perhaps from hiding as most men killed other men on the frontier. His voice scattered her thoughts.

"I reckon a man can live down mistakes, can't he?"

"Of course he can, Tom."

"You know, I've taken more baths since I've been back here than I ever took before."

She looked up, not understanding until he went on.

"I keep feeling dirty, Toni. And it won't wash off."

A shadow rushed over her face, or seemed to, but she very wisely held her tongue.

They came to the edge of the plank walk, stepped up onto it, and progressed slowly northward. Across the roadway Sheriff Tim Pollard, sitting on a bench in front of his office, leaned a little, the better to identify them. Then he rocked back and ran a thoughtful hand under his mustache.

There was the thinnest of sickle moons. Patches of lamplight made squares of diluted light along the walk and out into the road. Horsemen jogged past, trailing fragments of pleasant conversation. When they passed the Royal Antler, Gerald Finnerty doffed his hat at Antoinette and threw Tom a solemn wink. Farther along, near Beach's emporium, Jack Havestraw stood in the shadows, sighing; he scarcely saw Tom at all.

As they neared the Montgomery home, he said: "Toni, if I got a buggy from the livery barn . . . would you go for a drive with me . . . later on?"

Her eyes held a glowing deepness, a sudden sweetness that made her face even prettier. Her lips, soft and pliable, moved—red and full and kindly. "I'd love to, Tom," she murmured. He noticed quite suddenly that her hair seemed almost auburn in the night, that her skin was flawlessly smooth. He heard himself speaking and recognized only the voice, not the words. "Eight o'clock?"

She squeezed his arm and left.

He thought of the Royal Antler but there was no urge. Instead, he crossed the road, went to the livery barn, and made the arrangements, and for a moment he had trouble remembering the now smiling hulk of a hostler. Then it all came back and he handed the man a coin. "I reckon I've been reprieved," he said.

The man laughed. "The loft's full of hay," he said by way of answer. Then, as Tom was walking away, the night hawk added: "Your horse and that other feller's horse come back from Red Stone stage station today. I got 'em stalled for you."

Tom went back out into the night. He felt good, as though a heavy weight had fallen away from him, as though something had gushed out of a fester deep inside him. He could hear and understand the soft laughter that came along the roadway on the night air, each rising and falling note of it. A lanky silhouette came toward him, angling across the road and scuffing up grouts of dust with each step. "Where you bound?" he asked as Tex stopped and peered through the darkness at him.

"Oh, it's you. Well, y'see, Eloise got plumb roiled at me this evening and I figure to take her riding in the moonlight and sort of . . ."

"What moonlight?"

Tex cocked his head skyward, then looked down again. "In the cool of the evening then," he continued. "That way I figure she'll get over her notion of throwing things at me." A sudden thought struck Tex. "Y'know, for a female she's pretty good at aiming where she throws, too." He passed on into the barn, and Tom's attention was caught by four stalwart, striding men, moving noiselessly through the night toward the Royal Antler, their flat-heeled boots striking soundlessly against the earth beside the plank walk. Freighters. He searched out the tallest silhouette but could not recognize it in the gloom. It didn't matter, though; in a little while he would be driving out with Toni. There would be no meeting this night.

Tex came up beside him and halted, looking across the road at moving shadows. "Night hawk says you already got that top buggy with the yellow running gear."

"That's right."

"Hmmmmm. Driving out with no moon, Tom?"

A chuckle passed the big, dark man's lips as Tex stepped down into the roadway and trudged toward the Royal Antler. It was good when your partner kidded you because it only happened when he had no reservations in his mind about you.

XVIII

They drove through a pleasant night, breathing deeply of an atmosphere made fragrant by the scent of a sighing, cooling earth. The mare between her shafts plodded placidly with head hung and the yellow spokes threw back gyrating reflections of the thin moon. Beside him Antoinette murmured: "Tom, did you know it is possible to wait for something indefinitely without being conscious you were waiting at all?"

He leaned back with the lines slack in his hand. "Yes, I knew, Toni."

His jaw, she noticed, balanced his face. He had removed his hat and shafts of murky light touched his hair, making it darker, wavier; where it grew low upon his temples, it was pressed close. She had, in weeks past, made many private excuses for him, and it had been cruel the way things had worked out to rebuff them. It had not been an easy thing to take his part against the judge, nor had she done it openly, which was perhaps why the torment had been so scalding within her. But now, this night, it seemed to her that vindication had come. She had sensed it earlier when they had walked together through the twilight arm in arm, and the knowledge that her faith in him had not, after all, been misplaced was good knowledge. "When are you and Tex leaving, Tom?"

His head came up slightly as though he had seen something ahead of them. "We talked about pulling out in a week," he replied detachedly, as though speaking of two other men.

It was this tone that gave her a quick lift of the heart. She said no more. On both sides of them the land stretched off into a gradual merging lift and rise toward the distant hills. She recognized their direction, and, when the mesmerizing clop-clop-clop of the mare's hoofs had relaxed them both, she asked: "Where are we going?"

"Up by the creek," he answered. "Unless you'd rather go somewhere else."

"No," said Toni. "I was hoping you'd drive up there."

The mare was breathing deeply by the time Tom drew up and got down to loosen her check rein and tie her to a big willow. Somewhere behind him Toni could hear water tumbling over stones. He helped her down and led her to the base of an ancient cottonwood. She settled upon the ground, pulling him beside her. She laced her fingers together around drawn up knees, gazing at the high sky and its shimmering star fire. Silence settled around them in a soft, full wave.

Tom plucked a blade of dead grass, peeled it thoughtfully, and chewed it. He lay back loosely, legs thrust out, his body turning softly against the ground. He was, she thought, as thoroughly relaxed as a man could be; it was good to see him that way because she knew he hadn't often relaxed since returning to Beatty.

"This is mighty pleasant," he said around the drooping grass stem. "Damned pleasant."

It was her presence, she knew, that did this to him, but she was not a vain woman. Any woman's presence would have brought out this relaxed mood; he was a man with deep hungers, with strong emotions, a solid man, physically alive and strong. He had his desires, his thoughts, and his memories. Her gaze clouded over. It was the memories she would have to combat. "Don't go to sleep," she murmured, and he laughed up at her.

"I won't."

"Tom what does tomorrow hold?"

He kept his eyes on her face, her throat where the strong pulse was beating, and said: "Whatever you want it to hold. Tomorrow never comes, Toni, it's here. It's really today and it holds what you've made it yield."

This was a side of him she had not seen before. Their eyes met and held, then she looked skyward. He was also a deep man; one with private thoughts. "Tom?"

"Yes."

"I wish you had come back differently."

"You mean changed?"

"No. I wish you'd come back for a different reason."

He looked away from her, let his gaze wander along the base of the rising bald hills, and was silent for a while. Then he murmured: "I'll go away differently." And she heard the long sweep of an indrawn breath in his chest. "It's a strange life, Toni. You're driven to do things that you don't really understand until you're well into them . . . then they don't look as good as you'd thought they would."

"Isn't it better to see them in the right light, than not to see them that way, ever?"

"I reckon," he conceded. "Only it doesn't take away the shame."

"You've done nothing here to be really ashamed of."

"You don't know, Toni."

"I think I do. I've kept my eyes open."

He looked again at her, this time with a dry little smile. "And your ears as well?"

"Yes. Only I've never put any faith in gossip, Tom. Especially around Beatty. When there's not much else for folks to do, they talk about other folks."

His smile lingered. For a while neither of them spoke, then she asked about Tex.

"Tex? Oh, I've known him since a year or two after I left Beatty. We pardnered up and traveled from summer range to winter range and back again."

"No, I didn't mean his background. I meant . . . is he going away with you?"

"Yes."

"What about Eloise?"

How did you tell a girl like Antoinette that men, especially drifters like Tex Earle, took—they did not give? "I expect she'll forget him, Toni." It sounded resolved to him, the way he'd said it, until he caught her staring down at him, then it sounded callous. He threw the grass stem away. "Well, a man doesn't marry every woman he sparks. It's a sort of companionship thing, y'see."

"With us, too, Tom?"

"No, because that's different. We were kids together." His face softened. "You know, Toni, lots of nights I've lain in my soogans, remembering things we did. Climbing into the bell tower that time, and putting that skunk in Miz Grogan's geranium patch." His dark gaze brightened with reflection. "You didn't seem like a girl in those days. I didn't think of you as one." He cocked his head at her. "Did you know that?"

She smiled a trifle ruefully. "Sometimes it was pretty hard being your kind of a tomboy," she said, remembering, too, how she had mooned around the house when they were not together and recalling each little stab of pain he had brought to her heart when his words grew spiteful or scornful.

"Naw, you were always a tomboy, Toni."

She was silently hugging her knees and looking straight ahead. "That was so long ago, Tom."

"Not really."

"Could we ever go back?"

He looked at her profile. "No. I reckon you're right. It was a long time ago, at that." He was seeing her differently, the swelling fullness of her blouse, and her thigh where the skirt was drawn tightly around it. No, she wasn't the same person at all. He stirred and she spoke swiftly, fearful that he was becoming restless.

"Tim Pollard likes you, Tom."

He plucked another blade of grass. His feelings here were mixed. It was impossible not to like the sheriff, and it was impossible not to respect him, which of course meant much more. "He's a good man, Toni. I have nothing against him."

"But when you first came back you did."

"Yes. But I told you . . . that's all past now."

"Don't you want to be top lash any more?"

He bit down on the grass stem. "Who told you I wanted to be that?"

"No one had to tell me, Tom. You've changed a lot since we were kids, but basically you haven't changed. I just thought you had. Well . . . ?"

"No, I don't care about that any longer. It's part of something I'd like to forget."

She spoke in the gentlest, softest voice, looking fully down at him. "And the judge?"

"Him, too. Like I said, I want to forget all that."

"But you don't like the judge, Tom."

He had no ready answer because he actually did not like her father, had never liked him in fact, but as a youth the dislike had simply been because he was her father and used to bawl her out when they stayed away from home too long or were caught in some mischievous act. "I can forget that," he mumbled, and straightened up off the ground. "And he can have the damned hay."

"You'll lose money on those options."

"Not much. Anyway, the interest Finnerty paid me will make it up and then some."

He sat with his elbows on his knees, his head thrust forward, and his dark profile blending with the shadows. His lip corners had a tough set to them. Toni gazed at him with an interest that came only of deep personal interest. "I wish you weren't leaving," she said quietly. "I wish you'd stay, Tom."

He made no move but his jaw muscles rippled, his gaze gentled, and after a moment longer of hard concentration he turned to face her. There were no words on his lips. It was a difficult moment; the night around him was full of confused and confusing emotions. He changed expression, was on the verge of smiling at her. She did not smile back. Earnestness held her face dark and still. She put forth her hand; he took it. Her fingers closed around his palm suddenly strong, holding to him, pressing some of her thoughts into him. Abruptly she sought to draw her hand away, but he held her, drew her off balance toward him. But she braced against the pressure and freed her hand, jumping to her feet. "Maybe we'd better go back," she said in an unsteady, low voice.

The quick, sad call of a coyote broke upon the stillness. He got up more slowly and turned to swipe at the seat of his trousers. He felt uncomfortable and within him somewhere there stabbed a shaft of pain.

He went without another word to the buggy mare, untied her, left the check rein loose, and handed Toni up onto the seat, got in beside her, and flipped the lines. The mare turned instinctively and started the long trip back. After a mile of hush and discomfort he said: "Why do things have to happen like they do? It was so damned pleasant up there with you."

Her reply was warm and apologetic. "I'm sorry, Tom. I really am. It was my fault." She took his free hand in both hers and held it with her fingers curled tightly around it. "It was me. It was something I felt back there."

"But Toni, if I didn't go away . . . what then?"

She looked at him. "What do you mean, what then?"

"Well, hell, the judge doesn't like me. Pollard, he's not so easy to figure out. He's been kind to me . . ."

"He likes you. I know he does."

"Then he's the only one around who does."

"No, I do, Tom."

His hand in her lap twisted, caught at her fingers, and bruised them with unconscious feeling. "Thanks."

"Honestly, Tom, I think most people around Beatty like you." He shook his head at that. She drew up slightly on the seat and bent forward to emphasize her words. "The cowmen do, I know. They won't ever tell you so, Tom, but what you did for Gerald Finnerty is the kind of thing they judge a man by."

He understood this because he was also a man who judged other men by their actions. Still, he could not separate the bitterness that had driven him to return to Beatty with the hatred in his heart, from the things he had done since he had returned, and he was certain others saw in him, and in his actions, only the coldness, the hunger for vengeance that had governed everything he had done.

Toni's next words cut across his thoughts, driving them out. "Give Beatty a second chance, Tom. I can't explain away how you were treated years back. But I can tell you this. Not even the judge wishes you ill now."

He thought of his boyhood, of his days with Toni, of the fine days full of promise and golden sunlight, days that no other part of the land had ever successfully duplicated for him. And he thought of the soft, mellowed stone in the cemetery. He longed to belong, to forget what had happened twelve years earlier, and what had happened since he had returned. He longed only to put down roots and . . .

"Stop the buggy, Tom."

He obeyed. She was looking fully at him and her face was white, her eyes enormous, her lips slightly parted as though she had made some desperate decision. When next she spoke, the words were squeezed out, unreal sounding.

"Kiss me."

He drew her to him and found her mouth. A soft, stifled sob came from her throat; her breath beat savagely upon his cheek, and her hands felt for him, drew him even closer.

It was as though something exploded inside his skull. He bruised her with his strength and let the wild full run of his temper, the force of his will go free. It came out and broke over her, suddenly, this fierce hot longing that he had not known until this moment was within him for her, and it passed over them both. Deep down there in the hollow of the land, Beatty lay, a dark mass of irregularity in the warm blackness, touched less by moonlight than by its own squares of soft orange. All around was a loneliness, while circling the valley, chunked up heavily against the sky, were the bald hills.

XIX

He stepped to the bar with a pleasant tiredness in him, had his drink, took glass and bottle to the wall table, and dropped down. Roy the bartender kept looking at him. Tom Barker's face was a brooding mask, normally, but now Roy saw in it a kind of odd and unnatural beauty. This look fascinated Roy; it was not a thing men saw often in the faces of other men.

"Hey, Roy, you seen that Barker feller in here tonight?"

Roy looked around. "Right over there," he said matter-of-factly. "As plain as the nose on your face."

The cowboy crossed to Tom's side and stopped. "Mister," he said. "You got a pardner called Tex?"

Tom blinked out of his reverie. "I have. What about him?"

"'Pears he bit a chunk off he can't chew."

"A fight," Tom said swiftly, arising. "Where?"

"Out back o' the livery barn."

He asked no more and the cowboy rushed out of the saloon in his wake. It was beyond midnight now, with very little showing of Beatty in the darkness. There were a number of horses standing idly at the livery barn's outside rail and near them, blissfully asleep, lay a drunken drifter, head cradled in his arms.

He rushed the full-lighted distance of the barn's long main aisle and out into the cooling gloom beyond where motionless shapes of men stood, faces savagely intent upon a sprawled silhouette moving feebly in the dust of the back lot. It was Tex; he was down and he was hurt. Even in that bad light Tom could see the dilation of his pupils, the flung-back smear of blood along his cheek, and the scrabbling, numb gropings of his fingers in the dirt. He would have gone forward but a thick arm stopped him. It was Grogan, the liveryman. He said softly: "Better let 'em finish it, Mister Barker. There's three more of them freighters out there."

Tom raked the shadows with a hard look in his eyes. There were perhaps ten men in the darkness, all motionless. Some were cattlemen; he recognized their faces. Several were townsmen and three of them were freighters, lips skinned back, smiling at the big, taut figure bending above the downed man: Clint Ingersoll, shorn of belt and gun and with cocked fists at the ready.

"Get up," Ingersoll was snarling. "Y'dirty mother's son. Get up!"

Tex rolled over, got to his knees, and braced with both hands against the ground. He shook his head and bubbling sounds came from his throat.

"Put the boots to him," a freighter growled. "He ain't goin' to get up."

Ingersoll moved menacingly forward as though to comply and a soft, silken voice only slightly roughened by feeling said: "Keep it fair, Ingersoll. No boots."

Tom found the face; it was Gerald Finnerty. He had one hand resting lightly on his holstered gun. Around him were other cowmen, their faces closed down around a similar feeling for fairness.

Ingersoll drew up slightly, still holding his fists cocked. "Maybe you'd like some, too," he shot at the cowman.

Finnerty smiled very thinly. "Sure, put on your gun. I don't dog fight."

Ingersoll's gaze went back to Tex, who was getting clumsily to his feet. He waited only until Earle was staggering upright, then he went in. Fists crunched off bone and battered numb flesh, and Tex went down, rolled over, and lay breathing shallowly.

"He's out," a freighter crowed. "Dump some water on the whelp."

"He's had enough," an older man said, moving up into the reflected light of the barn. It was Tim Pollard. Tom stared in astonishment. "All right, it was a fair scrap. Now let's forget about it."

"The hell," Ingersoll said. "It's only just started."

"Dammit," Pollard snapped, "can't you see he's out?"

"Well, I ain't out, and I'm just gettin' warmed up."

Tom moved from behind Grogan's arm, stepped into the yellow glow facing Ingersoll. "I'd hate to see you go away unsatisfied," he said. "Anyway, I reckon your fight's more with me than with him."

Ingersoll turned heavily and glared. His lips parted. "Well, I'll be damned if it ain't top lash himself. Where you been hidin', Barker? We been all over town lookin' for you tonight."

There was a bloodshot brightness to the man's eyes and a flush of dark blood from throat to temple. Ingersoll had been drinking, yes, but more than that his blood was heated by the will to fight. Tom recognized this and a spasm of animal shock passed over him; it was an instantaneous flash that touched every nerve end, leaving him coldly calculating. An ancient, brutal eagerness flooded his mind. He knew what Ingersoll was going to do; it was as though they were thinking through one mind. The breath in his chest went deeper; his stomach pinched down, and the hard sloshing of his heart sounded loud in his own ears. His muscles turned loose and sweat ran under his clothing. Tim Pollard said in a high voice: "Hold it! You can't fight, Tom. Your lung ain't healed yet."

Then Ingersoll lunged for him, drove his big body forward, both fists flailing. Tom dug in his heels and shifted aside with a grunt. He grunted a second time as Ingersoll swept past and he threw a right fist at the freighter's ear, missed, and nearly lost his balance.

Ingersoll spun back and came on again. This time Tom settled himself and waited. But he missed again, and Ingersoll's momentum caught him, carried him back against the rough boards of the barn, and slammed him hard against wood. Through a roaring that did not altogether come from the bystanders he saw Ingersoll's big fists through a blur; he weaved away from them but caught one along the point of his jaw and his shoulders sagged; his arms partially dropped.

He turned away to take the beating along the side but each strike hurt him. It was like being struck with a pick handle; his ribs flashed pain into his skull and cleared that injured portion of his brain. He rolled along the wall, then dropped low, jammed his feet down hard, and shot forward, driving Ingersoll back, wrestling with him, their straining arms locked briefly, then he was clear to maneuver again, and he broke away, looping a hard blow to Ingersoll's chest that jarred the freighter and drove him off. They circled, weaving, ducking low, seeking openings. Ingersoll flung out a pawing hand and Tom knocked it aside. Ingersoll's next blow had the power of a lowered shoulder behind it. But Tom had seen him get set and moved farther out, leaving the freighter fanning air.

Next, the freighter feinted Tom closer and loosed a whipping uppercut. It grazed Tom's jaw raising an instantaneous red welt. But Ingersoll was off balance and still moving forward against his will. Tom's big arms fired twice, staggering the freighter with two hard strikes across the mouth. Ingersoll shuffled backward, great gulps of whistling breath gushing past torn lips, foamy and blood-flecked now. He circled, moving his shoulders and keeping his fists well forward, only slightly bent at the elbows. Someone was hanging a lantern near the barn's rear entrance; its light quickly found the fighters and made a pale circle around them. The bystanders were intently silent, mouths twisted and eyes glowing with battle lust. Blood dripped on Ingersoll's sweat-darkened shirt and Tom felt the throbbing cadenced beat of pain along the swelling side of his jaw.

Ingersoll leaped in close and swung. Tom met him with no inclination to move away. Big fists swung and meaty echoes mingled with grunts and torn snatches of hard breathing. Flesh and bone could not long stand this punishing exchange. Tom dropped flat onto his heels, head swimming and vision blurring. Then Ingersoll stumbled backward first, and the cowmen swore a fierce, common oath almost in unison. The freighters looked on, still and rock-faced.

They circled again and through battered lips Tom cursed Ingersoll in a bitter and steady undertone. "Fight," he said. "That's what you want to do, isn't it? Then quit backing up!"

Ingersoll jumped suddenly forward and struck Tom in the chest. Tom staggered. Ingersoll struck him again, and Gerald Finnerty grabbed Tim Pollard by the shirt front and shook him. "Argh!" he groaned, "he's going to open it up, damn him!"

Tom back-pedaled sluggishly, and Ingersoll rushed forward, sensing the kill, but he ran head-on into a massive blow that made his arms drop to his sides, made his mouth sag, and his eyes glaze over briefly. It had been a trick. He tried to get away. Barker's fist smashed him high across the bridge of the nose and claret spewed. The same fist, red and sticky, glanced across his cheek. Tom could feel the jolt of those solid blows all the way to his shoulder. It was like an electric shock. A faint mistiness swam before his eyes but he pinched them down nearly closed the better to see the twisting, graying face ahead. Then, in wildest desperation, Ingersoll rushed him with crooked fingers clawing for flesh or cloth. But he was too badly beaten; his co-ordination was numbed and Tom smashed him twice more across the face, bringing on a fresh spray of claret each time. Ingersoll suddenly stopped, planted his big legs wide apart, and stood there moving like a tree in a high wind. Tom struck him with all the strength remaining in him. Ingersoll absorbed the blow. Another blow, this one with a loud, sobbing grunt behind it, crashed into his face and Ingersoll's knees buckled; he bent slowly at the middle; his head dropped forward, and he fell full length into the weaving pattern of lantern light, pushing out to lie perfectly motionless. Into the deep stillness came his faint, broken breathing, a thinly bubbling sound.

Tom found someone facing him with a bucket of water. He plunged both bleeding hands into it, felt the sharp bite, and raised cupped hands to his face, dashed water into his eyes, and sucked back all the air he could get. Then he coughed and blood came, faintly pink, and he spat. Someone jostled him; he turned and gazed into the white and wide-eyed face of Tex; they attempted a grin at one another. "Guess I calculated wrong," Tex croaked. "The other time you done it, it looked so easy." Tex fingered his puffy face. "He caught you a couple of good ones, one there along the jaw. It's swelling up like a goose egg."

The freighters were helping Clint Ingersoll to his feet. They dumped water on him; he came out of it very groggily and slowly. Sheriff Pollard was talking aside to the cowmen. Someone handed Tom his belt gun and until he felt its coldness he did not know it had been knocked loose of its holster by the barn wall.

It was the night air as much as the water that revived him. His shirt was hanging in shreds and even the bandages across his chest were stained with blood and dirt. There was no sense of pain, really, but he ached in every muscle and joint.

"Hey, Barker," a gruff, angry-sullen voice called. "You got your gun . . . turn around here!"

Instantly Sheriff Pollard cried out. "Hold it! No gun play!"

The gruff voice snarled. "Who's goin' to stop it?"

Pollard's voice turned thinly dangerous. "Me! You fellers take Clint back to camp and get your wagons ready. I don't want to see a damned one of you around town come sunup."

Tom turned. The four freighters were glaring at Pollard. Each of them was armed and it was very clear that unless something stopped them they were going to precipitate a gunfight. "Wait!" Tom called. "Ingersoll . . . is that what you want?" The big freighter's eyes, nearly hidden in the swollen wreckage of his face, did not look straight at Tom, and Ingersoll said nothing. "Because if that's all you fellers'll settle for, I'll oblige you."

"Not alone you won't," Gerald Finnerty said succinctly. "Let 'em start it. I'd just as leave kill freighters tonight as not."

Pollard was protesting again but no one heeded him. Tom moved forward several steps, looking straight at Clint Ingersoll. "Well?" he demanded.

Ingersoll drew himself up; he pushed clear of his companions and faced Tom. He held out both hands; they were swollen nearly twice their normal size. His meaning was instantly clear to everyone; he could neither draw nor fire a gun.

Tom looked at the other freighters. "You fellers trying to get him killed? He fought a good fight. Isn't that enough for you?"

One of the freighters shouldered past Ingersoll. He was a massive and squatty man with an overhanging, low brow and a bully's massive, thick jaw. "Not for me it ain't," he said. "Now I suppose you're goin' t'say you can't draw a gun, either?"

Tom did not seem to move at all but there was a flash and a roar and the freighter was spun half around. He staggered and cursed and ran a hand down his side. No one spoke. Clearly visible in the lamplight his hip holster was hanging, ripped apart from the shell belt, and his pistol lay thirty feet behind him in the moving light.

"Hell," a man breathed into the hush.

Finnerty and Tim Pollard recovered first. "Anyone else?" The rancher asked, and Pollard said: "Move! Go on now, go back to your camp and get ready to hitch up! Beatty's closed to freighters from now. Pass that along the freight roads, too. No more freighters welcome in Beatty."

Men shuffled off into the night. Tim Pollard waited until they were all gone, then he went up to Tom and cleared his throat, but he did not speak, and eventually he, too, walked away, leaving Tom and Tex alone.

XX

Tom did not open his eyes until noon and he never afterward recalled clearly what it was that had awakened him, but he knew that his body ached all over and his chest felt feverish.

"Tom . . . ?"

It required an effort to lift his lids. When he saw her, there was movement in the background. He ignored it to concentrate full attention upon her face. "Toni."

"Are you all right, Tom?"

"I've felt somewhat better in my lifetime," he answered, propping himself up on one elbow. "I guess you heard . . ."

"Yes."

He saw the movement again and squinted beyond her.

It was Tex and beside him stood Tim Pollard, craning his neck. Next to the sheriff was Judge Montgomery, and grouped together behind the judge were Gerald Finnerty and six or eight men he knew only by sight, local cowmen and townsmen. Prominent in their foremost rank was Roy the bartender and Grogan the liveryman. His brows drew down. "Sorry to disappoint you boys," he said dryly. "But there'll be no wake today."

Tex grinned. Roy the bartender was slower to show appreciation of Tom's poor joke. The judge remained erectly impassive; a shadow passed across his face.

Toni sat upon the edge of the bed and took his hand in hers. He winced and looked quickly at his fingers. They were purple, scabbed over, and stiff with swelling. Toni bent a long glance upon the silent men, and Sheriff Pollard was the first to understand. He edged toward the door, gouging with a sharp elbow as he passed among the others. They were nearly all out of the room when Tom said: "Judge?"

"Yes?"

"I'd like to marry your daughter."

Montgomery inclined his head. "I think that's more in her jurisdiction than in mine, Mister Barker."

"No," said Tom, holding the older man's eyes with his glance. "What I mean is, I want your approval."

The judge stood alone in the room. It seemed that words would not come, but after a moment he said: "Tom, I am not a man who is governed by swiftly changing emotions. All I can say to that is that Antoinette's judgment in this matter is better than mine, and she's satisfied you're a good man. Personally I'll have to withhold an opinion until I know you better." His gray eyes flickered. "Thus far in our acquaintanceship, Tom, quite honestly I've found you honest . . . but hard and vengeful. Those are not things I like in any man." He stopped, waiting for Tom to speak. When he did not, the judge went on. "One thing I can say, though. After due consideration those of us who have stock in the bank have decided to ask you to take Elihu Gorman's place as manager. If you haven't convinced us of much else since your return to Beatty, you've shown us you have a good business head." The judge's tone turned dry. "In that matter of hay and loans, I, at least, am well convinced of that. Will you accept? Of course, that means you'll have to stay on here . . ."

"I accept," Tom replied.

The judge went out and softly closed the door. Toni bent fully forward and found his lips with her mouth. When she straightened up, he smiled; it was a boyish, full, and frank smile. "I'm home," he told her. "I'm back for good, Toni. Will he marry us?" She nodded through a rush of hot, unshed tears, and he lay back sighing. "Finnerty wants a neighbor. I'll take up the option next to him and give it to Tex."

"Tom?"

"Yes?"

"I suppose every woman feels this way at least once in her lifetime . . . Tom, I love you so terribly much."

THE END

About the Author

Lauran Paine who, under his own name and various pseudonyms has written over a thousand books, was born in Duluth, Minnesota. His family moved to California when he was at a young age and his apprenticeship as a Western writer came about through the years he spent in the livestock trade, rodeos, and even motion pictures where he served as an extra because of his expert horsemanship in several films starring movie cowboy Johnny Mack Brown. In the late 1930s, Paine trapped wild horses in northern Arizona and even, for a time, worked as a professional farrier. Paine came to know the Old West through the eyes of many who had been born in the previous century, and he learned that Western life had been very different from the way it was portrayed on the screen. "I knew men who had killed other men," he later recalled. "But they were the exceptions. Prior to and during the Depression, people were just too busy eking out an existence to indulge in Saturday-night brawls." He served in the U.S. Navy in the Second World War and began writing for Western pulp magazines following his discharge. It is interesting to note that all of his earliest novels (written under his own name and the pseudonym Mark Carrel) were published in the British market and he soon had as strong a following in that country as in the United States. Paine's Western fiction is characterized by strong plots, authenticity, an apparently effortless ability to construct situation and character, and a preference for building his stories upon a solid foundation of historical fact. Adobe Empire (1956), one of his best novels, is a fictionalized account of the last twenty years in the life of trader William Bent and, in an off-trail way, has a melancholy, bittersweet texture that is not easily forgotten. In later novels like The White Bird and Cache Cañon, he showed that the special magic and power of his stories and characters had only matured along with his basic themes of changing times, changing attitudes, learning from experience, respecting Nature, and the yearning for a simpler, more moderate way of life.